Glass Trilogy Book 2:
A Glass Darkly

By Max Overton and Ariana Overton

Writers Exchange E-Publishing
http://www.writers-exchange.com

Glass Trilogy Book 2: A Glass Darkly
Copyright 2013, 2024 Max Overton and Ariana Overton
Writers Exchange E-Publishing
PO Box 372
ATHERTON QLD 4883

Cover Art by: Julie Napier

Published by Writers Exchange E-Publishing
http://www.writers-exchange.com

1

Coal black shadows slithered across the cool green marble tiles surrounding the massive fireplace. Its heavy carvings of satin-finished mahogany glowed dully in the flickering light. Blood red glowed uncannily from the dead eyes of gargoyles, caressing their snarling lips, animating them, and making them appear to move with the shadows in silent conversation. Tendrils of ebony oozed up the dark carved wood of the walls surrounding the fireplace, giving the shifting patterns the look of pale-veined nightmares brought to life. Roaring flames, barely contained by a firebox large enough to roast an ox, gave birth to a ruddy glare that fought to overcome the shadows. The light and heat pouring out from the fireplace barely made an impression on the cavernous room, seeming to feed the shadows instead of subduing them.

Deeply ensconced within a high-backed Victorian armchair, Morgan Turner sat quietly, long fingers laced over his lean torso, his gaze fixed on the ornate burgundy and gold pattern of an antique Oriental rug under his feet. Dark curling hair, shot with streaks of grey, spiraled around his head like a wild thicket. His broad chest barely rose and fell under a heavy velvet dressing gown while his head lolled. His long chiseled nose involuntarily wrinkled with distaste when the odour of moldering earth and leaves assaulted it. The room, full of heavily carved antique furniture, seemed to be watching him expectantly as he arrogantly occupied their space and drifted, deep in thought and oblivious to his surroundings.

When a timid scratching of fingers sounded through the thick oak door, only Morgan's restless brown eyes moved in response. "What is it, Ehrich?" The heavy whispering bass of his voice carried around the room in spite of its lack of volume.

The heavy door silently swung open, allowing a bright square of light from the hallway to intrude upon the room's gloomy interior. The shadows fled before it. Morgan continued to stare into the flames as an elderly man with a balding head glided soundlessly into the room and stood patiently behind the chair, waiting to be acknowledged. Steele raised one ringed finger, the ring's ebony facets flashing multi-hued arrows of crystalline light around the room.

"Mr Turner, it is time for your meeting with the scientists." The old man's freckled head bowed slightly but his thin body, encased in an old-fashioned black suit, remained ramrod straight and at attention.

"Give me fifteen minutes then bring them into the conference room. Tell Travis I want a word with him afterward and to bring his latest report." Turner's voice was barely above a whisper but the tone of authority was one of absolute command.

Ehrich left the room as silently as he'd entered. When the heavy door softly closed behind his retreating back the shadows resumed their serpentine dance upon the walls and furniture. Turner rose slowly and deliberately, like a wary prey animal surrounded by ravenous predators. "What do you want from me?" he ground out between whitened lips.

The dry rustling whisper of ancient and crumbling paper filled the room.

Free us. Bring us to your world. We can offer power...immortality. The barriers must be breached. Free us. Free us. Free us....

The whispers faded, as if a great wind blew them away from Morgan's hearing. Morgan shuddered and quickly moved to turn on all the lights in the room.

I'm losing my mind. The sentence whirled around and around his brain until he grasped his temples with shaking fingers and clenched his eyes shut, praying that the litany would end. When it didn't, Morgan dropped his hands, ground his teeth and squared his shoulders.

But I won't let the bastards know it. I'm the king here. I'm one of the richest and most powerful men in the world. I can do anything...anything I want.

He threw his head back and stalked to the door. Hesitating with a death grip on the knob, he turned his face back toward the room, his eyes flashing like the black stone ring on his finger.

"Even you can't make me do what I don't want to do." He sneered, opened the door and left, slamming the heavy door behind him.

The shadows oozed out of the walls, undulating sensuously toward the portrait of Morgan Turner that dominated the wall above the fireplace. They converged upon the picture, caressing it with tenuous fingers. The low, brittle sound of contemptuous laughter echoed around the room, and then abruptly altered into something much worse. It permeated all, absorbed all colour and light from the room and reverberated through the walls like the muffled, desperate wailing of a lost soul buried deep within a cold, dark tomb.

2

The winter dusk is short in the Colorado Rockies and the last light of the day was fading rapidly when the mouse came hip-hopping across the crusted snow from the sanctuary of the tumbled woodpile. The snow-caked logs abutted the end of a small, one-room rough-plank cabin, its single window closed and shuttered against the cold, the only signs of life within its walls being the thin wisp of smoke curling from its covered stove pipe and the butter-yellow light that oozed from chinks in the shutters.

The mouse paused, whiskers quivering, as it sat up and peered myopically into the shadows under the pine trees that clustered closely around the cabin. Nothing stirred and the only scents that carried to its twitching nose were wood smoke and the ubiquitous stink of humans that emanated from the cramped construction behind it. Finding nothing to alarm it, the mouse hurried onward onto the cold covering of dead pine needles littering the forest floor. Food was still available this early in the season, with a little diligent searching, and after a few minutes it found a small pine nut overlooked by the foraging squirrels. Grasping the treasure in its forepaws, the tiny rodent sat up and nibbled at the morsel of food, the whispering rasp of its teeth against the nut masking another sound a few feet away in the shadows of a fallen log. A puff of displaced air swept over the mouse and it dropped the nut, turning and gathering its muscles to leap for safety even as a sleek body swept it off its feet. It uttered a despairing shriek of terror as sharp teeth closed on it, its pattering heart convulsing as its neck snapped.

A feral cat crouched at the edge of the trees where the first faint grasping fingers of snow reached out from the deep blanket that covered the open space around the cabin. Its jaws held the cooling body of the mouse and a single drop of ruby blood fell from the rumpled fur of the victim to stain the pristine snow. The lean predator growled, yellow eyes defying a silent world, as it waited and watched, alert for any movement, any sound, that spelled danger. After several minutes, the cat dropped its prey, licked the congealing blood from its fur, and started to eat, chewing delicately and stopping often to look and listen. When no more than the tail, the skull and a foot remained of its meal, the feral cat sat back and started cleaning itself, scrupulously removing every trace of blood and hair from its face, sleeking down its own ruffled fur before yawning widely and staring across the open expanse of snow to the cabin.

Inside the cabin, a potbellied stove radiated heat into the small room, and a single fabric-shaded table lamp cast a buttery glow over the furnishings. A young woman, closer to thirty than twenty, sat on a threadbare couch near the stove, her feet curled up under her, and her head, framed by raven wings of glossy hair, was bent over a battered paperback. Minutes passed and the woman's long fingers turned the page, then turned it back again and her eyes moved back to the start, moving over the words without making sense of them. She fidgeted and suddenly threw down the book and sprang to her feet.

"Damn it, Samantha. Where the hell are you?" she muttered, pacing the length of the cabin, a dozen paces one way, then a turn and a dozen more, the heels of her cowboy boots loud on the bare wood. A scratch, no more than the whisper of a pine branch on a window on a breezy night, distracted her. Three paces took her to the door and she flung it wide, a bolus of frigid air and a small cat sweeping in before she could close it again.

"Hi Pi," she greeted the cat. "Come in for some food, have you?" She bent to stroke the small creature but it bared its fangs and backed away. As soon as she straightened, the cat darted in again, rubbing against her jeans-clad legs. "Okay, Piwacket," she laughed. "Food it is." Crossing to her kitchen alcove, she took a small box of dry cat food from a cupboard and poured a half cupful into a bowl and set it on the floor. Piwacket rushed in, pushing her hand aside and started feeding, a rough, coughing rasp of sound indicating contentment.

She stood and watched the cat for a while as it ate, a smile on her lips, remembering the first time the starving feral kitten had arrived at her cabin. Normally, she was only in the cabin for one or two months in the year and fortuitously, her visit three years ago had coincided with the arrival of a vicious spitting ball of fur. Recently abandoned, the kitten was emaciated and torn from a struggle with a larger predator. At considerable expense to the skin on her hands and arms, she had nursed the tiny kitten back to health. Scarred by its experiences, it never allowed a human to get close to it but would, on sufferance, allow food and warmth to be provided at times of its own choosing. When she left after that first visit, she was sure she would never see it again, but six months later, it returned, lean and battle-hardened to demand food and a place by the stove on cold nights. She called it

Piwacket, after the witch's cat in a movie of which she had forgotten the name, though it never came to her call. Despite this, she came to look forward to its infrequent visits.

Piwacket finished eating and stalked over to the woollen rug in front of the stove and started to clean itself. The woman made herself a cup of coffee and took it over to a small table where a laptop computer sat, its screen blank in standby mode. She connected to her server and downloaded her emails, hoping for something from Samantha. "Come on," she muttered. "Where the hell are you?" She grimaced when the last of the messages popped up without any from her sister, and set about dealing with them. The last was from a friend and it was short and to the point.

"Andi," it read, "Call me. Marc." A phone number followed.

Andi made a face and looked across at the old black Bakelite land phone that had evidently been installed when the cabin had been built. She eschewed the use of a mobile as being invasive and demanding, content to have people leave a message that she could answer at her convenience. Picking up the handset, she hesitated, and then quickly called the number, letting the old-fashioned dial rotate after each numeral.

"Marc? It's Andi. What's so important it can't wait another month or so?" She engaged the speaker-phone unit connected to the old machine and stepped back to her desk and her coffee.

"I'm very well, thank you for asking," the voice from the phone crackled. "How are the mountains? Snowed in yet?"

"Have you heard from Sam? Is that why you're calling?"

There was a long silence from the other end of the phone. Only the continuing crackle of static told Andi the line was still open. "I've been remembering things," Marc said quietly.

"What sort of things?" Andi could almost hear the shrug from Marc. *Jeez, girl,* she thought. *Do you know him that well?*

"Nothing definite," Marc hedged. "Shapes in the forest, scary shadows, and some really ugly people."

"You're not living in Arkansas are you?"

Marc laughed bitterly. "Fuck you too."

"I'm sorry, Marc. My people skills are a bit rusty at the moment. Why did you want me to call you?"

"Do you want a job?"

"What sort of job?"

"Right up your alley. Physics with an electromagnetic flavour."

"Really?" Andi's interest was piqued. Those sorts of job were few and far between. "Who's it with?"

"A strong research element, I gather, but a bit of military involvement that'll bring in the big bucks."

"Who's it with?"

"Northern California, so the climate will be a bit better..."

"Marc! Stop dodging the question. Who is the job with?"

"Now don't get mad. It's Morgan Turner, but there's..."

Andi strode across to phone and hung up, cutting Marc off, then removed the receiver to prevent him calling back. She sat on the couch, letting the warmth from the stove envelop her, sooth her. *Damn the man*, she thought, uncertain whether she meant Marc or Morgan. Unwillingly, she let her mind slip back four years.

She had just graduated with a PhD in physics from M.I.T. and had taken a temporary position at a Minnesota laboratory working on a Defence research contract, while she looked for a university position. The research contract seemed far-fetched to her, involving an adaptation of the Tesla coil that, if successful, could deliver a blast of coherent, aimed electrical current at a target miles away. A year of testing had not moved the project any closer to success and though her own ideas were listened to, as far as she could tell, none of them were implemented.

Then, just as she contemplated quitting, one of the financial backers of the project had turned up, Morgan Turner, CEO of Turner Enterprises. He had listened attentively to the scientists involved with the Tesla weapon, watched a series of disappointing tests, and spent several hours ensconced with the military and the project leader. Emerging from the meeting, Turner had talked with every one of the research employees, arriving in Andi's lab just as she was packing up to go home.

Morgan Turner was--*and probably still is*, Andi thought--a tall, powerfully built man in his early forties with a shock of unruly black hair and an engaging smile. Impeccably dressed, he displayed few of the obnoxious traits so common to rich men used to getting their own way.

"I do apologise for getting here so late, Dr Jones," Morgan had said. "But I really would like to get your take on the project."

Andi nodded and started to take her street coat off. "Certainly, Mr Turner. What would you like to know?"

Morgan had hesitated, for a few moments appearing unsure of himself. "Look, I've been on the run since six this morning and I'm starved. I have to fly down to St Louis first thing in the morning, but I really do want to pick your brains. Would you consider having dinner with me this evening?"

"Thank you, Mr Turner..."

"Morgan, please."

"...Morgan, but I already have plans for this evening."

"Break them. I really need to talk to you."

Andi's eyes flashed ice. "I'm sorry, Mr Turner, but I couldn't do that."

Unexpectedly, Morgan nodded and smiled. "A pity. Your section leader apprised me of some of your ideas--yes, the ones he never implemented--and I'd like to pursue them. Unfortunately, I'm only in town for tonight and I was hoping to find out..." He shrugged and moved toward the door, then hesitated with his hand on the knob. "How about drinks before dinner? I'll only take an hour of your time."

Andi, who had been planning to curl up with a good book that evening, relented. "Okay."

Morgan glanced at his watch. "I'll pick you up at seven."

Andi shook her head. "Where are you staying? I'll meet you there."

Morgan nodded, studying Andi's face. "I'm at the Retzinger. I'll meet you in the bar at seven then."

Andi decided ten minutes was long enough to make him wait. She had considered longer but he was her boss--sort of. She did not want to get on his bad side, but neither was she planning on advancing her career by way of the bedroom, which unless she missed her guess, was his intention. Murmuring something about the traffic, she slipped quickly into the booth in the Retzinger's bar, taking her seat while he was still rising to greet her.

Sipping a vodka and orange juice, Andi listened absently while Morgan made small talk, but perked up when he switched to her work. He was well-informed and had a good working knowledge of electromagnetic field theory. On his prompting, Andi talked about her ideas of resonance and the use of a super-cooled crystal array to focus the energies before beaming them up into the ionosphere. Morgan listened attentively, prompting her when she flagged or strayed from the topic, leading her onward, and deftly turning the discussion away from the control of the raw energies of the atom and into the delicate realms of human brain wave manipulation.

"You've heard of Persinger's work in Canada?" Morgan asked.

Andi nodded. "He alters perception by fitting his subjects with a helmet wired up to stimulate the sensory parts of the brain."

"Mind you, that's only possible because his electrodes are almost in contact with the brain. If you tried that from even a foot or two away, the drop-off in stimulus would be too rapid for..."

"Nonsense. You've totally forgotten that the stimulus needed is...what?" Andi frowned at the amused expression on Morgan's craggy face.

"I believe it is more politic to say 'I think you might be mistaken', especially when talking to the person who controls the purse strings."

Andi flushed and looked away. "Sorry," she muttered. "I thought this was a government project."

"It was," Morgan said softly, "But we've passed from the Defence contract into other realms of possibility. I want you to come and work for me."

"I've already got a job."

"Not for much longer."

Andi stared at the older man. "You're firing me? For getting carried away and being rude?"

"Hell, no. I said I was offering you a job, not taking one away. Your project leader is the one who wants to get rid of you. I think he's a fool, but I want to take advantage of his stupidity."

"But you don't know anything about me."

"The hell I don't. You think I make offers like this to any pretty girl I see? Dr Andromeda Jones, I'm offering you a top position in my organisation."

"Doing what?"

"Whatever it takes."

Andi stared and then laughed. "You'll have to be a damn sight more specific than that."

"I'm sorry, Andi, but until you're mine, I can't tell you."

"Until I'm yours? What's that supposed to mean?"

"Professionally speaking, Andi. If you join me you'll be signing a whole slew of non-disclosure documents. I really can't tell you what you'll be working on but I can promise you it'll be right down your alley. The pay's good too. We can discuss it but we're looking six figures here."

"I...I'd have to think about it."

"Don't think too long. I'm putting my team together right now."

"Who else have you got?"

"You'll find out when you sign." Morgan stood. "I'd offer you dinner, Andi, but I respect your prior engagement. I'd like an answer tonight though. You can call me here at the hotel or come up and see me," he added softly.

He reached down and lightly touched the back of her hand. "Room six-oh-six." Turning, he strode across the room and disappeared into the hotel lobby.

Andi thought about the offer for the rest of the evening, sitting alone in her small apartment, nursing a glass or three of cold Australian Wolf Blass chardonnay. At midnight, she reached a decision and picked up the phone to call Morgan at the Retzinger Hotel.

"I'm sorry, ma'am," the hotel clerk said, "But Mr Turner checked out an hour ago."

Andi thanked the man and placed the receiver back on the hook. She felt let down and a little relieved at the same time. The job offer had been intriguing, and the pay would have been very welcome, but Morgan had also disturbed her. There was a hunger there, hidden mostly, but it had emerged briefly during their hour together--once when he'd referred to human brain waves and again when he'd touched her hand. She shivered and decided it was for the best--she would not try to find him by calling Turner Enterprises in California.

Morgan had not called her, and a month after his visit, Andi was let go from the project. She found work as a physics teacher at a high school in Aspen which allowed her to enjoy the mountains. It was here that she met Marc Lachlan, a freelance photographer holidaying on the snowfields, and found that he knew her half-sister Samantha Louis.

Andi sighed and picked up the phone again. "Marc, answer me one question. Why would I want to work for Morgan Turner?"

"To find your sister Sam."

"What? How are they connected?"

"I don't know, but he's looking for her. Not her specifically, you understand, but her husband James and, get this, exactly where they were in the Blue Mountains and Glass House Mountains. He even set a team of private detectives to follow up on their disappearance."

"But why? Why would he be interested?"

"I don't know."

"And he's offering me a job? How would you know about it?"

"Well, he's not exactly offering you a job, but there is one there for you, I'm sure. Wouldn't you like to be back in physics research, investigating electro-thingumy whatsits?"

Andi laughed. "Electromagnetic fields, moron. But how do you know that's my field? I certainly never told you."

Marc sighed. "We don't all live hidden away in a little cabin in the mountains. Some of us have real lives to live and we get to hear things. I do work for some big papers and magazines, you know, and one of them knows all about you and enough about Morgan Turner to be intrigued."

"And what's he heard about Turner?"

"He has a facility in Glass Mountain in northern California, near Medicine Lake. He's gathered quite a team of physicists, the US Army, and a pile of cash together, wrapped them up in Fort Knox and is building something."

"What?"

"Likely to be something nasty, but nobody knows for sure."

"Then how come you know so much?"

Marc hesitated. "If I don't tell you, you can't spill the beans."

"If you don't tell me, I'm hanging up."

Marc was silent for a long time. "Okay," he said at last, "But please don't let on where you heard this. Bob Gerhardt, Science Editor of the Mid-West Science and Technology Gazette, is a friend of mine. He came across a snippet of information that reveals Turner is building some sort of mind control device with unofficial elements of the US Army. I can't tell you what the information is, because I don't know. Bob wouldn't tell me."

"And where do I come into this?"

"Bob wants you to join the group at Glass Mountain and find out what's going on."

"You are kidding me. How am I supposed to do that? Does this Bob friend of yours have some sort of 'in' with Turner?"

"Nothing like that. There's an advertisement out for technicians with advanced bio-electromagnetic expertise at Turner Enterprises, and you fit the bill. The closing date is tomorrow so you need to get on board immediately."

"Marc, it doesn't work like that. This isn't some job I can just rock up to the front door about and get hired straight up. These things take weeks of detailed preparation."

"All done," Marc said with a satisfied tone. "Your resume, together with an application and glowing references, has already been submitted. My guess is you'll get a call for an interview by the end of the week."

"This is a load of crap!" Andi slammed the receiver down and stood staring at it, her mind churning. "Something doesn't add up here," she muttered. She turned at looked at Piwacket snoozing by the stove. "What do you reckon, Pi? Where does he get off putting in an application for me without telling me first? And why is he so damned interested in me getting this job anyway? What's in it for him?"

Piwacket's only comment was to stretch and yawn widely before going back to sleep. Andi smiled and picked up the phone again.

"Okay, Marc, put it on the line for me. Why are you doing this?"

"You're a friend, Andi. I hate to see you wasting your talents stuck..."

"Bullshit."

"And you'd be doing me a favour. There's a big story in this."

"How did you get hold of my resume?"

"Oh, I have contacts," Marc said vaguely. "Does it matter? You have a good opportunity to do some serious work in your field and help me on my way to a good story at the same time. It's a win-win situation."

"I'd only be a techie, Marc. That's not what I call doing serious work."

"You'd start as one," Marc admitted, "But when Turner finds out you're there, I'll bet he takes you on as a researcher."

"And what's it going to do to my career if I blow the lid on my employer? Always supposing there is something to blow."

There was silence from the other end of the phone, but Andi thought she could hear somebody talking in the background.

"Is there somebody there with you, Marc?"

"No...er, it's just the TV...why do you...hang on." There was silence again for about thirty seconds before Marc spoke again. "Someone wants to talk to you."

"Who..."

"Ms. Jones?" an unfamiliar voice asked. "Dr Andromeda Jones?"

"Who is this?"

"You don't know me, Dr Jones. You can call me Ted. I need to talk to you."

"Put Marc back on."

"Dr Jones, I need to talk to you, right now, so..."

"Put Marc back on or I hang up. I need to know he's all right."

There was a short pause before, "Andi?"

"Are you okay? Are you in danger?"

"No, I'm fine."

"Can they hear me at the moment?"

"No."

"Are you in danger?"

"No. Talk to him, Andi. Please."

11

Faint muffled sounds told Andi the receiver was being passed back to Ted, confirmed a moment later when he spoke again. "Satisfied, Dr Jones?"

"For the moment. What do you want?"

"Just to talk to you for about half an hour."

Andi shrugged. "Okay, go ahead."

"It will have to be in person. I am sending a helicopter to your cabin to pick you up so please be ready..."

"I'm not going anywhere, buster."

"Then I will come to you. My name is Ted Collins. Please ask to see my identification when I get there."

"ID can be faked," Andi said.

Ted paused. "It is a federal offence to fake this identification."

"Only if you're caught. I don't imagine that would stop you. You'll have to come up with some other form of ID."

A longer pause. "I will bring Marc Lachlan with me. He will vouch for my identity."

"Except I suppose he only knows you as Ted Collins because your possibly faked ID says that's who you are." Andi sighed. "Why do guys get off on playing games? Okay, come on out, and bring Marc."

"We will be there within an hour, Dr Jones." Ted rang off.

Andi frowned and looked around her small cabin, wondering what she should do to prepare for the mysterious Ted Collins. She had a shotgun tucked away in a safe place, and a box of shells, but she was not at all sure she wanted to go down that route. Collins had mentioned it was a federal offence to fake his ID, which implied he was a federal officer. That could mean anything though, from a tax official to an FBI agent or an officer of Homeland Security. In the end she decided to wait and see, putting on a fresh pot of coffee and breaking open a fresh pack of plain oatmeal biscuits.

She heard the whup-whupping of the helicopter blades fifty minutes after Collins had hung up. Piwacket was awake in an instant and raced to the door, scratching to be let out. When she opened the door, the cat raced for the shelter of the forest as a sleek black helicopter came racing up the valley before dipping and hovering above the field in front of the cabin. Powdered snow flew up in a blizzard, almost obscuring the aircraft and it settled, breaking through the thin crust and rolling forward a few feet. The engine idled back, the blades slowing and a door opened, allowing three men to jump out and run toward the cabin, bent over, and coats flapping. Andi recognised Marc in an instant, and saw he was flanked by two young men in dark suits and overcoats.

"Dr Jones?" the man in the lead said. Andi recognised the voice but let him introduce himself. "I'm Agent Collins and this..." he indicated the other suited man, "...is Agent Kowalski." He took a black leather billfold out of his pocket and flipped it open to reveal a picture of himself, his name, and the letters 'FBI' embossed on the half facing the photo. The other man revealed a similar billfold.

"They look like something you could pick up in a toy store," Andi said sourly. "Never mind, I guess I'm going to have to take you on trust."

"Thank you, Dr Jones," Collins said. "Could we go inside and talk?"

Andi stood aside to let them pass, and they entered the tiny cabin quickly and quietly, their eyes swiftly searching and passing on. She leaned close to Marc as he passed.

"What the hell have you got me into?" she hissed.

"Not his fault, Dr Jones," Collins said from inside the cabin. "We've had you in our files for some time and we approached Mr Lachlan for his assistance. We didn't really offer him a choice."

"Like you're not going to offer me a choice either," Andi said, following Marc inside and closing the door. "Coffee?" She indicated the pot on the stove.

"Thanks." Collins accepted a cup and passed it to Kowalski before taking another and sipping appreciatively. "Do you love your country, Dr Jones?"

"That's an odd question."

"Not really, we live in troubled times. Would you answer the question please? It's quite simple."

Andi frowned. "I have found that questions people describe as simple are often the most complex. I could ask you to define love." She held up a hand as Kowalski opened his mouth. "I am an American born and bred, I believe in the Constitution and the rule of law. I did not vote for our current President, nor do I support his war in Iraq and Iran, however, I will obey any legal command that comes from him. I pay my taxes, I obey the laws of the land, I am polite to policemen and I help little old ladies across the street. I do believe America is the best place to live, but I've never been outside its boundaries, so I can't really be sure. I think democracy is the best way to live, but we are not the only democracy in the world. So you tell me, do I love my country?"

Collins smiled thinly. "I think we can accept you are not an overt security risk."

"So what's this all about?"

"We have reason to believe the facility at Glass Mountain is manufacturing a weapon of mass destruction that will not be used in the best interests of the United States."

"So step in and stop it. You're the security people."

"It is not that simple. Morgan Turner has friends in high places--very high places--and our hands are tied unless we can show evidence of action against our country."

"Un-American activities," Marc quipped.

Agent Collins turned and stared at Marc until the young man dropped his eyes. "You could say that. I take a threat to my country very seriously and see no reason for levity."

"Sorry," Marc muttered.

"As I was saying, Dr Jones, neither we, nor the Department of Homeland Security can step in without the evidence. That is where you come in. We want to put you into the project so you can report back to us."

Andi raised her eyebrows in surprise. "Whose damn-fool notion was that? I'm a physicist, not a secret agent."

"Exactly. A physicist is what we need. We must have somebody that can properly evaluate what they see."

"And you don't have any physicists of your own?"

"Several, but you are known to Morgan Turner already. We know he tried to hire you three years ago. Dr Jones, this is perhaps the last opportunity to get someone into Turner's organisation. He is looking for a handful of trained technicians. You are more highly qualified than any of the other candidates and he knows you. I think you are our best bet."

"What would I be looking for?"

"I don't know. A weapon system of some sort. Something out of the ordinary. We will have to leave that up to you."

"And when--if--I find it? They're not going to just let me phone you."

"Don't worry about it. That can be arranged."

Andi smiled ruefully. "You want me to take a well-paying job, spy on my employer and ultimately bring my job to an end. What do I get out of it?"

"The satisfaction of having served your country."

"Oh, well in that case, do I have any choice?"

"No, not really," Agent Collins said. "But if it will help decide you, you may find out something about your sister, Samantha Hay."

"Sam? What's she got to do with all this?"

"We don't know, but Turner Enterprises is looking for her, or rather, for where she might be. She and her husband, Professor James Hay, disappeared under unusual circumstances in Australia. They are believed to be in the vicinity of either the Blue Mountains, near Sydney, the capital city..."

"Canberra," Marc said.

"What?"

"Canberra is the capital city; Sydney is just the largest one."

Collins gave Marc a long hard look before resuming. "Near Sydney, or else in the Glass House Mountains. Either way, Turner is looking for them and we don't know why. Do you have any idea, Dr Jones?"

Andi shook her head. "It doesn't make any sense. They've never met nor had any sort of contact."

"Then maybe you could find out what that is about at the same time," Collins said softly.

"Okay, say I decide to do this, how do I even know I'll be given the job?"

Agent Collins took an envelope out of his inside jacket pocket and handed it to Andi. "This came for you. You have an interview at ten tomorrow morning at the Turner building in Oakland, California. We will fly you out of here this evening, and arrange for an overnight flight to San Francisco. A driver will make sure you get..."

Andi turned the envelope over in her hands. "It's been opened." She looked up at the two agents. "Isn't tampering with the US mail a federal offence?"

"Unless you have a court order."

"And you have one?"

"I can have one here within three hours--backdated to cover that letter."

"Shit," Andi muttered.

"Dr Jones, I really do not see what your problem is." A touch of impatience crept into Collins' voice. "Your country is asking you to perform a small task, for which you will get paid, and through which you may find some answers concerning the disappearance of your sister. Is that too much to ask?"

"You could have just said 'please'."

Agent Collins stared, the corner of his mouth lifting a fraction. "Dr Jones, will you please help us?"

Andi grinned. "Okay."

3

Glass Mountain in northern California is a strange, rather spectacular, steep-sided flow of dacite and rhyolite obsidian, or volcanic glass that sits on the eastern rim of the Medicine Lake caldera. It is the result of a recent eruption, perhaps only a thousand years ago, and its nearly treeless slopes offer little in the way of cover for any sort of research installation. In fact, tourists regularly tramp the slopes of the mountain and surrounding countryside without any hint of the intense activity taking place hundreds of feet below them.

Echo-soundings taken nearly forty years before revealed the presence of chambers in the solidified magma throat of the volcanic vent and Turner Enterprises had invested in a costly mining operation from a site on an unnamed island on nearby Medicine Lake, under the waters of the lake, running down through caverns and excavated shafts to the heart of Glass Mountain. Exactly why Morgan Turner had wanted to build in such a remote and inaccessible location was not clear, even to him, but he was well satisfied with the installation when completed.

The island in the lake could be reached by helicopter or by boat, and Morgan had installed a helipad and docks surrounded by an island-wide security fence and electronic system. A large hunting lodge on the highest point of the wooded island was little more than a façade, though a number of bedrooms were available for the few guests who visited his retreat. In the basement, a steel door opened into a chamber with a ramp that spiralled down another hundred feet before heading in a north-east direction toward Glass Mountain. In order to carry large amounts of building materials, a small electric rail system was installed, and as a fail-safe, a parallel tunnel was built for foot traffic. Both tunnels ended in a large chamber, from which several corridors led to accommodation, living facilities and laboratories. Morgan had puzzled over the need for living quarters for large numbers of people--a hundred could be housed at a pinch--but he had gone ahead with the plans. A year later, the need arose, when the US Army became involved and an infantry unit was billeted in the caverns to act as security. Another tunnel, smaller and less well-appointed, ran from the part of the living quarters that housed Morgan's own suite of rooms, rising rapidly to debouch within a dense stand of pines about two kilometres from the Glass Mountain laboratories.

Numerous ventilation shafts kept the air sweet and fans circulated the air efficiently, keeping the temperature stable. Power was available through the West Coast grid, and also from banks of emergency generators. There was also a complex geothermal power station, with the lake water pumped deep below the dormant volcano to generate steam to drive turbines. Morgan had never seen the need for this source of power, but the plans called for it and his mind was easier, his sleep less troubled, if he followed the plans as he had originally written them.

The laboratories were well equipped and large enough to accommodate the building of the particular piece of equipment Morgan had in mind. The idea had sprung fully formed into his mind four years before, but he had looked around for a long time to find exactly the right location, and scientists that were leaders in their field but not overly concerned with ethics. Morgan could foresee circumstances where single-minded determination would win through while humanitarian concerns would lead to failure. Glass Mountain was the perfect site, and his team of researchers would provide the expertise. His machine would come into being, and its use would ensure that his country became a benevolent guide and mentor to the world, but he could not shake the feeling that there was another possible use for the device, a darker, more sinister use. Morgan sometimes tried to contemplate this other use, but every time he did so, he would find his thoughts sliding toward more mundane topics. He would shrug off the uneasy feeling it gave him and turn his energies elsewhere.

The heart of the Glass Mountain facility was a long room which housed the growing device. Access to the passageways that led to the room was by key card and code number only, and work was under way to provide a retinal scanner. In the meantime, the US Army provided men to guard the device and the men and women who worked on it.

The long room was windowless, and almost devoid of shadows. Fluorescent lights blazed throughout its length and covered the high ceiling, casting a diffuse white light into every nook and cranny, under every bench, and even illuminating the vast array of equipment that filled shelves and bins, or was stacked in tidy arrangements at the far end of the room. Frosted glass paneling ran the length of the room and from the movement of shapes behind the glass it was obvious that a passage or hallway was on the other side. Benches ran along both long sides of the room, wooden and recently polished though their shiny surfaces were now marred by stains, burns and a scattering of nuts and bolts, electronic cards and crystals, wire and sundry tools. A plain painted wooden door at either end of the room allowed access to the structure taking shape in the middle of the smooth concrete floor.

The structure was elongate and covered with shiny surfaces, though the overall shape was anything but streamlined. Basically, massive coils of cable snaked from one wall and disappeared into a massive box that hummed and crackled. A copper column a meter in length emerged from the top and ended in a doughnut shaped coil of tightly wound copper wires. A long tube also sprang from the box at an angle of about twenty degrees from the horizontal and was surrounded by arrays of crystals, brackets holding loops of wire, electrical cables and glass fibres, and a plethora of strangely shaped ceramic, glass and metal objects that had no obvious function. Standing around the structure, delving into its parts, were two men in white coats.

Jacob Spindler was the older of the two men, a stoop-shoulder individual with a shock of white hair and a rheumy, distant look to his pale blue eyes that disguised an adamantine will and a fierce determination. His wrinkled, blotched hands trembled slightly and the thin skin of his face barely hid the skull beneath. Now in his eighties, he could at last see the goal that had eluded him all his life, a goal that had been snatched from him in the dying days of the war--for him, there was only one--when the Allies had closed in on a shattered Berlin. After two years in prison for his beliefs, he had changed his identity and disappeared, re-emerging in America in the fifties as a physics student, forced to earn his doctorate all over again. A lifetime spent researching the effects of radiation on living tissue and working minds had evaporated five years before when an investigative reporter, checking on Spindler as a possible recipient of a humanitarian award, had stumbled on his past and revealed his long-held and well-camouflaged political leanings. Research money dried up and forced retirement left him bitter and penniless--until he came to the attention of Morgan Turner. Turner was concerned only with the future, not the past, and Spindler found a new outlet for his dreams.

The younger of the two men working on the machine was Kenneth Braun, a tall gangling man of early middle age, whose hair was as retiring as his personality, having withdrawn to the periphery of his high-domed skull. Twenty years previously, he had been a promising young research student on the brink of fame in his chosen field of bioenergetics. Passed over for an award that he believed he richly deserved, Professor Braun had fiddled his findings, massaging the data delicately to reveal exciting results. Nobody picked up on his cheating, and a year later, Braun invented data to push the boundaries of his field still further. His peers could not duplicate his results and questions were asked, but as his reputation was impeccable, the controversy died down. Next he fed data to scientists of dubious reputation in developing countries, counting on their desire to make a name for themselves. For the next few years, Braun's work was duplicated elsewhere and his own reputation grew, until someone grew too greedy and, through sloppy editing, revealed the source of his data. Braun's fall was swift and hard. He was lucky to escape prison when his financiers decided discretion would be more profitable than disclosure. Reputation and livelihood in tatters, Braun lived a hand to mouth existence until rescued by Morgan Turner.

Spindler muttered to himself as he delved into the wiring inside the machine. "The damned connections are all wrong." He pulled his head out of the wiring box and glared across at Braun. "Are you responsible for this pig's breakfast?"

Braun shrugged and looked away. "Nothing to do with me. My concern is the crystal lens array. Talk to Parker about it. He has overall control of the electronics part of the project."

"Idiot." Spindler went back to work without making it plain to whom he was referring.

Braun shot the older man a look of hatred and returned to his examination of the fused quartz elements of his array. He unlocked another shaped segment and carefully withdrew it before carrying it over to the bench and subjecting it to a battery of tests. The shaped elements had been very carefully cast and machined to exacting specifications by another of Turner Enterprise's corporations, but inevitably, there were minor differences in a number of properties. Most important among these were tensile strength, the rigidity modulus, the coefficient of thermal expansion, electrical resistivity, the index of refraction and sonic attenuation. Other factors played a part, but these were the hardest to balance. The manipulation of three or four elements in an array was hard enough, but this machine called for a total of one hundred and twenty shaped segments that interlocked to produce, hopefully, a coherent whole. *Why do there have to be so many?* he wondered, not for the first time. *We manage well enough in the miniature model with only six.* He sighed and made a notation in the open notebook beside his testing instruments.

The miniature model was a shortened imitation of the main machine. It stood at the far end of the laboratory under a tarpaulin. A few feet from it was a large reclining chair not unlike a dentist's chair--if the dentist concerned was particularly sadistic and needed restraints to hold his patients immobile. Both chair and machine had been employed in a series of highly successful tests that had led to the inception of the full scale model, though the patients had been volunteers from among the junior staff on the project.

Spindler swore loudly and threw a screwdriver across the room. "Where is the dumkopf who wired this thing?" he screeched. He turned and made his way over to a telephone by the door and lifted the handset, punching in numbers with savage jabs of his finger. "Ver is Parker?" he screamed into the receiver. "You tell him I vant to see him now, verstehen sie mich?" As he got angrier, his accent thickened and German words crept into his speech. "Ja, tell him."

"Is that wise?" Braun asked mildly from across the room. "He won't like it and you know how he gets when..."

"I do not care. I am the **führer**...the leader of this project, and I will not be treated mit such disrespect. Vy, I vill haf him dismissed." Spindler nodded to himself, muttering as he retrieved the screwdriver and returned to a contemplation of the wiring in the machine. "Dese are colour coded. Vy can he not do it properly? Is he perhaps farbenblind?"

Minutes passed, in which Spindler continued to fulminate and Braun quietly got on with his measurements, his shoulders already hunched against the storm he knew was coming. It came swiftly, the first distant peals of thunder being the slamming of the security doors that connected the living quarters with the laboratory suite. Footsteps sounded in the concrete corridor, amplified slaps of rubber-soled shoes, as the storm approached. The door to the laboratory slammed open and Braun flinched, though he knew he was not the target today.

A small, thin-faced young man of sallow complexion and fastidious dress stood framed in the doorway. Travis Parker had sometimes, behind his back, been compared to a ferret, but this comparison greatly maligned the fun-loving mustelid. Parker was often pleased with himself but seldom with others, and it was doubtful he knew how to laugh. He had a competent but pedestrian mind and had developed one talent above all others--a talent which had stood him in good stead during his rapid rise through the ranks of technical science. He could take an idea, usually somebody else's, and twist and turn it so that everybody thought it was his, even the person who dreamt it up in the first place. This had become so natural to him that he no longer knew he was doing it. As far as he was concerned, he had a brilliant mind and fully deserved any praise or reward that came his way. The only thing that held him back, he knew, was the envy and stupidity of others. He should have been the project leader here in Morgan Turner's underground base, but for some reason it had been given to the stupid old Nazi standing in front of him. Well, he would show Turner what a mistake he had made, but first he would deal with this ancient fart named Spindler.

"What the hell do you want, Spindler? I've got better things to do with my time than play nursemaid to a senile old man."

Spindler's yellowed and veined eyes bulged and his mouth twitched. "H...how dare you talk to me that way? I am the **führer**, the leader of this team and you answer to me. When I..."

Parker's eyes glittered. "So, you are the **führer** are you?" He slipped his left fore-finger horizontally underneath his nose and raised his right hand in a Nazi salute. "You pathetic idiot. You are living in the past, in a time when people actually listened to you. Well, they don't here, they listen to me." He walked forward and pulled at the jumble of multi-coloured wires spilling out of the machine. "What have you been doing here?"

Spindler shook with anger and he elbowed the smaller man aside. "I haf been trying to correct your damage, you dumkopf. These vires are in the wrong positions. The machine vill not verk like zis."

"Speak English, Nazi," Parker muttered. He peered into the entrails of the machine and followed a few wires from their connections and through the tangle. "What's wrong with this one? Or this?"

"There!" Spindler yelled, flecks of spittle spraying the machine casing. "Look at zat one, und zer. They are mix up. Are you farbenblind?"

Parker grimaced and stepped back, pointedly wiping his face. "Well, they are now, but that's not how I connected them. You must have been playing around with them."

"I do not play," Spindler retorted. "I try to fix your mistakes, dumkopf."

"You be very careful how you talk to me, Nazi. I don't like you and I don't think you are pulling your weight on this project."

"Alvays mit zis Nazi crap," Spindler whined. He took a deep breath and struggled to control his anger and his tongue. "I am not a Nazi and have not been for fifty years. It was an aberration of my youth. I was foolish then, but even so, not as foolish as you are now. And Mr Turner saw fit to make me project leader, so you will afford me the respect due to my position."

"Respect? For what? If it wasn't for me, this project would have fallen over two years ago." Parker thrust his slight body close to the taller man, forcing him to step back. "I've had it with you, Spindler. I'm going to Turner right now to get you fired."

"Please, gentlemen," Braun pleaded. "Let us not do anything we'll regret later. We can work as a team, we have..."

"Shut up," Parker snapped. "Or you'll be next. Your work has been pretty abysmal too."

"That's not fair. I've been doing the best I can. I can't help it if you've increased the complexity of the quartz crystal array beyond all reasonable limits. The small machine works fine on just six segments, but this..." Braun slapped the barrel of the large machine, "...needs twenty times that number. It's not just twenty times harder to align them; it's thousands of times harder."

"If you're not up to the task, you can always leave," Parker sneered. "I'm sure I could find more competent technicians to do the job."

"That's nonsense and you know it, Parker." Braun gulped, astounded that he had stood up for himself so strongly. "I...I'm a theoretician, not a mere technician, and I'm precisely what is needed to achieve success. The six-segment array works well in the small one. Why can we not just increase the power and maybe double the focussing...?"

"Don't think, Braun, it doesn't suit you. The small machine works well within the confines of the laboratory, but we need one that will work over much greater distances."

Braun frowned. "How much greater? Why am I not told these things? I could achieve more if I had a firm idea of the purpose behind this work."

"That is only dispensed on a need to know basis. You do not need to know."

"But I do," Spindler said forcefully. "I am in charge. If anyone knows, I should."

"You are a security risk," Parker said, a cruel smile on his face. "I advised against you being told."

"You did no such thing, Dr Parker."

Parker whirled to face the doorway. Standing in the doorway was a tall, muscular man with a shock of black hair streaked with grey, and an irritated look on his tired and lined face. Parker refused to consider he could be at fault, so his response was not so much bluff as serene confidence. "Ah, Morgan," he said. "You have happened along at a most opportune time. I was just explaining to my colleagues the need to work smarter, rather than just working harder."

"You really do live in a world of your own, don't you?" Turner shook his head and advanced into the room, revealing a willowy, dark-haired young woman standing behind him. "Gentlemen, let me introduce you to..."

"I wish to register a complaint," Spindler cut in. "This person here..." he indicated Parker, "...continually tries to undermine my authority as leader of this project. I want him chastised severely or fired, if you prefer."

"That is nonsense," Parker snorted. "I don't know where he gets this notion that he is in charge. Tell him who really commands, Morgan."

"Neither of you are in charge," Turner said wearily. "I don't know how often I have to say it."

"I expressly remember you telling me I headed up the project," Spindler complained.

"I said you were in charge of the wiring, not the whole thing. And as for you," Turner nodded at Parker, "You need to recognise that not everything revolves around you. This continual bickering is extremely tiring and is not helping the project."

Parker sneered but said nothing.

"Now, as I was saying," Turner went on, "Let me introduce you to Dr Andromeda Jones. Dr Jones, this is Dr Jacob Spindler, Dr Kenneth Braun, and Dr Travis Parker. Dr Jones is joining our little team. I will expect you all..." he looked slowly round at the scientists as if daring them to comment, "...to make her welcome."

Andi shook hands with the three men.

"What is your area of expertise, Dr Jones?" Spindler asked.

"Bioelectrical fields, in particular, the effects of imbalance on health."

"Interesting," Braun said. "I, myself, am in the area of bioenergetics. In this project, I am attempting to manipulate the fields created by the laser unit, modulating them through a crystal array..."

"Yes, yes," Parker interrupted. "I am sure that is all very interesting, but I am more interested in what you can bring to our group, young lady. Morgan said he was advertising for technical staff, so I assume you will be helping one or other of us." He leered at Andi, as if he could judge her mind by her outward appearance. "I think you would fit most suitably into my group."

"Let me disabuse you of that right now," Turner said sharply. "Dr Jones obtained her doctorate at MIT and I have seen the quality of work of which she is capable. I have no intention of wasting her considerable talents on the mundane work of any single group. Dr Jones will have oversight of the whole project--not to make command decisions, but to troubleshoot on all aspects of the construction and testing. She will be answerable to me alone, and I will decide exactly what it is she will be doing."

Spindler and Braun greeted the news with stony expressions, but Parker grinned and winked. "We won't be seeing too much of you then," he commented. "Or at least, not nearly as much as Morgan here. So don't you worry about a thing, and if you need anything, just come and see me."

Andi thanked him coolly and, following Morgan's lead, took her leave of Spindler and Braun.

"I'll come with you two," Parker said affably.

Morgan scowled. "Don't you have work to do here?"

"No, I was called out to fix something some idiot had got wrong. I can reasonably leave it in Spindler's hands for now. Now that he knows what is wrong, he should be able to fix it. After you, Miss..." Parker gestured toward the open door.

Morgan Turner followed Andi out of the laboratory and did his best to prevent her being harassed by Parker, shepherding her down to the living quarters where he pointedly waited for the little man to leave them, explaining he had other duties for Dr Jones at that time. Parker smirked but left.

"Do you really have a job for me or was that just to get rid of him?" Andi asked.

"We need to talk. Do you feel like a drink?"

Andi hesitated. "I thought this place was alcohol-free."

"It is. There are only two places you can get a decent drink around here-- my suite and the lodge." Morgan smiled wearily. "I won't invite you to my rooms just yet, so I guess it's the lodge."

Morgan and Andi walked to the rail terminus and the attendant on duty opened the doors on one of the small electric cars that sat astride the shiny rails leading up the brightly lit passage. Morgan sat at the simple controls and started them toward the lodge at a sedate twenty kilometres an hour. The trip took a little under fifteen minutes, and Morgan filled in the time by asking inconsequential questions about what Andi had done in the intervening years. In turn, he talked in generalities of his own life, turning aside from any hint of his present purpose or the Glass Mountain facility.

"Soon," he promised.

They left the terminus at the lake end and took the elevator up to ground level, moving from what looked like the lobby of a hunting lodge to a private room overlooking a magnificent view of Medicine Lake framed by old pine trees.

While Andi admired the view, Morgan poured the drinks. "Those are old pines," he said with a measure of pride. "Somehow they got missed in the logging that swept through here early last century. My grandfather bought the island in fifty-seven and had the foresight to maintain the forest. I've owned it for nearly twenty years now and no tree gets cut down. I leave the dead ones standing to act as nesting sites for birds." He handed Andi her rum and coke and gestured to the overstuffed armchairs. "We need to talk."

Morgan sipped his own single malt Scotch and looked at Andi appreciatively. "It's good to see you after all these years, but how did you find out about this position?"

Andi sipped her own drink, looking away as she answered. "I just answered the ad."

"Where did you see it? I didn't use many places."

"A friend emailed me the application forms. He thought I might be interested."

Morgan nodded. "He didn't say where he saw it?"

Andi shook her head. "Is it important?"

"Perhaps. Certainly curious. You see, I never actually got around to advertising the position. I notified Personnel in Turner Enterprises, drew up the ad, and arranged for it to go out in the next employment supplements--all open and above board." Morgan sipped again, savouring the smoky tang of the aged liquor. "I stopped the ad at the last minute for reasons that are neither here nor there, yet somehow you still saw it somewhere and applied. Now I wonder how that happened."

Andi sat silently, not looking at Morgan, waiting for the blow to fall. He had discovered she was a plant and she would be fired before she had even started.

"I'd like to think you were here because you wanted to get to know me better, or at the very least because you were trying to take up that offer of a job I made you years ago, but we know differently, don't we, Andi?"

Andi still did not say anything and Morgan sighed.

"Who was it? Police? Army? FBI? Homeland Security? Some other security agency?"

"FBI," Andi said quietly.

"Why?"

Andi shrugged. "I guess they made the proverbial offer--the one you can't refuse."

"That's not what I mean. I assume they would lean on you somehow, we all have sensitive sides and things we don't want to come out--or did they appeal to your loyalty? It doesn't matter; what I'm interested in is why they want to investigate me."

"They didn't say. They just wanted me to report back on what was happening."

"Nothing specific?"

"No." Andi hesitated and searched Morgan's face. "What happens now? Will you let me go, or...or...?"

Morgan stared back. "Good God, Andi, what do you take me for? This isn't some lurid pulp novel where the villain tries to kill the heroine."

"I'm sorry, I didn't mean to imply that...well actually I suppose I did, but this whole business has me on edge." Andi put down her drink and stood up. "I'll get out of your hair if you can have someone take me back across the lake."

"I'd like you to stay."

Andi frowned, looking down at Morgan's upturned face and seeing a fleeting glimpse of uncertainty in his eyes. "In...in what capacity? Am I to be a prisoner after all?"

"Nothing like that."

"Then what? You can't think that on the basis of a drink and a job...I don't respond well to force."

Morgan looked away, seeming to shrink down upon himself. "I...I am in need of a friend, but if you can't be that, then be a spy." He looked up and met her gaze. "Andi, stay and do your job for the FBI."

"What? Why?"

Morgan sipped on his drink and stared out of the window at the old pines. "I own all this, and I have funded this project, but sometimes I wonder just how much real control I have. I feel as if I'm being manipulated." Andi said nothing, and after a few minutes, Morgan continued. "Spy for the FBI by all means, but keep me in the loop. I'd like to know what's going on too."

4

James Hay woke in the night and rolled over onto his back, his eyes wide, staring into utter blackness. Not for the first time, he raised his hand in front of his face and waggled it, but his eyes failed to detect anything, though his proprioreceptors assured him his hand was there. He listened, and thought he could detect a faint hum, deep and resonant but so soft he was not sure if it was heard or felt. It was reassuring, he thought, like a ship's engine heard in the darkness of one's cabin, telling you the ship had not yet hit an iceberg.

What made me think of an iceberg? James lay naked, as he always did, beneath a single sheet. The room in which he lay was temperature controlled and was on the cool side, as he preferred. His wife Samantha, who lay next to him, was curled into as much of a foetal position as her advanced pregnancy allowed, and had a sheet, a blanket and a quilt covering her, as well as a voluminous frog-patterned nightdress. She snored, as James had found to his amusement in the months after their wedding, and though it was loud, it never kept him awake. At the moment, her breathing was low and regular, her sleep seemingly untroubled. Whatever it was that had roused him had not disturbed her.

He thought back over the last few months, marvelling afresh at the things that had happened to them. The arrival of the black rock had started it all--started the modern phase, he corrected himself. According to Amaru and Garagh it had started thirty thousand years ago, though they were still vague about exactly what it was that had gone wrong. James wondered if they really knew, or whether the whole thing was just an act to make themselves seem more in control. They were Neanderthals, cousins of modern humans, though now a separate species, yet their actions were often curiously human. *There needs to be another word to describe humanity that includes other intelligent species,* he thought. *Intelligencity? That would preclude many humans.* He snorted derisively then held his breath as Sam stopped snoring and rolled over. After a few moments her deep, even breathing resumed, and he relaxed.

It's been a bugger of a few months for Sam. I've lived a lifetime with such things, but she's had this all landed on her in a few months. She's been remarkably resilient. I wonder if I would be in her place.

But it was no longer just humans and Neanderthals. Garagh and his tribe had genetically engineered half a dozen other species, mixing their own genes with animals, producing the fearsome-looking Yowies, the ubiquitous technical-minded Greys, what he called the Blue-greys--*doctors and scientists*-- and a few other curious mixtures he had caught glimpses of around the complex under the Glass House Mountains.

James and Samantha were not there now, and in fact, not really even in Australia, though still close. Despite having bases worldwide, the Neanderthals were centred on the Australian region. When the Greys had come for them on Magnetic Island, with the assistance of half a dozen yowies to carry baggage--*isn't it amazing how many clothes a woman can gather in a few short weeks*--they had been brought to the central base under the Glass House Mountains first.

Amaru had then explained that the two of them would remain there for a few days until their permanent accommodation could be readied. She was evasive about staying in the Central Base and eventually revealed that the shadow creatures were growing in strength and that Gaia was too important to put at risk.

"Ernie didn't seem to have much trouble with them," James had said.

"The one you call Ernie is not here," Amaru had replied. "We do not have his...er, expertise in these matters."

"I'm surprised. I thought with all your knowledge you'd know all about them and be able to cope."

Amaru had looked uncomfortable. "We do not know what they are or where they come from, so we are unable to counter them effectively."

"I thought they were Quinkan. Surely the Dreamtime Lore has knowledge of them? The same knowledge that Ernie has must be available to you too."

"Quinkan is only the name you gave them. They resemble those mythical beings, but they are something else. Even the 'Others' cannot help."

James found his thoughts sliding off at a tangent but did not resist as the subject of these mysterious 'Others' was one he had pursued before. Amaru and Garagh were reticent about their nature, but as James' telepathic powers grew, he sometimes caught a few unguarded thoughts. The 'Others' lived in the sky and had guided the Neanderthal tribe for over thirty thousand years, teaching it and leading it out of Ice Age Europe and down to Australia. As near as he could work out they were aliens but what form they took was anyone's guess. No one had even seen one, or even knew if there was more than one, or if it was the same one over the millennia. Gradually, James pieced together a picture of a spacecraft in earth orbit, somehow cloaked from NASA and the other space agencies around the world. He was not sure whether that comforted him or not. Maybe it was good to have beings that powerful on your side, but what if you were only test subjects in an experiment of theirs? *I don't want to be a lab rat for anyone...anything. Mind you, just because Amaru and Garagh believe in them doesn't mean they really exist.*

Whether or not they existed, Amaru used their supposed advice as an excuse to move James and Sam to another base. They knew nothing of this one save the fact that it was underground somewhere. It consisted of a series of small caverns--a large living area, a bedroom, kitchen, bathroom, and a combination doctor's surgery and exercise room. There were doors between the rooms, but no exits from the base. Amaru had pointed out the portal to James and Sam as soon as they arrived.

"You see the faint oval on the surgery wall?" Amaru asked, tracing the outline with one finger. She slapped the rock within the oval with her hand. "Solid rock. Nothing can get at you here except through Central Base and two way-stations. We control the portals so there is no way they can reach you."

"And can we get out if we want to?" Sam had asked. "I feel claustrophobic here already. Where are we?"

"We are under Lord Howe Island."

"I think I'm going to regret asking," James had said, "But how far under?"

"About a kilometre. I will show you a setting for this portal that will deliver you to the top of Mount Gower on Lord Howe about once a day if you decide you want some fresh air, or to stretch your legs. It will not be the same time every day as we must make sure of your safety first. If the island is being observed or there are humans nearby, the portal will not work."

"And how do we get back to Central Base if we need to?"

"You do not," Amaru had said firmly. "We will cycle you through the system if it is needed. Greys will come through to clean and also replenish your stores every night, and I will show you both the code that will summon assistance should you need it."

"Sounds like we're prisoners," Sam grumbled.

"Think of yourselves as treasured guests. Gaia is important to all of us."

29

Amaru had left them and for the next five months they had lived in their underground cavern, making only brief forays to the summit of isolated Mount Gower to enjoy a sunset, feel the rain on their faces, or to sunbake, replenishing their vitamin D levels. Inside the caverns they had a plentiful supply of books, CDs and DVDs, internet connection, and tutors on any subject under the sun was available should they require it. Everything they needed for their own amusement and Gaia's education was provided--even visitors from time to time. Nathan and Ratana had dropped by often in the weeks leading up to their wedding. James smiled at the memory. *Honorary uncle, but I feel like a father to both those kids. I'm glad they decided to tie the knot.*

The Greys kept the place spotless, behaving much like the Brownies or Elves of European folktales, creeping in at the dead of night to soundlessly clean the rooms or replenish the food stores. James had only seen them once when, in the early hours of the morning, he had gone to the kitchen for water and surprised one in the act of wiping down the refrigerator. It had blinked its huge black eyes and backed away, twittering softly, before fading into the wall. James had rushed forward but the wall was once more featureless rock. Apparently, Amaru had misled them into thinking the surgery portal was the only one.

Not that it really matters. Whether it's for our own protection or because we're pawns in an Alien/Neanderthal game, we're still prisoners--though minimum security ones. James had little doubt they could escape down the sides of Mount Gower, should they ever need to.

Sam moaned softly beside him and James turned his mind toward hers, probing delicately. Distorted images floated across the surface of her brain, forming a coherent picture for a few moments before dissolving into something quite different. *She's dreaming.* He withdrew after satisfying himself the dream was unlikely to degenerate into a nightmare. If that happened he would wake her at once and hold her, soothing the night terrors. A nightmare seldom returned upon re-entering the dream state. The nightmares were all one thing--Gaia and the Shadows. James grinned in the dark. *Sounds like some pop group.*

Not that he blamed Sam for having nightmares about the shadows. They were scary things. He had never fully shared his experience in the Landcruiser outside Emerald when the shadow beings had invaded him. It had felt as if he was being enveloped in cobwebs, choking as they swept into his throat and lungs, but the truly horrific thing was the realisation that they were sentient creatures, for he had heard them, seem them within his mind as they assaulted him. It would not be strange if he had nightmares, but James never had them. Something about his brain turned a potentially frightening dream sequence into something innocuous, or if it couldn't, woke him up.

What are they? Amaru had said they were not Quinkan, those thin, shadowy beings from Australian Aboriginal Dreamtime that inhabited cracks and hollows, emerging at night to wreak mischief. As a biologist, James knew there was no natural part of the animal world that matched their description--but then neither did Neanderthals, Yowies and Greys. Despite the surrounding darkness, James set himself to thinking about the Shadows, sorting out everything he knew.

They are humanoid but not physical--no, strike that, they are almost insubstantial but I felt them--cobwebby. I could hear them too--a thin rustling sound like paper...no, like snakeskin...snakeskin on dry leaves...or the rushing patter of a million cockroaches. James shivered and drew the sheet up over his waist. He was a biologist, but that did not mean he was automatically immune to the prejudices of his species. *Okay, what else? I caught a glimpse of eyes and a mouth, which makes them look like people but...that's it for physical attributes. What about mental? There they're less human, intent on invading my mind and attempting to do...what?* James cast his mind back, not only to the road outside Emerald, but also what Nathan had told him. It seemed the Shadows could not do much themselves, but needed to enter a human and take over his actions. But for the timely arrival of the one called Ernie, James had little doubt the Landcruiser would have gone into the ravine, where they would have died or been severely injured. *But to what purpose? Why would they do that?*

Gaia. The thought came unbidden into his mind. *But she hadn't been conceived yet.* For a moment, James' thoughts turned to other, more pleasant things and he grinned in the darkness. *Okay,* he thought, forcing his mind back to the shadows. *Did they want to prevent her conception by killing one or other of us? But how could they possibly know about her? What threat could she possibly be to beings like that? 'The healing of the world,'* Amaru said, *but how could a baby heal the world?* James shook his head. There were too many unknowns.

Sam groaned again, louder, and threw out an arm, catching James across the chest. *What's up, love?* he asked, not expecting any answer from the sleeping woman.

I think it is nearly time, daddy.

Gaia?

Yes, daddy. I'm being pushed downward, gently now but I think it is starting.

Oh my god! James sat up suddenly. "Lights," he called out, and as the automatic system kicked in, quickly added "Dim," squinting as the blaze of light dropped to comfortable levels. "Amaru!" he yelled, then leapt naked from the bed and ran to the door, before returning to his wife. "Sam, get up. It's starting."

Sam struggled to wake up, yawning and stretching. "Go watch your rugby," she mumbled. "I'll give it a miss."

"Wake up Sam, Gaia's coming."

Sam opened her eyes and stared suspiciously at her husband for a moment before closing her eyes again. "I think I'd know, you silly man."

Sam. Wake up. The baby is coming. Gaia told me.

The soundless shout got through where words had failed. Sam's eyes flew open but her vision was turned inward.

It's true, mummy. Your uterus walls are contracting gently...it's quite exciting.

"James, don't just stand there, hand me my clothes." *Why is it men always seem to go to pieces at a birth?* "Have you signalled Amaru yet?"

"I was just on my way, but I thought I'd better tell you first." James grinned. "I thought you might be interested."

Silly man. Sam turned her mind to her baby to sooth her. *Poor baby, poor Gaia, it will be all right. This is all natural, my little baby, a little discomfort..."*

I know, mummy. I know everything you know on the subject and a bit more. I've talked to Amaru and Bisnia and Uta--most of the mothers..."

James hurried to the portal and punched in the code that signalled an emergency. He was not sure how this would work as he'd never had occasion to use it before. Seconds passed and James tapped his foot, willing it to hurry, and just as he reached out to punch it in again, the oval of rock shimmered and two small Greys stepped through into the surgery. They stared at him and one trilled questioningly.

"My wife. The baby's coming. Gaia." James felt his patience unravelling. "In there, for God's sake." He pointed toward the bedroom.

One of the Grey's scampered across the living room and disappeared, popping back into sight a few minutes later uttering a series of warbling cries. The one waiting by the portal stabbed in a code and stepped through, leaving the other one to take James' hand and start to drag him back to the bedroom.

*Plis. Bring mate. Hurry you to...*There followed an unfamiliar word.

James stopped dead and stared. "You can talk!" he exclaimed. *I mean, you can talk. Why have we not heard you before?*

No need. Plis bring mate to...to room with instruments.

Aren't we going back to Central Base?

Plis to go instrument room.

Sam waddled out of the bedroom wearing a maternity dress and a cardigan and clasping a packed overnight case and a large make up bag. She saw James standing in the living room with one of the Greys.

"Tell them I'll be there in a few minutes. There's no way I'm seeing anyone without my 'face' on."

"He says we are to go to the surgery, but not through the portal," James said.

Sam stopped dead and stared. "What? I thought we'd be going to a hospital."

"Apparently not," James said. "Look, you go and get gussied up or whatever women do, then come through to the surgery. I'll go and try to get through to Amaru again."

"Okay." Sam put a hand on her belly and winced. "Just get a move on. Gaia's in a hurry."

Not me, mummy, it's you. Ooh, that was a strong one.

Sam disappeared into the bathroom and James went through to the surgery to call Amaru. He punched in the alarm code he'd been given, but though the wall shimmered and shook, nobody came through in response. Shrugging, he looked at his attendant Grey. *I don't suppose you know where she is?*

Plis?

Amaru? The doctors? For the baby.

They come. You wait.

"What else?" James muttered. He started to pace.

Sam came into the surgery, having artfully applied powders and paints in sufficient quantity to look as if she was going out to dinner rather than facing a gruelling session of giving birth. She opened her mouth to ask what was going on, and shut it again as Amaru and two white-coated Blue-Greys stepped out of the surgery wall.

"You took your time," James growled.

Amaru raised one eyebrow. "Really? Samantha looks as if she has yet to give birth."

Sam tut-tutted. "Be nice, James." She hugged Amaru, towering over the squat Neanderthal woman. "Greetings, Amaru."

Hello Amaru.

Hello Gaia. How are you feeling? Ready to join us?

Oh yes! I'm very excited but a little apprehensive.

Don't concern yourself, little one. The birth process is largely automatic.

It's not that that worries me. There's a whole world out there to experience. So far I've only seen it through the filters of mummy and daddy and you of course, Amaru. Soon I'll have to do it all by myself.

You'll manage, kid, James broke in.

Baby goat again?

They all laughed, and Amaru called the Blue-Grey doctors over. "You remember Dr Qeretu and Dr Yttru."

"Yes, of course," Sam said with a smile.

"How arrre you feeling?" Qeretu trilled.

"Have the watersss broken?" Yttru added.

"I'm feeling fine, and not yet..." Sam winced as another contraction rippled through her.

"Pleassse," Yttru said, pointing to the table. "Let usss examine you."

Sam undressed a trifle self-consciously and slipped on a hospital gown. She lay down on the table and let the doctors busy themselves examining her, while James held her hand and tried to look calm.

"Verrry good," Qeretu said. "It will not be long."

Sam's waters broke about three hours later and events moved rapidly thereafter. As the contractions became stronger and longer, Sam contorted her arms and legs, striving vainly to find a comfortable position. Sweat broke out on her face and body and despite herself, her grunts and groans occasionally slipped into screams. James tried to soothe her as much as he could, but some of his well-intentioned platitudes only served to shorten Sam's temper.

"Can't she have something for the pain, Amaru?" James asked after being verbally abused once more.

"Chemicals, you mean?" Amaru shook her head. "We cannot risk it harming the child. I'm sorry, Samantha, but you must suffer through it."

I could neutralise the chemicals, I think, Gaia said. *But there is a better way.*

Sam could feel her baby doing something but she could not concentrate, as another wave of contractions threatened to eviscerate her. She started to scream again and then suddenly gulped. Though she could feel the contraction continuing, the muscles of her uterus rippling and pushing, the pain had suddenly cut off as if a switch had been flipped.

"What happened?" she gasped.

"What did you do, Gaia?" Amaru asked, displaying agitation. The Blue-Grey doctors trilled and warbled, speaking a language of their own as their long fingers probed.

I switched off mummy's noisy receptors, Gaia said. *Is that the right word, daddy?*

34

Close enough, kid. Nociceptors are the pain receptors. How did you do that?

I don't know. I just told them not to and they stopped leaking a chemical at the fringy bits on the ends of the cells.

"The synapses," James muttered. "Is that okay?" he asked the doctors. "That won't harm her, will it?"

"Jussst a moment, pleassse," Yttru said, holding up a hand. He concentrated and James could feel his mind slipping past Gaia's into Sam's brain. "It isss sssafe," he said, after a few moments.

"The cerrrvix is dilating nicely," Qeretu interrupted. "Push, Ms Samantha. Yourrr baby wishes to be borrrn."

Sam could feel a terrible pressure building inside her, but the pain was no more than a faint tickling sensation as Gaia manipulated her mother's sensory receptors. The uterus contracted again, long and hard, and Gaia switched her focus from her mother's nociceptors to her hypothalamus and pituitary, stimulating a rush of endorphins as her control slipped.

With a slippery rush, Sam felt her baby push through the last barriers and out of her body into the large hands of Amaru. She heard within her mind a cry of wonder and love as her baby was born, and she burst into tears.

"The motherrr of the worrrld is borrrn."

"Yesss, ssshe hasss come."

Oh God, she's so beautiful, Sam. Gaia, my lovely daughter.

Gaia? Where are you? Let me hold her. I love you, Gaia.

Love you, mummy, daddy. Hold me close, it is...is...cold? Gaia focused on Sam's face and her tiny fingers gripped one of her mother's.

"I didn't think newborns could do that," James murmured in wonderment.

I'm not just any newborn, daddy. Gaia turned her head to look in her father's eyes. *My motor control is still shaky, but I know how to do it.*

Amaru wrapped a small blanket around the baby girl and contacted Garagh, far off in the Glass House Mountains Base. *She is born, Garagh, and the resemblance is strong.*

Good. Clean up and withdraw, Amaru. Give them some time together. They will not have long.

5

"You want me to spy on you for the FBI?" Andi looked at Morgan incredulously.

"Sounds insane, doesn't it?" Morgan smiled wryly.

"Just a bit."

Morgan sat in silence for a few minutes, sipping his drink and staring out of the window at the tree-framed lake. "I'm supposed to get you to sign a confidentiality agreement, threatening you with incarceration for an indeterminate period should you ever leak what I am about to tell you. I think I'm going to forget to do that, so you may not be held liable for breaking it when you tell the FBI."

"Thank you, I think."

"Okay, have you heard of the work of Michael Persinger?"

"The Canadian researcher who worked on magnetic fields and the brain?"

"Yes, though he is American, only working in Canada. Back in the eighties, he found that if you stimulate the temporal lobes with a weak magnetic field, you can induce a religious state. People sometimes felt a presence in the room, and once or twice had hallucinations. He also developed a concurrent theory that seismic activity produced an intense electromagnetic field which in turn created a body of light that people interpreted as a UFO. Possibly the two phenomena are related. Anyway, in the nineties, I was approached by--well, let's just call them representatives of the US military--to investigate the possibility of inducing hallucinations at will."

Andi nodded. "Yes, I've read up on some of that. The problem is that Persinger's subjects had to wear a hat of electrodes--I think it was called a 'God helmet'--and the fields were so weak that some people argued that electrical appliances should produce the same effect. Critics asked why we don't all have a religious experience every time we switch the coffee pot on."

Morgan smiled briefly. "Maybe it depends on the type of coffee. But no, that's perfectly correct. The effect is slight and there are many variables involved. If you believe his theories, everyone should have them because we are all awash in electromagnetic radiation."

"I can't see that wearing a helmet would be much use for the military either. Not if you want to induce hallucinations in the enemy. I suppose you could cheer your own troops up by feeding them a religious experience as they went into battle."

"It was definitely the enemy they wanted to confuse. And you're right that Persinger needed the helmet to get the electrodes close to the right parts of the temporal lobe to induce hallucinations. So we had three main concerns. First, we had to find a way to deliver the electromagnetic field to a person at a distance. Second, we had to 'tickle' the right part of the brain without direct contact, and third, we had to control the nature of the hallucination."

Andi's eyebrows lifted. "Boy, you had your work cut out for you. You seriously thought you could succeed?"

"We did succeed," Morgan said calmly.

"The hell you say!"

"Let me qualify that a bit. We found we did not have to have the electrodes exactly right. As it stands, we can induce the hallucinogenic experience across a room. We no longer need a 'God helmet'; we can bathe the subject in a modulated electromagnetic field from a short distance and while the whole brain is bathed, for a reason we don't fully understand, the temporal lobes are affected most. The subjects hallucinate."

"Incredible. You can control the hallucination?"

"After a fashion. The easiest way is to influence the mind of the subject by a suggestion just before the field is turned on. I've experienced it myself." Morgan shook his head and grinned. "We've all tried it, using pleasant experiences where possible; though I've no doubt you could use any suggestion. I concentrated on the memory of an old mutt I had as a kid and there the damn thing was, sitting at my feet. I could even smell him."

"There are no ill effects of bathing a person in this field?"

"None that we can tell. You'll understand, of course, that we haven't had the time to fully test it, though we also have not been restrained ethically. That's one good reason for military involvement. No shortage of volunteers."

"I'd like to try it."

"You shall. We decided early on that anyone involved in the project would have to experience the phenomenon first hand."

"So all the scientists I met have done it? Even Parker?"

Morgan nodded, a look of distaste crossing his eyes. "They each conjured up their own memory. I'm not sure what it was they saw but Parker had the most evil look on his face and as for April Newman...well, it was like watching a porno movie, or walking in on someone masturbating."

Andi thought about this while sipping at her drink. "Okay, you've achieved something quite incredible here already. How much further do you intend to take it?"

"That was essentially as far as my original mandate from the military ran. This was in early 2003. In December that year I was contacted again, by...by a General Thaddeus Spader, with a new proposal. He wanted me to expand the capabilities somewhat."

Andi regarded Morgan's drawn face with concern. "Expand it how?" she asked quietly.

"The code-name for the instrument—the one you saw in the lab—is 'Vox Dei', the Voice of God. The smaller instrument which we have been using for laboratory tests is now known affectionately as Baby Vox."

"Voice of God? Why is it always ominous when military people talk about God?"

"It seemed reasonable enough at the time," Morgan said. "The United States had just been attacked and this was a means to get back at the enemy hiding out in the hills of Afghanistan and Iraq. Imagine being able to send an enticing hallucination into the minds of the enemy, so they would pour out of their hiding places and get cut to pieces by our troops."

"Did it work?"

"Not yet. That's where you come in."

"I'm not sure what you think I'll be able to do."

"I have the greatest respect for your capabilities, Andi. I tried to recruit you, remember? I think your insights could solve the problem for us."

Andi thought about it. "Okay, let's suppose I can help. Why do you want me to? If you want me to bring the FBI in on this, then why go to all the trouble of solving the problem first?"

"Let's just say I like to see a project through to the end, even if it gets shut down afterward."

"You're saying that as a shrewd businessman you'd pour more good money after bad to complete this project, while making sure you gain no monetary benefit from it? Forgive me if I find that a little hard to swallow."

"All right, that's a fair enough comment. But if I bring the authorities in now, I can only show a possibility, not an actual Weapon of Mass Deception. What if they don't believe there's a threat? The FBI could just walk away and leave me to the not so tender mercies of Spader and...others. I'd rather have something definite to show them."

Andi nodded. "I can see that, but our armed forces don't act that way. This General Spader of yours has his own superiors, all the way up to the Commander-in-Chief, the President. Even if he is pushing his own agenda with this machine, he would not be able to deploy it without being found out and stopped. Uncle Sam may be a bit hide-bound at times, but it is not criminal."

"Ordinarily, I'd agree, but there's another factor involved and when I tell you what it is, you are going to really think I've lost my mind." Morgan got up and fixed another drink. He gulped half of it down before looking wryly at the rest of the amber liquid in his glass. "Sacrilege to treat a good malt that way, but by God, it helps."

"You...you haven't got foreign involvement, have you? Nothing...terrorist related?"

"God, no! I'm not a traitor, but...shit, perhaps I am. I've got myself thoroughly entangled in something I don't like and I can't see how to extricate myself. That's why I'm clutching at this FBI straw of yours."

"If it's not foreign or terrorist, then what? Some sort of shady business deal? Selling houses out from under widows and orphans?" Andi smiled faintly, trying to encourage Morgan.

"Do you believe in the supernatural?"

Andi's jaw dropped. "You mean God? I don't know."

"God, the devil, good and evil...especially evil."

Andi frowned, and picked her words with care. "I was raised a Catholic, but my college education broadened my outlook somewhat and I lapsed. If you're asking whether I believe in an old bearded man on a cloud and a horned man in red with a pitchfork, then no, I don't. But if you mean some essence of good and evil in the world, then possibly, yes."

"I didn't think you'd understand," Morgan muttered.

"You're not giving me much of a chance. What exactly do you mean by supernatural and how does it relate to this Vox Dei project of yours?"

Morgan shrugged. "Back up a few steps and answer another question first. Have you heard of the Nine?"

"Nine what?"

"Just the 'Nine'," Morgan repeated, emphasizing the capital letter. "Originally, they were a group that represented themselves as the Ennead of Heliopolis, the nine ancient Egyptian gods and goddesses that basically represented the whole world and everything in it—earth, air, water, fire, life and death. In more modern times they represent tremendous forces in the business world. Like the Fortune 500 is a register of the top five hundred public companies in the country, imagine the equivalent of that wealth and power--and probably much more--concentrated in just nine men. That is the 'Nine'."

"And you are one of them?"

Morgan threw back his head and laughed, but his mirth quickly dried up. "My fortune is almost beneath their consideration, but I have one thing they want--the Vox Dei."

"But you said this was an Army project, so how can they get it?"

"The Nine could probably buy and sell the US Army, but Spader is one of them--not one of the Nine itself, but an agent. I have every reason to believe they set this whole thing up on the back of my previous success."

Andi got up and fixed herself another rum and coke, making it stronger this time. *I think I need it.* "Where does the supernatural come into this story?"

"In a moment. There is another link in the chain--Ehrich Mannheim."

"Your butler?"

Morgan grimaced. "He was my grandfather's butler, my father's body servant and confidante, and the bane of my existence. If Spader is an agent of the Nine, Ehrich is the superintendent. Also not one of the Nine, but closer to the power. I am sure the Nine heard about my successes through him."

"But if he's your family servant, why not just fire him?"

"You think I haven't wanted to? He holds a double-edged sword over my head--knowledge of some insider trading I did when I was a lot younger, and the threat of violence to my nearest and dearest."

"So you want the FBI in as protection?"

"And maybe they can get me off the insider trading charge."

"Maybe," Andi said uncertainly.

"That's why I need something really good to show them. That's why I want a fully operational Vox Dei."

"And the supernatural?"

Morgan hesitated and Andi was astonished to see a haunted, fearful look creep over his strong features. "I think the Nine have dabbled in demonism and raised something terrible. Through Ehrich, they have sent these things to me to control me through fear."

"What things?"

"Shadows."

"Shadows?"

Morgan nodded. He drained the remnants of his single malt whiskey and obviously thought about refilling the glass. "It doesn't sound like much, does it? When the first one appeared, I dismissed it as a trick of the light, a corner-of-the-eye thing, a product of leaping flames in a fireplace on a winter's night." He decided more single malt would be a good idea and walked across to the bar. "But a normal shadow is cast by some solid object, whereas these things just appeared on a wall, a ceiling, a bookcase--anywhere."

"What were they a shadow of?"

"Nothing, I tell you. They exist alone, without anything to cast the shadow."

"Sorry. What I meant was--what do they look like?"

"Humanoid. Thin, gangly, with long arms and legs and eyes that glow like a banked flame."

"Holy shit. Do...do they do anything?"

Morgan poured another drink, the neck of the bottle clattering against the glass. He turned back to face Andi, his face pale and drawn. "Oh, yes," he whispered. "They do things." He gulped at his drink, spilling some of the amber fluid down his shirt. "They talk to me, inside my head, and they sound like the sibilant whisper of a grave shroud slipping from a rotting corpse."

"Very poetic," Andi said dryly. "You had me going there for a moment, but that sounds altogether too rehearsed."

"Of course it's fucking rehearsed!" Morgan snapped. He gulped liquor again and wiped his mouth on his sleeve. "Sorry, I didn't mean to use foul language, but I've been living with this horror for over a year. I have thought often about how I would describe them to somebody else--dry leaves, snake scales, insect legs--but those descriptions seem too commonplace. I wanted to try and convey the utter loathsomeness of these things."

"Okay, so these things talk to you. What do they say?"

"They ask me to free them and in return they offer power and wealth."

"Hardly original. Any jinni worth his salt offers that to get out of his bottle. Are you sure it wasn't three wishes?"

"You don't believe me," Morgan said flatly.

Andi sighed. "You're not giving me much to rationally believe. You tell me you have furthered Persinger's work and that the army wants you to develop it into a weapon. That's fine, but then you say the army--this General Spader--has teamed up with your butler to raise shadow demons from hell who are offering you power and money to free them." She looked earnestly at the older man. "Morgan, are you sure that the electromagnetic fields from your machine haven't done something to your brain?"

Morgan's glass thumped to the carpeted floor and he groaned and put his head in his hands. "Then I'm fucked. I hoped you might help me, but you think I've gone crazy. Shit, shit, shit..." He started sobbing.

Andi sat and stared at her employer, disquieted by his breakdown. *What the hell do I do? He's gone completely ape-shit. I should get outa here.* She half rose from her chair, hesitated, and sat down again. *I can't just abandon him. He needs a shrink. Perhaps the FBI would get him one...but they won't come in unless I have something to report...*"Morgan, let's say I believe you. What do you want me to do?"

Morgan ceased his despairing sobs and looked up, wiping his cheeks with one hand. "You do? You're not just saying that?"

"Look, I'll be straight with you," Andi said. "You think you are infested with demons. Well, I really think you need to see a psychiatrist, but I will admit that there might be another possibility. Maybe someone--Spader or Ehrich--is playing around with your mind, your perceptions. You've already told me your Baby Vox can induce very real hallucinations. Is it possible someone is using it without your knowledge to make you see things?"

Morgan sniffed and blew his nose. "I never thought of that, but Spader has never seen the Baby Vox in operation." He thought for a few moments. "Ehrich has though, and it is possible one or more of my scientists have talked too freely. By God, it's possible." A smile cracked Morgan's face. "You know, I'll bet you're right, Andi. That's one hell of a relief. I thought I was going mad--or worse."

"What will you do?" Andi asked cautiously.

"Act as if nothing has happened. Whoever it is that is trying to manipulate me via these shadow hallucinations will have to reveal what they really want. When that happens, I'll know who's behind it. Then I kick some ass."

"What do you want me to do?"

"Stay with me. Work with the others to get the Vox Dei working, then when I give the word, bring in the FBI to close me down and arrest Spader and Ehrich Mannheim."

"It's not going to be easy to get word out. I've seen your security set up now and I'm worried."

"How were you going to do it when you were just spying on me? The FBI must have given you a means."

"The idea was that I would write to Marc and he would liaise with the authorities."

Morgan grunted. "Ordinarily, that's just so damned simple it might work, but given the secrecy involved on the project, every single piece of paper leaving the site passes through Spader's hands."

"I meant by email, or texting."

"No external calls or access allowed. The only way out is by snail-mail and that is censored."

"Well, I wasn't going to just say 'Villains at work; bring in the cavalry,' you know. We had a series of code words and phrases that could be worked into the conversation--for instance, 'give my love to Auntie Flo' means 'everything is fine, no suspicious activities' and reminiscing about Uncle Dave would be an alarm call."

"Shit." Morgan shook his head. "Here I was thinking the FBI would have the latest technology and cryptic codes."

"Sometimes less is more. I've always believed in the adage 'hide it in plain view'. Something so commonplace and obvious could not possibly be a code."

"What if Spader's done some research on you and knows you don't have an Auntie Flo or an Uncle Dave?"

"Ah, but I do. Not blood relatives but close enough to warrant the titles. Don't worry; all my contact phrases have a basis in reality."

"Okay, well, I suppose it will have to do," Morgan said reluctantly. "You'd better send a letter to your Marc then, about Auntie Flo."

Andi nodded. "When do I start work on Vox Dei?"

"Tomorrow. Spader will have to issue you with the necessary passes first." Morgan picked up his glass from the floor and got to his feet. "Come on. No time like the present. Let's get you started."

The door closed behind them and a kilometre away, Ehrich took the earphones from his head and switched off the cassette recorder. He sat back and thought about what he had heard, a thin smile creasing the aged skin of his face.

6

They gathered in the underground laboratory at midnight, not because that time held any special significance, but because the West Coast power grids now had the least drain on them from commercial and residential usage. The apparatus had its own generators, but nobody could be sure how much energy would be needed. Spindler made a great show of uncovering the elongate machine and pointing it at the granite target situated at the far end of the long laboratory. Braun fussed over the placement of the complex array of glass and crystal within the 'barrel' of the device, and Newman made some last minute adjustments to her controls. Parker insisted on flicking the switch that fed power from the massive turbines deep within the glassy core of the mountain into the newly completed Vox Dei.

For the last three months, the team of four scientists and Andi Jones, together with an impressive array of technicians, had worked on the great machine, slowly ironing out its problems. Andi's role as trouble-shooter had annoyed the other scientists and it was with ill grace that they allowed her access to the apparatus. Only Morgan's forthright intervention had allowed the project to proceed with a full complement of scientists. They all had different reasons for loathing the presence of the young physicist, reasons which ranged from insecurity to misogyny and from jealousy to self-detestation. None of them wanted her working alongside them, but as the weeks passed, each came to realise that Andi's contributions were making them all look less than perfect.

The whine of the secondary generators beneath the floor of the laboratory grew rapidly louder, the coils of wire wrapped around them pulsing with enough energy to power a small city. A series of lasers fed off the external energies, the increasingly complex makeup of the gain media, or optical cavities, altering the qualities of the emitted beam by degrees. Dysprosium and niobium, tantalum and micromanaged mixtures incorporating rare earths and transuranic elements in trace amounts subtly altered the nature of the electromagnetic output, giving it properties that were yet to be described in the scientific journals. Spindler and Parker each dreamed of writing the papers that would describe their methodology, though each was also determined that the other would have no share of the resultant fame.

Finely machined lenses with exotic coatings and magnetic fields of a hundred Tesla or more, contained, focused and propagated the beam of coherent collimated light up the long tube. Halfway up, the tight, hair-thin beam, invisible to the naked eye, entered the information box, where the laser was de-energized to become a simple, visible guidance beam and the monumental energies bled off and converted into a magnetic carrier beam. Information was added to the carrier and the thin laser with its surrounding vortex of magnetic lines of force. The machine became something startlingly new--a Magnaser, an acronym for Magnetic Amplification by Stimulated Emission of Radiation.

Dr April Newman twirled guidance knobs, made delicate adjustments to the controls in front of her, and gradually focused the guidance beam on a huge slab of granite at the far end of the laboratory. "Are we ready?" she asked, licking her coral-red lips with the tip of her tongue. Her eyes sparkled with an excitement that was, for her, borderline orgasmic. She punched a button and the thin guidance beam strengthened momentarily. A thin wisp of vaporised granite appeared, dissipating as the guidance beam shut off automatically. Invisibly, the magnetic vortex bathed the target, vainly subjecting it to the information carried within its complex structure.

"Is it working?" Braun asked, after a few moments. "I can't see anything."

"Well, you wouldn't, would you?" Parker sneered. "Where the hell were you educated if you think you can see magnetic lines of force?"

"There's no need to be nasty about it," Braun muttered. "I only meant how can we know it is working?"

"Go stand in the beam," Parker replied with a grin.

"Piss off," Braun snarled.

"Please, this is most unprofessional," Spindler said primly. "Dr Braun is right though. How can we be sure the beam is in place and functioning correctly?"

"The first is easy enough," Andi said from her observational seat to one side of the granite slab. "Put a gauss meter in the beam. It will also tell you if the flux intensity matches the settings."

"You see," Spindler beamed. "Perfectly simple. Thank you Miss Jones."

"Okay, Jones, hop to it," Parker snapped. "Get that gauss meter in place."

Andi swallowed a retort and walked across to the target, holding the probe from the meter in line with the hole in the granite burned by the guidance beam. The digital readout flickered and beeped as it went into overload. "Too strong," she called. "Turn it down."

April made an adjustment and the meter came back to life, giving a measurement at the high end of the scale.

"Again." The reading dropped again, then again, until the value was only about twice the earth's normal magnetic field for Northern California. "That'll do," Andi said, before switching off the meter and walking back to her chair.

"Now what?" April asked.

"Now we test it on human perceptions," Parker said. "Spindler, you're the oldest and would be missed the least. Go and stick your head in the beam."

The old man grimaced. "You are a thoroughly objectionable piece of shit, Parker. Why do you not do it yourself?"

"Because I'm too valuable to the project," Parker sneered. "Okay, go find one of the techies, they're expendable."

"Jeez, you guys. I'll do it," Andi said. She got up and moved over to April and looked down at the control panel. "Start it off at about ten percent of background and make sure it is direct current and not fluctuating."

"I know my job," April said sulkily. "You just do yours." She turned the dials and fed in a set of figures through the computerized keypad.

Andi nodded and moved back to the target. "What's the coded information in the vortex?"

"Just a few sensory perceptions I whipped up," April said vaguely, studying her computer screen. "Colours, textures, shapes. That sort of thing."

Andi raised her hand and moved it into the beam. She felt nothing, and after a few moments, she held her breath and stepped into it, letting the invisible lines of force envelop her head. Her hair prickled, particularly the short hairs on her neck, but that was the only effect. No extraneous thoughts came to her, nor impressions of anything that had not been there before. "Nothing. Raise the level to fifty percent background, DC." The static effects on her hair intensified, but little else, though she thought she could detect a slight feeling of warmth. *That could be subjective.*

"Take it to background levels."

"Get on with it, Jones. You're way too cautious."

"You come and do it then, Parker. Raise it to double background," she added to April. Now Andi felt something, a slight tingling behind her eyeballs. "There's an effect," she said, "But not much. Up another fifty percent."

Warmth flooded through her and Andi became suddenly conscious of her own body, the way her dark hair fell about her face, the texture of her shirt caressing her breasts as she moved; heat in her belly. She panted and closed her eyes, fighting back an almost overwhelming surge of sexual feeling. She did not see April's smile or the movement of her hand.

Andi staggered as her body went into spasm. Her back arched, her jaw clenched and she fell to the concrete floor, her muscles suddenly relaxing as she passed from the machine's invisible beam. She lay on the floor groaning, blood trickling from the corners of her mouth.

"What the shit happened?" Parker yelped. He slammed the switch off at the wall, cutting power to the Vox Dei abruptly.

"Not that way," Braun yelled, too late to stop him. "You'll blow the...damn." There was a muffled thump from within the electronics and a wisp of smoke issued out from the casings. "Now look what you've done." He reached across to the wall and hit the silent alarm.

"I told you I shouldn't stand in the beam," Spindler said, staring avidly at the prostrate girl on the floor. "What if that had been me?"

"No great loss," Parker muttered. "What happened, April?" he asked. "You were responsible for the imagery and strength of signal. Did you fuck it up?"

"That's right, blame me," April whined. "I just did as I was told. I can't help it if the bitch can't take it."

"Well, pick her up. You knocked her down."

April grumbled but helped Andi to her feet and over to a chair. The other scientists gathered round, staring at Andi's pale face with trickles of blood down her chin.

"How are you feeling?" Braun asked.

"Groggy," Andi croaked. "And I've bitten my tongue." She shuddered and closed her eyes. "What the hell was in that beam? April, you said it was just shapes and colours."

"Well, nothing you should get upset about," Dr Newman said defensively. "I just thought I'd make it a bit more interesting with a few erotic images."

"Hell!" Parker grinned and looked across at the machine.

"Yes, just that," April confirmed. "Everyone likes a bit of sex, so where's the harm? I can't help it if Miss Jones here is a bloody nun."

"You're a maniac," Andi muttered. "You couldn't think to warn me?"

The sound of running feet came from the corridor and a junior army officer, with side arm in hand, came through the door with a small squad of soldiers. They immediately spread out and covered every person in the laboratory, but after a few moments, when no obvious threat eventuated, the officer holstered his pistol and stood his men down.

"Who sounded the alarm, and why?" demanded the officer.

"I did," Braun said. He pointed at Andi. "She fell over while testing the machine."

The officer stared. "She fell over. And you thought that warranted putting the whole base on stand-by?"

"Given the circumstances, I thought it..." Braun's voice trailed off.

Parker pushed his way forward. "Dr Travis Parker. I'm in charge. Lieutenant...?"

"Evans, Dr Parker. Is the situation serious?"

"No, not at all, but it's better to be safe than sorry, don't you think? The test subject there, Miss Jones, felt a bit dizzy and fell, but she's all right now."

Evans looked dubious. "Is that blood on her face?"

"She bit her tongue when she fell. Perhaps your men could take her to the sick bay?"

"I'm okay," Andi said, getting to her feet.

"Nonsense. You need to get yourself checked out." Parker grabbed Andi by an elbow and half dragged her over to Lieutenant Evans. "Please make sure she gets medical attention. You'll understand that we do not have the time to attend to her injuries. We must repair the damage her accident caused to the project."

"Hey, my fall had nothing to do..."

"It was your damn shut off that did the damage," Braun snorted.

"We don't know that," Parker said, "But even if it did, my action possibly saved worse damage or injury."

Spindler laughed and Parker flushed, ushering Andi to the door. "Lieutenant, if you please."

Evans nodded and rapped out commands to his squad. They formed up around Andi and, despite her protests, walked her out into the corridor and closed the door behind them.

"Very well, we have got rid of the annoyance, so tell me—what went wrong? Report to me in turn—Spindler, you first."

"Vat gives you the right to conduct this enquiry, hein?" Spindler snapped. "I am in charge, as you know. Shall I bring Mr Turner down again to confirm this? No? Then shut up." He glared at April. "You, Dr Newman. Your actions precipitated this debacle. Vat is it you did, und vy?"

April shrugged. "How the hell should I know? My task was to prepare a small amount of information to be carried by the magnetic beam, if you recall. I did this, apparently very successfully." She smiled smugly.

"Dr Braun, you are next," Spindler said. "Will you please open the casing..."

"Wait up, buddy," Parker broke in. "I want to hear more about this image. What did you choose, Newman?"

"An encounter," April said, staring Parker down. "She wanted something like a puppy and Turner wanted a vase with flowers. Shit, something like that can be imagined. If she was expecting a puppy and saw one, who's to say it wasn't just a trick of the mind? No, I wanted to put something in her mind that could not be faked, something she definitely wasn't thinking about."

"An encounter? What the hell do you mean by that?" Parker muttered.

April tossed her head, her eyes sparkling. "Come on, Parker. Surely even you can remember what a man and a woman do together."

"And you..."

"Played over some of my memories, some of my feelings and gave her a thrill."

"Jesus. Your encounters must be hair-raising if they have that effect on someone. She damn near had a seizure and bit her tongue off."

"So I ramped up the power a bit." April shrugged, a sulky look on her face. "How was I to know the bitch was so sensitive?"

"Please," Spindler implored. "Let us observe the proprieties and keep this discussion on scientific matters. We must learn what has happened to the apparatus after it was improperly shut down and determine the appropriate levels for dissemination of the information in the magnetic beam."

"Pompous old fart," Parker snarled, but he turned away from his confrontation with April Newman and started dismantling the cover plates of the power source.

Braun sidled over to April and leaned close, whispering. "So where did you get the images? What encounter did you use? Us?"

April smiled. "Something before your time, buddy, and a whole lot better." She laughed as Braun scowled and stalked away, then pulled up the information program in the computer, making subtle alterations as she consulted her notebook.

Spindler stood and watched his team working for a few minutes. He hummed an old German tune and felt very pleased with himself for having dealt with a potentially troublesome incident so efficiently.

Lieutenant Evans delivered Andi, protesting, to the base infirmary and left her in the care of the doctors, using one of the telephones there to make a verbal report to General Spader and to Morgan Turner. He waited until Morgan turned up and excused himself.

Morgan talked to Andi as soon as the doctors had examined her and given her a clean bill of health. He noted the spots of dried blood on Andi's tee shirt, but decided to wait for her explanation.

Andi sat on the edge of the bed and watched one of the doctors cleaning up and as soon as the man left the room, raised an eyebrow enquiringly and mouthed the words, "Is the room bugged?"

Morgan shook his head. "Not that I know. How are you feeling?"

"Fine. I only bit my tongue."

"Ah, I wondered about the blood."

"What blood?" Andi peered awkwardly at the collar of her shirt, and frowned at the small brown stains. She shrugged. "I'd better get back to work."

"Not before you tell me what the hell happened. Lieutenant Evans said you got in the way of the Vox Dei beam and it knocked you down."

"Not quite. The test went well, the machine fired up beautifully; the guidance beam was spot on and the carrier held steady. It needed to be tested, so I had the energy levels dropped and I stood in the target area while the level was raised again on my command. That's where it went wrong."

"Jesus, Andi, you could have been hurt or had your brain scrambled. We have army volunteers for dangerous duties like that."

Andi made a chopping motion with her hand. "Nothing dangerous about it. The levels are in the same order of magnitude as Persinger's work and that was shown to be harmless. All we were intending was to conjure up an ordinary hallucination."

"The vase with flowers?"

"That's what you wanted. I wanted a puppy, but that vicious bitch Newman fed in one of her own warped sexual adventures. I found myself experiencing a flood of emotions entirely foreign to me." Andi blushed. "Don't get me wrong, I know what love feels like, but I feel dirty after that experience."

"Shit. Look, I...I'll talk to her. She won't do it again." Morgan showed unusual hesitancy.

"No. I have not gone running to you, and I don't want them to get that idea." She brooded for a few minutes, swinging her legs. "You really couldn't have picked a worse bunch of people if you'd tried, Morgan. What on earth possessed you?"

Morgan sighed and turned away, pulling an upright chair out from a desk and sitting down. "They are all brilliant in their own fields..."

"Agreed," Andi interrupted, "But so goddamn dysfunctional. They're borderline psychotic."

"I found and hired Braun and Spindler, and the two of them worked well for six months. Then Newman turned up as a recommendation from Ehrich and a little later, Parker, at the behest of General Spader. I didn't like them but I had no real grounds to deny them."

"You pay them, don't you?"

"Yes, but the money comes from...elsewhere." Morgan did not elaborate and hurried on. "The arrival of Parker signalled our first breakthrough with the Baby Vox and Newman has done wonders with the coding for the carrier beam. I don't like either of them, but I can't deny their abilities." Morgan looked carefully around the infirmary, got up from his chair and crossed to the bed, sitting down beside Andi. "Look," he said in a low voice. "I appreciate the degradation that bitch has put you through, but do you really want me to fire her? We are getting close to finishing the machine and then we can call the FBI in."

"Hell, I don't want you to fire her. How would that look? The 'team' may be at each other's throats, but they'd close ranks if they thought I was your favourite." Andi shook her head and grinned. "You leave Newman to me. I've worked with worse than her."

"You're sure?"

"Absolutely, so buzz off and let me get back to work." Andi jumped to her feet, threw Morgan a mock salute and marched to the door.

Parker was the first to see her when Andi slipped back into the laboratory. "All better?" he called out. "If you've quite recovered from your girlish fainting spell, you can give me a hand over here."

"Pay no attention to him, Dr Jones," Spindler said primly. "He is not in charge. Be so good as to assist me with this wiring."

"In a minute," Andi said, not looking at either man. "There's something I need to sort out first." She walked slowly across to where April Newman stood at the computer console, examining the programs she had built.

The three men stopped their work and watched Andi's progress. The sudden cessation of noise brought April's head up and she paled as she saw the other woman's expression. She backed away, but Andi cut her off and leaned close over her, using her height to dominate her.

"Y...you stay away from me," April stammered. "I'll complain to Mr Mannheim and he'll have you fired if you touch me."

"Touching you is the farthest thing from my mind," Andi said coolly. "Your juvenile sexuality does not interest me in the slightest. I just want you to be aware of one thing, Dr Newman. What you did constitutes sexual harassment and if anything--and I mean anything--like that happens again, I will go to the authorities immediately. I know Ehrich Mannheim hired you, but Morgan Turner is his boss and General Spader is in overall charge, so think very carefully. Sexual harassment is grounds for dismissal." Andi stepped away and smiled. "Now, let's see those computer settings, Dr Newman. The content of the beam may have been utter crap, but the technique was brilliant. Let's see how you did it." Andi moved to the computer keyboard and started calling up the programs.

April hesitated, and then shouldered her way past the other woman. "Let me do it," she muttered. "You'll just fuck up the programs."

Andi stood back and watched, taking careful note of April's methodology. Once or twice she made suggestions, which April ignored but incorporated variations a little later.

The three male scientists returned to their work, disappointed that the two women had apparently resolved their differences amicably. In the armed camp that was the scientific team, any blood-letting that involved others was to be encouraged and enjoyed. The potential cat-fight between the two women had not eventuated, so the others worked, biding their time, and waiting for the next opportunity to slip the knife into a colleague.

7

The hot Australian sun hammered the dense *Eucalyptus* forest of a nameless valley in the Warrumbungle ranges, west of Coonabarabran in northern New South Wales, making the landscape ripple and tremble. Volatile oils blasted from the leaves by the heat hung like a blue haze over the valley and permeated the air with a sharp citrus smell. Cicadas called from the undergrowth, their incessant rasping combining with the dry rustle of unseen animals among the fallen leaves, and the raucous cries of crows to form an irritating cacophony. A lone kookaburra sat hunched in the shade on a branch, watching the ground below for incautious reptiles and listlessly grooming its feathers in between glimpses down at the activity next to the water.

A stream still ran through the rocky bed of the valley though the continuing drought had reduced its tumbling presence to a turgid gurgling between dry algae-encrusted rocks. Reeds and grass clung to tiny pockets of sandy soil or mud between the boulders, their root systems eagerly sucking life from the lowering water.

An old man crouched beside the stream, a battered hat shading his stubbled face as he trailed two fingers slowly round an impression in the dried mud a pace or two from the water's edge. He sat back, dusting his fingers off on his jeans and grimaced as a twinge of pain shot through his lower back. "Getting too old to be wandering round the countryside like this," he mumbled. His nose twitched at a stray scent that wafted over him and he smiled.

He relaxed slowly and scraped up a handful of pebbles, sorting them in his hand absently. He picked out a shiny one, looked at it for a moment then tossed it lightly into the stream. A small freshwater crustacean, a yabbie, darted out from the shelter of a rock and moved towards the pebble, investigating this addition to his cool world. The old man searched for, and found another glinting piece of gravel and flicked it away into the stream. The yabbie raised its claws and, suddenly arching its back, flicked away into the cover of its retreat.

The bushes at the tree line, several paces from the stream, parted slowly and a pair of huge hairy hands gently pushed the leaves and branches aside. Two large, intelligent eyes set in an extremely hairy face regarded the man for several minutes. The creature rose silently and stepped out of the undergrowth, approaching the man slowly from behind. Long brown hair covered its body and glinted in the sunlight. Its long arms swung gently by its side, and huge feet rose and fell as it moved toward the sitting figure.

The old man sat quietly, contemplating the ripples in the stream and the dance of a red dragonfly dipping and flitting above the water. A faint odour of garlic and sewage drifted in the light breeze. His nostrils flared slightly and he smiled without turning. "You took your time, Wulgu."

A low rumble like distant thunder answered him and a thought bounded across his mind like a young wallaby. *You have nothing better to do than throw pretty rocks, old man?*

Spence turned and grinned up at the towering form of the yowie. "By God, Wulgu, I'll never understand how you can move a body as large as yours so quietly. I smelt you long before I heard you." He rose to his feet, brushing the seat of his pants. A tall man himself, Spence craned his neck to look up at the expressive though hair-covered face of the yowie.

The yowie frowned, a sight that would terrify most humans. *You are making fun of me again? I have told you, every creature has its own smell. It is how we identify each other. Even you would have a proper smell if you did not wash so much.* An amused look entered Wulgu's eyes, his lips drawing back to reveal enormous canines. His nose snuffed the air gently. *Actually, your smell develops nicely, old friend. Another few days out here and you will be fit for any decent company.*

Spence chuckled and took out his water bottle, drinking thirstily. "Did you find any sign?"

"*Yes. About a mile...*" The thought had popped into Spence's head as an entirely different measurement, but his mind automatically translated it into the old imperial measurements of his youth. "*...upstream. I have left Munda and Oonoo there to watch for it.*" The yowie hunkered down beside the stream, scooping water into its hand and drinking. *I know we must find out about these creatures but I do not like to get close to them. They are wrong somehow.*

"What do you mean 'wrong'? Out of place, I'll grant you, but these big cats most likely are just escaped pumas or something. You know what a puma is, my friend?"

Wulgu nodded silently. *I know of these pumas, but any animal that has lived with man carries the taint of man with it. These cats do not. They smell wrong, they look wrong, they behave wrong.* He shook his head, a troubled look on his face, then rose and stretched. *Come, old man, let us find these things for you.*

Spence nodded and fell into step behind the yowie as it crossed the stream and walked slowly up the valley. *Interesting,* he thought. *When I came out here to investigate that report I was sure it was just another case of mistaken identity, a large dog--just possibly an escaped puma from...where? What does Wulgu know of them?*

His mind recalled the brief newspaper report. A couple out tramping the Warrumbungle ranges had been surprised at dusk by a large black cat. They had stood petrified as it crouched in the trail, snarling at them before bounding off into the bushes. They beat a hasty retreat and notified the papers from a park ranger's office. They had described it as being as big as a lion, jet-black and with large glowing eyes.

Even allowing for natural exaggeration, Spence thought, *it sounds impressive.* An impressive sounding story could be far removed from reality though. Spence had, in a lifetime of searching for strange animals, found that the bulk of them had little basis in fact. One never knew though, which kept him looking for the odd gemstone in the piles of pebbles. The yowies themselves were one of the brightest diamonds in his jewel box.

Spence bumped into Wulgu as he stood motionless on the faint track leading through the bush. "Sorry," he muttered.

Please be quiet, now, old friend. We near the place. Talk only with your mind. Wulgu's nostrils twitched and he pointed off to one side.

Spence searched the undergrowth with his eyes. Excitement mounted as he picked up on a slight movement. For long seconds he stared at a dark form crouched beneath a dense stand of paperbarks and tried to identify the shape. A hand moved and he suddenly recognised the shape as that of Oonoo, a young female yowie. Wulgu moved slowly over to the paperbarks and crouched beside Oonoo. Spence reached out and laid his hand on her hairy shoulder briefly. *Gidday, Oonoo,* he thought.

A pair of inky eyes set in dark, almost black hair stared back at him. *I see you, old man. Wulgu told us you would join us. Are your friends here too? Gaia?* She peered hopefully over his shoulder.

Not this time, Oonoo. I come to see these creatures you have found. Spence shifted his weight, rustling the leaves under him gently.

Wulgu stiffened and raised his hand, pointing across a small clearing. *Munda has seen the beast. It killed a wallaby an hour ago but did not feed.* He scowled, his hands clenching. *All creatures must eat, even meat-eaters, but this thing kills for pleasure. It destroys but does not eat. It is not natural.* The huge male yowie paused again, listening to his unseen companion. *It has entered a vine thicket.* He rose abruptly and gestured. *Come, we shall observe it.*

Spence followed Wulgu and Oonoo towards the side of the valley. A small dry creek bed opened up in front of them as they silently climbed upward, clambering across boulders and logs. A huge, shaggy cloud of golden hair detached itself from the clay walls ahead of them and padded over. The yowie nodded briefly at Spence and pointed into the shadows of a dense vine thicket a hundred metres further up the valley.

Wulgu turned to Spence. *Munda says it is still there.* He hesitated, looking deep into Spence's eyes. *Old friend, we do not try to kill this thing, or capture it. We will only show it to you. You understand? If it lives it has a right to freedom, though we may disapprove of its actions. We only seek to know it.*

I understand. Spence nodded and smiled at the three huge hairy faces.

Wulgu nodded. *Wait here beside this boulder. We will drive it out, down the creek.*

The yowies turned and silently melted into the undergrowth. Minutes passed. Spence shifted from one foot to another impatiently, wiping sweat from his brow, feeling his shirt sticking to his back. He scanned the edges of the vine thicket, watching for the slightest movement. His mind remembered some pictures he had seen recently of a strange beast photographed on Dartmoor in England. It had been labeled a large cat, but its body seemed to morph between successive frames, resembling a wild boar, a panther, or a hyena. *What sort of animal looks so very different only seconds apart?*

Abruptly a series of screams and hoots rent the still, hot air. Trees shook. A shadow slipped silently from the vine thicket and flowed over the boulders in the streambed toward him. Spence sucked in his breath as the black form rushed down upon him and silently slipped past him. *A cat,* he thought, *a bloody huge cat!*

As if he had spoken aloud, the cat stopped in its tracks and turned its head toward him. Its eyes flashed green and it snarled, a low rumble starting deep in its chest and rising sharply in pitch to a yowling scream. The long black tail slashed at the air as it fixed Spence with a predatory stare. It stepped toward the old man, slowly and deliberately.

Spence froze. His mind struggled to wrap itself around the sight of a huge black cat stalking him. *This cannot be. There are no large cats in this land of marsupials. And it...it's not a puma, the body's all wrong...*

A rock shattered on a boulder beside the cat and it flinched. It swung its head back up the creek bed and spat, its ears flattening in rage at the sight of three huge yowies crashing through the undergrowth toward it. The cat turned and sprang, leaping lithely downstream. It raced over a flat sandy area and, just before it reached the bushes on the far side, abruptly faded from sight, disappearing between one step and the next.

Wulgu loped up to Spence and laid a hand on his shoulder. *It has gone, old friend.* He smiled, showing white fangs. *You are unhurt?*

Spence breathed out noisily and sat down on a boulder. *I will be when my heart stops thumping.* He looked downstream to the sandy area where Munda and Oonoo were cautiously investigating. *Where did it go? I could have sworn it just faded out before it reached the trees. It certainly didn't crash into them.*

Wulgu frowned and nodded. *It has 'gone over', old friend. We do not know where it goes but it ceases to be 'here'. We can no longer feel the presence of its mind.* He shrugged, a surprisingly human gesture. *Perhaps you should ask your friend Amaru, she knows many things of this and other worlds.*

Spence nodded and stood shakily. "I will. That thing was incredible! I'd call it a cat but it wasn't any species of cat I've seen. If only I'd had my camera..."

Would your camera have worked?

Spence nodded, grimacing. "You're right of course. The chances are good that the camera would not have worked." *It's strange how that happens. UFOs, ghosts, big cats, Nessie--anything paranormal plays merry hell with electronic equipment. Most photos of oddities are hoaxes, and most of the rest are hopelessly blurred or out of focus.* "I'd still like to have tried though."

His voice trailed off as Munda loped over to Wulgu.

We are recalled, Wulgu. They did not say why, but old friend here must return immediately. Amaru sends an urgent plea.

Wulgu turned to Spence. *You must obey.* He looked around, orienting himself with the sun. *Come, there is a portal two hours from here.*

The giant yowie set off down the creek bed, the other two falling into step behind him. Their long legs and limber stride ate up ground at an amazing pace. Spence groaned and staggered after them. "For God's sake, slow down you chaps. I'm too old to be running in this heat."

8

The old man walked out of the pine forests to the northwest of Medicine Lake and, shading his eyes against the glare of the early morning sun off the clear waters of the lake, regarded the island and its security fences with distaste and concern written on his lined face. Tiny in the distance, he made out the figures of men walking the perimeter and the arrow wake of a boat speeding toward the island's dock. He closed his eyes, but the image of the lake and island remained in his mind as he concentrated on things not readily discerned by the normal senses. Somewhere here was wrongness and he meant to find it and see what he could do to correct it, bring it back into balance.

The old man, who was sometimes known as Moon Wolf to those few men he came in contact with, had seen many wrongs over the years, especially since the coming of the white man. His people had, after the first heady days of exploration, when they found themselves entering a rich land teeming with wild life, lived in harmony with nature. They had moved south between two huge ice sheets as the great cold drew back, wandering across the broad land bridge to the west and down into the North American continent. The People found a feast of food after long years of famine and for a generation or two had spread out across the great plains and wooded hills in an orgy of destruction, killing and burning. In those days he had gone by the name Olelbis, the creator spirit of the people who were later known as the Wintun. Great had been Moon Wolf's anger when faced by the disrespect of the tribes, and he had withdrawn his favour from the People. They heeded the lesson and as time passed, the tribes learned balance and worked with the land, claiming ownership over nothing, harvesting the beasts and the plants, the rocks and the water as needed, cherishing every object as the habitation of a spirit to be respected and praised, a fragment of Wokwuk, Olelbis' own son. The one who was called Olelbis, in the days before he took a man's name, had been something different from these nature spirits. He could become spirit or man at will and held sway over the lesser spirits, guiding them, teaching them and responding to their needs. In time, Olelbis became known as the Great Spirit, though he was not the Supreme Creator Spirit others thought him to be. His aegis was the west, from the towering mountains to the sea, and little took place within his realm of which he was not aware. He made his home on Mount Shasta, or as it was known then, Bulyum-pui-yuk.

The white men came in ships from over the ocean, then overland, and within the space of a hundred years or so, an eye blink in time to one such as he, overran the tribes and destroyed the land. Almost too late, a handful of the white men saw their error and tried to save something of what was left, but their hearts were not in it, being ruled by greed and self-interest. Moon Wolf had sought out the spirits of these new pale people, but was shocked to find that even their spirits were warped by dark thoughts. Their Great Spirit apparently had given the land and its bounty into the white man's hand, to do with as they pleased. Once the destruction of their own lands had robbed them of all balance, they sought to do the same to the lands of others, sparing no regard for the rights of the indigenous peoples.

The situation was little better now, even though the white man was at last learning responsibility. Moon Wolf had withdrawn almost completely from the great cities that sprawled across the southern parts of his western realm, finding little balance in the concrete hills and valleys, the choking air and filthy water. The lesser spirits had withdrawn also, leaving the white men to the not-so-gentle ministrations of their own dark spirits. He withdrew to the snow-capped mountains, wooded hills and grassy meadows sprinkled with wildflowers, to clean air and crystal water, where nature spirits were so abundant you could not walk through the forests without the babble of their joyful cries and the jostle of their insubstantial being. Their presence brought joy to the heart and uplifted the spirit, a fact which was becoming known even to the white men who, in increasing numbers, sought to escape the cities and seek out the unspoiled wilderness for a short time. Some came to stay longer, however--men still wedded to the soulless cities but feeling the need of something pure in their lives.

Morgan Turner was one of these. His grandfather had come to Medicine Lake, bought the island and set up his home, excluding others who also sought its peace, and passed on ownership of the island to his son and grandson. For many years Morgan Turner lived in harmony with the spirits of the island before darkness entered his mind and he burrowed beneath the earth, building things that reeked of wrongness. The Turner man preserved the forest and allowed the birds to nest where they had for generations, but the spirits of the island withdrew into silence, fearful of the growing shadow.

Moon Wolf heard their cry and came, but what he found was worse than he had feared. The darkness was no longer just on the island in Medicine Lake-- it had spread to nearby Glass Mountain.

Glass Mountain was sacred to all the tribes of the Medicine Lake highlands and was a valuable supply of sharp-sided volcanic glass that could be used locally or traded up and down the coast. Turner's burrowing had taken him deep below the sacred site and awoken or provoked dark forces. Moon Wolf had striven to get to grips with these forces but had to acknowledge defeat in the end. Their feel and flavour was alien, like nothing he had ever encountered, and his magic slid off them, leaving them unharmed. He had returned to Mount Shasta to think and prepare, but now was back at Medicine Lake again.

Moon Wolf sat down on a mossy stump on a knoll overlooking the lake, and coaxed his old man's body into a cross-legged position. Being a spirit, he was not subject to time and entropy, and he could just as well have adopted the form of a young man, but in his dealings with men, he had found them much more likely to do his bidding if he appeared as an elder, an ancient man with all the authority of long experience. So he folded his jeans-clad legs slowly and tugged at the sleeves of his plaid shirt, getting comfortable. A bluebottle fly winged out of the forest and settled on one worn boot. Moon Wolf concentrated on it, seeing himself reflected a thousand times in the tiny facets of its compound eyes. A lined, sun-darkened face topped with long white hair drawn back and fastened with a carved bone clasp stared back as he contemplated the insect.

"Greetings, Brother Fly," he said softly. "What news have you for me?"

Moon Wolf sat in silence, as if listening. The sounds of the forest merged with the drone of the boat on the lake and the distant whisper of a jet passing far overhead. Sunshine bathed him in warmth and the lake surface reflected shards of dancing light.

"Your news is heavy," Moon Wolf murmured. "Be assured I will do what I can. Be ready if I should call."

The bluebottle fly buzzed off into the depths of the forest and the old man looked out toward the island again, probing beyond sight and into the passages that ran beneath the lake and under Glass Mountain. He saw men and women, soldiers and scientists, and a large machine, but could not determine its use. The stain of wrongness lay not on the machine, but on the spirits of many of the men and women who tended it, but still he could not see...aah, there...Moon Wolf saw a flicker of movement, a shape, a shadow in the darkness, an uncleanness that was alien to the touch...and it saw him.

Moon Wolf broke the connection quickly and snapped his consciousness back across the lake to his waiting body. With his physical eyes he saw a faint beam of darkness stab through the brightness of the day, roiling as if composed of smoke. It swept swiftly over the countryside before concentrating on the lake and its surrounding forests. He closed his eyes. Children close their eyes in the belief that if they cannot see the danger it cannot see them, but Moon wolf closed his for a different reason. He knew that his consciousness provided a connection that the enemy could use, so he deliberately turned his mind elsewhere. The shadow beam swept over him and away, dissipating like vapour on a hot day.

Moon Wolf withdrew into the cool dimness of the pine forest where the whisper of air through myriad pine needles soothed him with a fragrant susurration. He admitted to himself that he was worried, for the strength of the shadows beneath the mountain was far greater than he had supposed. Men called him Olelbis, the Creator Spirit, but he knew that identification was false. He never claimed to be the Creator but sometimes things could be accomplished with the right amount of authority, so he did not always correct mistaken assumptions. It was an innocent fiction for the most part as he was a powerful spirit, even if not the supreme one. But not powerful enough, he feared--at least, not alone.

What resources do I have? Moon Wolf considered first the many nature spirits that would answer his call with varying degrees of enthusiasm. Nature spirits were not his to command by right, but could generally be relied upon to render service if presented with a cogent argument. Of course, the majority of spirits inhabited small things--pebbles, plants, insects and tiny creatures. Their assistance would be of no more than nuisance value, a distraction whilst the real blow came from another quarter.

The Great Spirits? Hard to persuade and harder still to control. Beings like the Sasquatch, the Thunderbird or the Black Beasts could surely cope with a menace such as that under Glass Mountain but what would they want in return? Moon Wolf knew of shamans who had raised these spirits and then could not control them, unleashing them on their fellow men until their energy ran out and they returned to the spirit realm. He would not deal there except as a last resort.

What of men? Men were like the Great Spirits in that they were unreliable. Having great strength of purpose and possessing bravery out of all proportion to the strength of their bodies, they could be very useful, particularly in combating other humans, like those who lived beneath the mountain. However, they had a strong attachment to their mates and offspring and had, in the past, deserted a cause for no greater reason than loneliness. Humans could be used judiciously, and Moon wolf knew of men on whom he could call. The indigenous population had suffered enormously with the advent of the white man, but there was one tribe who had not accepted the White Great Spirit, but clung stubbornly to their native ways, gods and language. They were very few now, and mostly too old for physical combat, but Moon Wolf knew of a handful of young men of the Wintun tribe who would rally to him.

Who else? There is another--face it. Moon Wolf's mind had shied away from this alternative at the start, but he kept returning to it like a blowfly to rotten meat. What was happening under Glass Mountain was within his jurisdiction. It affected the spirits and people of the Medicine Lake highlands, No one else. Therefore he should only involve the spirits and people of the highlands...*yet, I am tempted.* On an impulse, he concentrated and broadcast a summons. In physical terms it went out south and west, though in terms of its spiritual nature, Moon Wolf thoughts did not have to travel to circle the globe. Almost instantly, he got his answer.

Olelbis? Moon Wolf? It has been a long time, my friend...

Wandjina. I...I have a problem.

Wait a moment, please. Moon Wolf became aware that Wandjina was talking to others close by, though he could not hear what was said. After a few minutes, the mental voice returned.

Sorry, what was it you wanted to discuss, Olelbis?

I have a problem.

*So do I. The elder humans...*an image of hairy, muscular humans with prognathous features drifted into Moon Wolf's mind...*are under attack.*

The old man hesitated. *I am sorry for your troubles but I cannot offer assistance. Rather, I need your help.*

Now the mind of the one called Wandjina displayed hesitation. *I do not need your assistance, Olelbis, but I cannot spare the time right now to help you. Can you wait half a year?*

No. Moon Wolf felt almost relieved at being turned down. *I will seek help elsewhere.*

Silence dragged on for many minutes before Wandjina spoke again. *Maybe I can offer advice?*

Perhaps. I, too, am under attack.

You, Olelbis? What could possibly attack you?

I am not Olelbis, as well you know.

I know, Moon Wolf, yet even so, what could attack you?

Shadows.

Shadows?

Yes. Human-shaped, black, having no substance, wrong.

I know them.

You do? How?

They attacked the humans, both elder and new, here in Australia.

How did you prevail?

With difficulty. As you say, they are without substance, yet are not spirit, as you and I.

What was their purpose?

An edge of grim humour tinged Wandjina's thoughts. *They did not say. However, I have my thoughts on the matter.*

Yes?

I will not say just yet. We can be overheard and I do not want them to know I suspect.

You can give me no clue? Your insights may help me combat them here.

That is what I cannot understand, Moon Wolf. I believe their purpose is local, intimately connected with the elder humans, so why are they troubling you?

Perhaps you should come over here and see for yourself.

To Mount Shasta? The spiritual coordinates of the Californian volcano leaked around the edges of his thoughts. *I do not know why they should be there, but I cannot believe it is of pressing importance. My first concern must be with the elder humans and my tribes.*

That is as it should be, Wandjina. However, it is not Mount Shasta they attack, but Glass Mountain.

Glass Mountain? Wandjina was silent for a time. *I do not believe in coincidences. What is this mountain that they should attack it?*

Not the mountain itself, but a human excavation beneath it where men are building a machine.

What is the purpose of the machine?

I do not know. You said you do not believe in coincidences--why do you say that?

All events in the universe are connected. You know that.

Yes, but what is the significance of this one?

The place they attack in Australia is the Glass House Mountains, Wandjina said. *Beneath it, a group of elder humans have excavated a base and are working...well, toward their purpose. This purpose the shadows oppose. I cannot believe it is coincidence that two places named for glass are both targeted by these creatures. There must be a connection.*

Then you will come?

I will come...but not yet. There are things I must see to here. It would not do to leave this place undefended.

Of course not. Tell me when you are coming, Wandjina. Until then, I shall muster what forces I can.

I cannot tell you what to do in your own realm, Olelbis, but be cautious. These creatures are not to be taken lightly.

Moon Wolf stretched and got to his feet, moving slowly as worn joints protested. He laughed at his own conceit and at once his body flowed and changed, becoming younger and stronger. White hair darkened and the lines in his face and hands vanished as if rubbed away. It was many miles to the Wintun village and though Moon Wolf could have travelled as a spirit, he preferred the way of a human. *I must not forget to age again before I see the young men; else they will not know me.*

He set off through the sighing pine forest, a bluebottle fly accompanying him half a hundred paces. A careful observer, miles away across the forest, might have noted the shaft of sunlight that lit the treetops as he walked. The brightness followed him as if clouds refused to hide the sun when he passed, though that same observer might have marvelled at the way the clouds moved contrary to the wind. Unseen, the fragments of Wokwuk that were fly and squirrel, pine and cloud, water and earth, the myriad elements that made up the world, followed Moon Wolf, ready to do his bidding.

9

Nathan shifted uncomfortably as he sat cross-legged on the ground. His skin felt hot and damp, the air still and suffocating in the clearing of the Far North Queensland rainforest. Cicadas whirred in the trees and butterflies danced around a cascade of red blossoms at the far end of the clearing, the only movement to disturb the forest. Somewhere nearby was a pool of stagnant water, judging by the number of mosquitoes whining around his head. He swatted at them viciously, wishing he'd never come on this trip. *I shouldn't be here. I have important things to do, more important than chasing through the rainforest after some deluded old man.* He looked over at his young wife Ratana, who sat near the entrance of the little bark lean-to. She wore jeans and a tee shirt, with heavy bush boots, yet appeared calm and relaxed--cool almost; as if on a photo shoot rather than on an arduous trek through rugged country. *How does she manage to look so neat and happy?* he wondered.

He slapped his forearm, noting with satisfaction the smear of blood from the dead mosquito. "Ratana, this is pointless. I don't believe he is coming at all. We should go home."

Ratana looked round with a smile. "He will be here, my beloved. We must be patient." She got lightly to her feet and stepped away from the shelter, sitting down beside him. She put her hand on his arm and leaned over to kiss his cheek. "It is a great honour to learn from Wandjina himself and we..."

"Why do you insist on using that name? Do you think he is literally one of the Creator Spirits of our people's Dreamtime?" Nathan snorted and got to his feet. "He is just an old man who likes to feel important. But there are better, more direct ways to further our cause."

"Nathan, have you forgotten the things we saw and did in the Glass House Mountains? You were there. You know he sent James and Sam through the portal to the Blue Mountains. You saw him scatter the shadows outside Emerald and talk to the wild ones of the forest, the Yowies. How did he do those things if he is just an old man?"

Nathan shuffled his feet and avoided Ratana's gaze. "I'm sure there is a rational explanation for all of those things. Would you have me believe in myths and spirits?"

Ratana sighed as she rose. "My love, you have spent too much time at the university and not enough of it with your people. You have learnt the lesson of the white man too well. You deny the evidence of your own eyes."

"Listen to her, my son. She speaks the truth." A whisper came from the forest, causing Nathan to swing round, searching for the source.

"Ernie, is that you?" Nathan strode out into the middle of the small clearing, turning his head back and forth. "Where are you?"

Ratana smiled gently and pointed to the side of the bark shelter. "See, he comes." Nathan stared in that direction but saw nothing. He frowned, and then spun on his heel, searching the forest edges again.

"I am here." The air shimmered and the figure of an old Aboriginal man stepped out of the air from beside the shelter. "Greetings, daughter." He smiled and nodded as Ratana bobbed her head and knelt submissively in front of him.

Nathan shook his head. *For a moment there I could have sworn he just stepped out of thin air. He must have been in the forest behind the shelter.* He nodded perfunctorily at the old man and spread his feet, folding his arms defensively in front of him. "So what do you want with us, Ernie? I should be with my friends, the young men of our tribe, preventing the miners from raping our land."

"There are more important things for you to do, my son. Come, sit beside me. We must talk." He gestured at the ground beside him as he folded his legs gracefully and sat beside Ratana.

Nathan walked over reluctantly and stood above the pair. "Even your attitude to women is antiquated and insulting. Do you truly expect the women of today to kneel at your feet and do your every bidding?" he sneered.

Ernie looked up, his eyes hardening. Nathan flinched involuntarily. "I expect the honour due to an elder of the tribe. I expect a civil tongue from a youth, and I expect a mind that is open instead of filled with the white man's modern theories." He gestured quickly with his hand and barked a command. "Sit!"

Nathan was sitting before he realised he had moved. He made a feeble attempt to rise, and then thought better of it. Ratana smiled encouragingly, reaching over to take his hand. Nathan shrugged away from his wife, muttering, "You could at least back me up."

Ernie sat silently, observing the young couple. As the silence drew out he noted with approval that Ratana sat quietly, waiting, and her eyes downcast. Nathan however, fidgeted, picking at twigs on the ground, snapping them and flicking the bits away. He glanced around constantly, looked at his watch or swatted at the ever-present mosquitoes. Ernie sighed gently. "Do they trouble you?" He gestured and the whining stopped abruptly.

Nathan snapped his head up to stare at Ernie. "How the hell did you do...?"

"How do you think I did it? Tell me."

Nathan squirmed. "Er...you probably, er...some sort of repellent I suppose." When Ernie shook his head, he shrugged. "They probably just stopped anyway. Insects come and go as they please."

"I asked them to stop."

Nathan laughed uneasily. "You're kidding, right?"

Ernie shook his head again. "You could do that as easily as I, were you to bend your mind to it." The old man paused and searched the younger man's face before continuing. "Nathan, you trained as a scientist, did you not? Then tell me of your beliefs as a scientist. I want to know."

Nathan shrugged and looked away. "I believe in what I can prove. Anything worthy of belief must be testable, must be able to be measured, be quantifiable. I cannot believe in this idea that the things of myth that old women chatter about round the campfire have any reality." He shook his head. "There must always be a logical, scientific explanation."

"But you were there in the Glass House Mountains, at the feet of the Twins. You experienced what we all did; you even talked to a hairy one of the forest. Do you not believe in your own eyes?"

"I remember bits of a vision." Nathan put his hand to his head. "I have dreams but I cannot remember them completely. I know we went down to the mountains and trekked into the bush, looking for Doctor Hay's black stone. I...I remember a cavern, I think, and...and ugly people. I have nightmares of choking, of being chased by...by things, and of searching. But we found nothing..." he looked imploringly at Ratana. "Did we?"

Ratana looked worried. "I don't think he remembers, Wandjina. You told us not to speak of it and we never have, not even to each other. But I remember it all vividly."

Ernie pursed his lips. "This should not have happened to you, Nathan. Forgetfulness was necessary for our companion, Marc. He could not handle what he saw and besides, he was not of our kind." The old man reached over and touched Nathan's forehead lightly with his forefinger. "There is darkness here," he muttered. "I had not thought them so strong."

"Who is strong, Wandjina?" inquired Ratana. "What do you mean?"

"The Shadow People. They go by many names, child. Think back to the tales of the Dreamtime. Do you remember tales of the Quinkan? You saw them at Tunbubudla."

Ratana gasped. "I don't...yes, I remember now. They attacked us at Emerald, I know, I can remember that...and...and again at Tunbubudla. How could I forget that second time? It was even more horrible than the first."

"You put them from your mind, Ratana. It was a protection for you. Now you must remember."

Nathan screwed up his face in concentration. "The Quinkan? They are supposed to be evil spirits that live in rock crevices, aren't they? How does a Dreamtime myth affect me?"

"Tell me, Nathan. What is an evil spirit?"

Nathan snorted, and then shrugged. "Okay, I'll play along. Let me see...an evil spirit would be a supernatural creature of great power that tries to harm people. Right?"

Ernie smiled. "Right. Except they are not supernatural. I believe the Quinkan are a race of beings that come from outside our world. Somehow, the barrier between our world and the world of the Quinkan weakens from time to time. The last time it happened the effect was so horrific that they entered our stories as evil spirits."

The old man drew a hand slowly across his face and sighed. "The barriers are again weakening and the Quinkan return. For some reason they are attracted to you, Nathan, and have clouded your mind. It is strange how they twist the minds of men of science, ones that do not believe in the higher, unseen things. Your university education works against you here. I must try to remedy this."

"Wandjina, father...how can these...things, know my husband?" Ratana gripped Nathan's hand hard, a look of anguish on her face.

"On the slopes of Tunbubudla, daughter. The Shadows attacked you and apparently invaded Nathan, getting into his body. I thought they had been expelled when he passed through the rock portal. Only physical things should be able to pass through those portals."

"But why? Why do they target my husband?"

"I do not know. There must be something within his mind that attracts them, that allows them access. Through him, the Shadow People have infiltrated the Neanderthal base and perhaps learned of our purpose."

"What purpose is that, Wandjina?"

"That is not for you to know," Ernie reproved. "Well, that cannot be corrected, but I must ensure it cannot happen again. Now stay very still, Nathan. I must summon extraordinary power."

Ernie placed his hands on either side of Nathan's head, gripping his hair firmly in his fingers. "Close your eyes, boy. Try to think of nothing." The old man closed his own eyes and became very still. After a few moments he groaned, a sweat starting on his forehead.

Ratana listened closely as Ernie started a low chant. His voice deepened and the words became clearer, but they remained meaningless to her. Some of them had a vague resemblance to her tribal dialect, or Nathan's, but others just seemed like gibberish. Her mouth dropped slightly as a faint glow appeared around the old man's head, a white nimbus that quickly grew stronger. Little flecks of coloured light burst from his body and swirled about him, drifting like fireflies on a warm summer's night or darting like sparks carried in the strong updraft of a fire.

Ernie's voice started getting louder, the tempo quickening. The white light expanded to envelop Nathan's head, pouring in through nostrils and mouth like smoke. The young man groaned then his mouth flew open and he cried out loud--an incoherent cry of loss and despair. A vague, half-formed shadow flitted out of his mouth, rushed across the clearing, and disappeared into the green gloom under the forest trees. The white light snapped out and Ernie released Nathan's head. The young man fell backwards onto the ground and lay still, his only sign of life being the regular rise and fall of his chest.

"He will be all right in a few minutes, daughter. He is strong."

Ratana knelt beside her husband, stroking his brow and squeezing his hand. "Has the thing left him, father?"

Ernie nodded. "I have cleansed him of the Shadow that remained within."

Nathan groaned again and stirred at the sound of his voice. His eyes opened, looking in astonishment at the two people bending over him. "What happened?" He sat up and looked around him, puzzled. "This is tropical forest. How did we get here? I can't remember."

Ernie leaned forward and peered into Nathan's eyes. "What did I do with the ring of black stones, Nathan?"

Nathan frowned. "What black stones, Wandjina?"

"The ones on the slopes of Tunbubudla."

"Oh, those ones. You opened a portal, Wandjina. Did we get here through a portal?" Nathan looked around for the ring of black stones.

Ernie smiled and turned to Ratana. "His mind is whole again. You must tell him what has happened, beloved daughter. I must leave you for a while as I have been summoned by...well, let us say by a person far away. I will return as soon as I can. Then we must talk seriously. You two have a lot to learn, a lot of training if you are to take your places as leaders of our people. I fear the time grows short."

The old man got up fluidly and walked toward the bark shelter. As Nathan and Ratana watched, Ernie abruptly vanished, stepping through air to another place.

Nathan smiled. "He loves making spectacular entrances and exits." He turned to Ratana. "So, my love, what must you tell me? What has been happening here?"

10

N early two months passed before Dr Spindler was satisfied the Vox Dei was working again. Travis Parker had howled that the 'old Nazi' was dragging his feet, insisting on everything being absolutely perfect rather than just workable. Parker was over-ruled though, and the team gathered a few weeks later in the cavernous laboratory to witness the final screwing on of the last control panel cover.

Morgan Turner was there to see it and watched carefully as the last bolts were tightened. "It's all finished then?" he asked Spindler.

"Ja. It is finished," the old scientist replied.

"It could have been ready weeks ago," Parker grumbled. "Except someone wanted not only triple but quadruple checks of every system. It's all positively Teutonic."

"Could have been worse," Braun said with a sneer. "You might have had to do some work."

"But it is working?" Morgan asked. "Fully functional? You've done tests?"

"We've done all the tests necessary," Andi said quietly. "Vox Dei is operational."

"Ja, it vill vork," confirmed Spindler.

Morgan nodded. "Good. Then I want you to dismantle it, carefully, and reassemble it in the north cavern."

"What?" Parker screamed. "Are you out of your mind?"

Spindler gaped, the shut his mouth and frowned. "Vy do you vant it moved? It vill vork here as vell as anyvere else."

"It really is not a good idea," Braun observed. "The apparatus is quite delicate and to take it apart and reassemble will involve many days, possibly weeks."

"Well, I'm sorry about that," Morgan said, "But it needs to be done, so please let's have no temper tantrums. Just get the job done."

"Ve are scientists. Ve do not do the temper tantrums," Spindler said coldly.

"Speak for yourself," Braun muttered under his breath. "That's Parker's normal state."

"Why do we need to shift it?" April asked, a pleasant smile on her face. "We were told that this laboratory was the ideal place."

"I'm sorry, but I don't really know the answer to that question," Morgan replied. He looked around at the assembled scientists. "Look, I'll level with you. I'm the man who holds the purse strings of this project, but the men behind it are General Spader and...well, somebody who wishes to remain anonymous for the time being." He glanced at Andi's face but his own revealed nothing. "This laboratory was ideal when we started, but I have been told that the north cavern is better for the next phase."

"And what is the next phase?"

"We are to test it on an external target."

"External?" April asked.

Morgan nodded. "Outside the base. We are fortunate to have the army involved. We can use military personnel as targets."

"Vereabouts? Vat is this target ve are to use?"

"You'll be told that when you have everything ready. Now, can you please get started on the move?"

"It's not as easy as that," Parker snapped. "It's not just the machine itself, but all the ancillary equipment, the power source, the..."

"All taken care of. I've had technicians duplicating everything you have here."

"How long have you known about this move?" April asked.

"A few weeks," Morgan replied vaguely. "We still had to make sure the Vox worked properly, so there didn't seem much point in telling you."

"The north cavern is a storage area," Braun said. "It's full of supplies. We can't work in a janitor's closet."

"Not any longer. It is empty except for the power supply and laboratory equipment."

"Well, that's okay then," Andi said with a grin. "The sooner started the sooner finished, guys." She picked up a spanner and started loosening the bolts on an access panel.

"How to rise to the top of your profession with a brown nose," Braun muttered.

"Flat on your back, more like," Parker sneered.

Morgan's jaw clenched and he stared at Parker for a few moments before whirling on his heel and stalking from the room.

The scientists worked quickly but carefully, dismantling the Vox Dei, breaking it down into small enough pieces to negotiate the corridors and doorways of the underground base. The taking apart only took two days, and the transport to the north cavern another day, but then started the long and laborious task of putting it all together. The vast array of lenses and shaped quartz crystals, the delicately shaped fibres and conduits required precision fitting and constant testing. The addition of each segment of the array called for nanometric placement and individual adjustment. Each new piece added meant all those that had gone before needed to be measured again and realigned. Slowly, the long crystal-filled tube took shape, while the electronic and magnetic components grew apace.

After two weeks, it was ready for testing. The electricity poured in, the laser fired up to maximum efficiency, and the magnetic fields initiated, but all that came out the end was a blast of laser energy that split the target slab of granite and filled the cavern with a cacophony of electronic noise. Every circuit was checked and every refractive crystal was realigned and tested individually and in concert, and then again, before Andi noticed a hairline crack in one of the niobium impregnated crystals in the quaternary array. With that one replaced and calibrated, they tried again.

This time, the guidance laser stabbed out for a nanosecond, lightly singeing the crosspiece of the paper target stuck to the granite slab. With the laser switched off, the carrier beam bathed the target in invisible energies, only detectable by the array of tiny electrodes packed closely around the target.

"How much spread have we got?" Braun asked.

"The beam has a diameter of just over a millimetre," Andi said. "Is that on the 'broad' setting?"

"Of course. I'd be bloody incompetent if that was the level of accuracy at the narrowest."

"Very good then, Doctor. Please narrow the focus."

Braun made some cautious adjustments. "Mid-range," he stated.

"That's better, we're down to a tenth of a millimetre diameter at a target distance of ten metres."

"What sort of target distance is needed?" April asked.

Spindler shrugged. "It is an army project, so I vood imagine vithin a battle situation. Say ten kilometres or so."

Parker did some quick calculations. "That would be out to ten metres wide by then, maybe more if environmental conditions like cloud or dust spread the beam."

Andi laughed out loud. "Haven't you been looking at the specifications of this carrier beam? Forget about the laser finder--that'll spread like you say--but the carrier's something totally different."

"What the hell are you talking about, Jones?"

"She's right," Spindler said. "The carrier beam isn't attenuated by anything--not cloud, not dust, not even solid rock. You could send that beam right through a range of mountains and it would still be as narrow as...as..."

"As your mind," April crowed.

"Of course, you'd need more power than we have on the base," Braun added. "But it could be done."

Parker flushed scarlet, and muttered incoherently. "How was I supposed to know that?"

"Try reading the project reports," Braun sneered.

"Please," Spindler interrupted. "Can we continue with the test? Mister Turner and General Spader are impatient to start the next phase."

"Sure, no skin off my nose," Parker said with a shrug. "Braun, be so good as to narrow the focus still further, will you."

Braun muttered to himself but made some careful adjustments to the controls. "There, that's about as good as we can get. What's the spread like, Jones?"

"Zero point zero-five-two of a millimetre," Andi said, reading off the displays from the sensors.

"Is that all? That's not much better than at mid-range. I'd hoped for more--or rather, less."

"Try looking at it another way. The aperture through which the beam exits the array is precisely zero point zero-five millimetre in diameter. That means that over a ten meter range it has only expanded point zero-zero-two millimetres. I'd say that's pretty damn good by any standard."

Parker's fingers were dancing over the keys of his calculator. "You are only looking at a few millimetres dispersion at ten kilometres. You could pinpoint an enemy soldier."

"And do what to him?" Andi asked.

"That is for others to decide," Spindler said primly. "We do our job and our superiors make the decisions."

"Maybe you could feed him April's encounter," Parker grinned. "That would confuse the hell out of him."

"These jokes are not appropriate," Spindler stated. "We will run through these tests once more to be sure before I notify Mister Turner that we are ready."

It was another hour before Spindler was satisfied that everything was in readiness. He telephoned Turner and listened intently to a series of instructions before hanging up.

"Mister Turner vants the little machine as vell for the demonstration. He and General Spader vill be here in about half an hour. So, Braun and Parker, please bring through the little machine from the laboratory. Newman, you vill bring chairs for our guests and Jones, you vill please organise coffee from the canteen."

April complained about her menial task, but Andi just shrugged and got on with it.

"And what are you going to be doing while we run around like your servants?" Parker asked.

"Someone must lead," Spindler replied, "And it has been given to me to do so. I vill go over the machine one last time vile you are making the other things ready."

Forty minutes later, when Morgan stepped through into the north cavern with General Spader, his aide Captain Anders and Lieutenant Evans, everything was ready for them. Morgan and Spader accepted a seat and a cup of coffee, while the other officers stood to one side.

"So, what have you got for me?" Spader growled.

Morgan nodded to the team of scientists. "Great things, General. Dr Spindler, would you please, without unnecessary scientific terminology, introduce the machine."

"Certainly, Mr Turner. General Spader, we call this machine the Vox Dei because it can be thought of literally as the 'Voice of God'--God speaking quietly and convincingly into a man's mind. We have built a device that is capable of targeting a group of people at almost any distance and implanting in their minds an idea, a thought, a vision, so intense that they would be unable to distinguish it from reality. We can, with this machine, literally control the thoughts of people, and by controlling the thoughts, we influence their actions."

Jacob Spindler walked over to the Vox Dei and put his hand on the long barrel. "We have here a powerful laser which we use to fire up the main beam. It also serves as a sighting mechanism in that we can aim it with incredible precision at a nearby target, knowing that it is also precisely fixed on the main target which may be ten or even a hundred kilometres away..."

General Spader stirred and opened his mouth to speak before thinking better of it and signing for Spindler to continue.

"As I was saying, General," Spindler continued, "The laser beam has a dual purpose--to energise the magnetic beam and to sight it in. The magnetic beam is the real weapon though. Potentially millions of times stronger than the earth's magnetic field, the field within the Vox Dei is like no other field you have ever seen. In fact, it is like no other field anyone has ever seen. We have controlled it and fashioned it into the magnetic equivalent of a laser. The word 'laser' is an acronym for Light Amplification by Stimulated Emission of Radiation. We have used magnetism instead of visible light and created the world's first Magnetaser."

"Clumsy name," Spader's aide commented. "If 'magnet' is replacing 'light' in the name, wouldn't 'maser' be a catchier name."

"Indeed it would, captain, but 'maser' is already taken. It is a laser using microwave radiation." Spindler pursed his lips as if he had taken a bite of a lemon. "To continue, the coherent magnetic beam is used to carry information in sufficient detail to convince the target person of the utter reality of the information being carried."

"I have read the reports," General Spader said, "But surely this is no more than a sophisticated television broadcast. I fail to see how even an extremely lifelike representation is going to convince anyone."

"Television? Faugh, that is nothing," Spindler almost spat the words out. "But let us use that analogy if it is something your mind can grasp. Imagine a dog, your own dog if you have one..." Spader nodded. "Gute, so I send you a television picture of your dog--what do you think? It is really your dog? Nein," Spindler waved his hands vigorously in case anyone had the temerity to interrupt him again. "Of course not, only a fool would think so. So, I add sound--is it now your dog? Nein! I add in smell perhaps--is it your dog? Here perhaps some people might think their dog was somewhere near. I then add touch. You can feel your dog's head under your hand, he licks your face. Is this reality? Nein! You know--know in your mind--that the dog is not there, so I add in that conviction that he is present and your mind accepts the presence of your friend. Ja? Of course, ja."

"Very impassioned, Dr Spindler, but not very convincing," Spader said. "Sight and sound can be conveyed easily enough, they are only photons and pressure waves in the air, but an odour is made up of molecules. There is no way you could send molecules in any beam to convey that information accurately."

"I see, you wish to be convinced. Shall I demonstrate?" Spindler pulled a plastic chair over and stood it in front of the target. "Please, sit there."

"There is no way I'm sitting in front of an untested laser."

Spindler shrugged. "If you are afraid, then send one of your men."

Andi stepped forward as Spader rose from his chair, his face scarlet with suppressed rage. "Dr Spindler, General Spader, please. There is a far better way to demonstrate this. We can use Baby Vox."

Spader turned to face Andi. "You are Dr Andromeda Jones, are you not? You know about this machine?"

"Yes sir. I agree with you actually. We should not be testing the Vox Dei on test subjects yet, but we could certainly use the small machine." She smiled. "We call it Baby Vox, and we've all sat in front of it. There is nothing harmful about its energies." She walked over to the small version and swung it into position. "I think too, we should show you the effect it has on someone else before you try it. Perhaps Lieutenant Evans here?"

Evans looked extremely uncomfortable, but at Spader's order, went and sat on the plastic chair, looking nervously at the open barrel of the small machine.

"There is no need to be fearful, Lieutenant," Andi said. "The machine itself carries no information. It merely provides a concentrated magnetic field that will stimulate portions of your own brain. Your mind will experience a reality that is a construct of your own memories. Think of something pleasant from your childhood. Did you own a dog as a boy?"

Evans nodded. "Yes, a labrador."

"Good. Think of your dog. Keep an image of him in your mind." Andi reached out and turned the Baby Vox on, waited a few moments for the field to build, then released the energies.

Evans gave a cry of delight and dropped to his knees, embracing thin air. "Good boy, Rex, good boy. Where have you been, eh? You want to play?" The man rolled over on his back, laughing, wrestling with something unseen. Andi let the scene continue for a minute, and then snapped the power off.

Lieutenant Evans' laughter cut off abruptly, and he sat up, looking around in apparent bewilderment. "Where'd he go? Rex, Rex, where are you?" To Andi's horror, his face crumpled and the army lieutenant started to weep.

Spader shot to his feet. "Evans, control yourself," he barked. "Good god, man, it was only a...a dream."

Evans sighed deeply and wiped his eyes with his fingers, getting to his feet. He saluted shakily and stumbled back to join the other officer.

"What the hell was that all about?" Parker demanded.

"Never mind." Spader stared at the Baby Vox. "It was that real to him? He actually saw his childhood dog?"

Spindler nodded. "Ja, and we should have realised, if it was a childhood dog, the animal is dead now. We brought the pain of its loss back to him. Lieutenant Evans, you have our sympathies."

"Okay," Spader said. "I want to try it." He walked over to the chair. "My dog is still alive, so I won't be unmanned by the experience," he added with a smile. "Switch on the machine, Dr Jones."

"One moment." Parker held up a hand. "May I ask you a question, General Spader?"

"Yes. What is it?"

Parker smiled. "Area fifty-one, General. Where they keep the alien spacecraft and bodies. What are they really like, those aliens?"

Spader stared at the scientist. "They don't exist, Parker. You've been reading too many comics." He nodded at Andi. "You may proceed, Dr Jones."

As Andi's finger touched the button to switch on the Baby Vox, Parker grinned and said, "Aliens!"

General Spader's jaw dropped and his eyes bulged. He stared at a corner of the room, where stacked boxes threw deep shadows, and made gurgling noises in his throat. "Nooo. Keep them away. Why are they loose? Why aren't they in their containment cages?" The General scrabbled backward, tipping the chair over and scrambling away, horror written all over his sweating face. He passed out of the beam of the machine and he stiffened, staring around wildly, though the terror in his voice quickly became anger. "Where are they? What have you done...where is...was that the fucking beam?"

Andi switched off the Baby Vox. "General, are you okay? I had no idea...what were you thinking?"

Spader rose to his feet and dusted off his jacket and trousers. "It does not matter. Shall we continue with the demonstration?"

"You saw aliens, didn't you?" Parker crowed. "They do exist. What are they like?"

Spader looked at Parker coldly. "They do not exist. You merely put the idea into my mind."

"Yeah, right. I saw the look on your face. You recognised them. You do..."

"Captain Anders," Spader snapped. "You will take this man into custody and hold him in solitary confinement until I say otherwise."

"What? Hang on, you can't do that. I'm not under your command."

"Actually, he can," Morgan said. "If you paid a bit more attention, you'd know that General Spader is in overall charge of this project, which is under Army control." He got to his feet and faced the two men. "General Spader, I urge you to reconsider. We are not yet at a stage where we can dispense with this man's expertise. Dr Parker, please apologise to the General for your ill-considered remarks."

"The hell I will."

"Then I cannot help you," Morgan stated firmly. "You will be removed from the project and Dr Jones will take your place."

"The hell she will!"

"The choice is yours."

Parker ground his teeth and flushed. "This is blackmail." Nobody said anything and after a few moments he dropped his gaze to the floor. "I'm sorry if I caused offence, General, I was overcome with curiosity, that's all."

Spader nodded. "Captain Anders, ignore my last order." He turned to Morgan and inclined his head slightly, still frowning. "Mr Turner, shall we continue with the demonstration?"

"Certainly, General. If you would care to take your seat."

Turning his back on Parker, he sat down facing the larger machine. "One question before we start. Dr Jones, this small machine is extraordinarily powerful. Why do you not just use it? Why build the larger version at such huge expense?"

"Because while powerful," Andi explained, "It has an extremely short range--no more than a kilometre or so--and it can carry no information beyond a few metres. Generally, what a person sees is what is already in their mind. We influence that by suggestion," she added.

"But it can carry some information over a short distance?"

"Yes, but only a few metres."

"Could it be used on the battlefield as a hand-held weapon?"

"The power needed would be prohibitive."

General Spader digested this information for a few moments. "Very well. Carry on."

Spindler resumed his lecturing pose. "Now, what Dr Jones says is correct, General. The prototype is very limited with regard to range and information content. I cannot envisage its use as a field weapon, but I can perhaps see it as a tool of interrogation. I have been thinking about this aspect..."

"I'm sure you have," Spader interrupted, "And another time I would be delighted to hear your ideas, but for now I would like to hear about the capabilities of the larger device. I believe you have a demonstration planned?"

"Yes. You will recall that Mr Turner asked you to send a squad of men out to the lake shore at Indian Head? Well, we have set up cameras on that spot to record the actions of your men. Dr Newman, will you switch the monitors on please?"

April wheeled a large wide-screen television monitor in front of the seated men and switched it on. A panoramic view of the lake front flickered into view, framed by pine trees and small wavelets lapping on a pebbled shore. In the foreground sat or lounged half a dozen soldiers, talking and smoking cigarettes. Their weapons lay on the grass beside them and only the sergeant paid even a modicum of attention to keeping a watch on the surroundings.

"What the hell is his name, Anders?" Spader growled. "I'll have them all up on a charge."

"Before you get carried away, General," Morgan said quietly. "I told them they could take it easy. I wanted them relaxed for the demonstration."

"Okay. Get on with it then."

Spindler took over the talking again. "You see on the picture this object lying about fifty metres offshore? That is a log we had tethered on that spot. It does not move, attract attention, or cause ripples in the lake. No doubt the men saw it when they first arrived, but now it has sunk into their subconscious and they pay no attention to it. Until we aim our beam at them, that is."

"You have a machine out there on the island?" Spader asked, his voice tinged with concern. "Who is guarding it?"

Spindler smiled. "No one, General. We will use this machine."

"But how? We are deep underground. How can you use any weapon from within a cavern?"

"The magnetic beam passes through rock and soil as easily as through air. First of all, we feed the coordinates of the men into the Vox Dei..."

"Not the log?"

"No, General. We are attempting to alter the perceptions of the men, not the log." Spader grunted. "Then we fire up the laser and energise the magnetaser beam. There." The Vox Dei swung round and raised its barrel toward the ceiling. A deep humming filled the chamber and the brilliant but narrow beam of light that had stabbed from the barrel suddenly shut off.

"The men are being bathed in the energies of the magnetaser," Andi said. "It will do them no harm, but neither will it influence them in any way. For that to happen, we must feed in a prepared program--instructions to the brains of the soldiers that will enable them to see what we want."

"What will they see?" Spader asked.

"Something outlandish. The log will seem to morph into a threatening creature and we will watch the reactions of your men."

"Can you be a bit more precise? What sort of threat are we talking about? Terrorists? A man with a gun?"

"A huge alligator."

Spader stared at Andi. "You don't get alligators in California."

"Precisely. It's not something they expect."

"But you expect trained soldiers to believe an alligator is coming out of the water and menacing them?"

Andi grinned. "Remember Baby Vox, General. Watch and learn." She tapped commands in through the computer keyboard and flipped the switch to allow the information to stream into the magnetic beam.

For a few moments nothing happened on the screen. The log bobbled up and down on the sun-dappled lake and the soldiers continued smoking their cigarettes and talking. Now even the sergeant joined his men.

"It's not working," Spader complained. "The log's just a log."

"You won't see anything, General; you're not in the beam. But they...there, see? Someone has seen something."

A soldier leapt to his feet, dropping his cigarette and pointing at the lake. They could see his mouth working but had to guess at the shouts coming from it. Others joined him and within seconds, every soldier had snatched up their weapons and had them trained on an unseen target slowly moving toward the shore. The sergeant said something and one soldier stitched a short burst of automatic fire across the path of the creature. It did not seem to be affected as the soldiers edged away from the water. Another command and the same soldier raised his weapon and put a single round into the approaching hallucination. Moments later, the water of the lake erupted as every man fired his weapon on full automatic, the waters churning as rounds kicked up a curtain of spray.

"No sense in panicking them," Andi murmured. She cut the computer link to the Vox Dei. "The image has disappeared from their minds and they'll think they shot it and it sank."

Spader shook his head. "They can't honestly think they saw some huge alligator rise up out of the lake. They were firing at nothing."

"Like your aliens?" Parker asked with a grin.

Spader shot him a warning look and the scientist turned away.

"They really saw something?"

"Ask them," Spindler said. "Interrogate them when they report in. You vill see they all saw the same thing."

"Is there any limit to what things you can create in men's minds?"

"The simpler the better," Spindler said.

"Especially for men," April whispered to Andi.

"A complex thought may be confusing but simple things can be grasped by all," Spindler continued.

"And range?"

"For a battle situation, I vould imagine ten to fifty kilometres vould be sufficient, and the Vox can handle that easily."

"What about further than that? A thousand kilometres? Ten thousand?"

Spindler hesitated. "Vell, it is possible, I suppose..."

"Anything's possible, General," Andi cut in. "The problem is finding enough energy. The base generators can produce enough power to cut through a few kilometres of rock, but for hundreds, or thousands of kilometres, you'd need more energy than we can produce."

"What if we took it to the surface so there is no rock to go through?"

"Wouldn't work. The beam is straight line and to reach a place beyond the horizon you would have to aim it through the curve of the earth. The further away the target is, the steeper the angle and the more rock. For that you need much more energy."

Spader nodded, frowning. He got up and shook hands with Morgan before addressing the scientists once more. "You have done well, very well. I would like you to think about the problems involved in targeting an area twelve thousand kilometres away. Work out how much energy we would need." He turned and, accompanied by his aide and Lieutenant Evans, marched out of the cavern.

"What's twelve thousand kilometres away?" Parker asked.

"Does it matter?" Morgan asked. "We'll be told when we need to know. In the meantime, well done, all of you. That demonstration was most impressive."

11

The baby clung to the front of Sam's chest like a monkey. The special sling that Amaru's people had made as a present held her tiny body gently and comfortably where awake or asleep, she could hear her mother's comforting heartbeat. Sam concentrated on her studies, readjusting the computer monitor and punching a sequence on her keyboard that accessed a whole new databank of information. She nuzzled the top of Gaia's fuzzy head absently as her eyes followed the rows of data.

Are you hungry, darling?

The baby peered up at Sam with large, turquoise-coloured eyes and replied in turn. *Not yet, mum, this is too interesting. Can you shift the screen a bit so I can see with my own eyes?*

A huge humanoid, completely covered with long golden brown hair and looking very much like a relative of King Kong, stepped forward from the cavern walls where it had been waiting patiently and leaned down to face the baby. The creature had large, soft brown eyes and an affectionate inquiring look on its expressive face.

Do you want me to take her? The creature waited with outstretched arms for an answer to her silent plea for the baby to come to her.

The baby's mind responded instantly. *Yes! Rima, come put me up on your shoulder. That way I can see everything!*

The yowie tilted her head and looked at Sam with twinkling eyes, searching for consent after the fact. When Sam nodded, the nine-foot tall being, Sam's companion during the expedition to the Glass House Mountains and now Gaia's self-appointed personal bodyguard, delicately plucked the baby from her sling and hoisted the tiny body up to a wide shoulder. Gaia poked her head up and turned it from side to side like a radar scope.

Sam chuckled at Gaia's obvious delight. *Cindy, you're spoiling her--sorry, Rima, I forget.* Sam still had difficulty in thinking of the yowie in terms of her real name rather than the alias she had used when disguised as a human. When Rima moved toward the centre of the complex, Sam sent a silent message to both the yowie and her daughter. *Now, Rima, don't let her tire you out. You know how demanding and voracious for information she is.*

Amaru, clad in her gown of gauzy white, bare feet, no jewelry and looking for all the world like the proverbial heavy-browed cavewoman, glided into the cubicle shaking her head of long silvery-blonde hair. *She's come a long way in six months hasn't she?*

Sam nodded in agreement but continued to watch Rima moving gracefully through the large information centre, stopping in turn at every working terminal so Gaia could observe the computer screens. Every time Rima stopped, Gaia's head of gleaming red hair would pop up further on the big yowie's shoulder in anticipation. The assorted humanoids working at the computers--mixtures of tiny Greys, tall slim Blue-greys, crosses of animal species with human-like forms and others--had long since gotten used to the baby's insatiable curiosity and warmly indulged her hunger for knowledge. When Rima graced each work station with the baby's presence, the operator hastily stopped his or her work and gladly showed the infant anything new stored up since her last visit. It was obvious they all loved her and she soaked it up like a sponge.

Amaru touched Sam lightly on the shoulder. *My dear, I know you're justifiably proud of your daughter and can watch her all day.* She smiled and added, *So can I.* Then she paused before finishing with, *But there is something of grave importance happening now and your presence is needed. James is already in the conference room awaiting us...and others are on their way.*

Her attention now fully on Amaru, Sam noted the tiny woman's worried look and the dullness of her usually bright blue eyes. Sam nodded and rose to follow.

When Sam and Amaru walked into the large room where James lounged at the table, comfortably tilted back in a huge chair and his feet on the metal desk, the room still felt empty. It could easily hold two hundred life forms and still have plenty of room to spare. James, at the head of the table, appeared small and childlike from the doorway. He waved gaily at them as they approached.

Amaru retained her standard emotionless demeanour but Sam waved back and shouted, "Hey, lazy! Why aren't you working?"

His lopsided grin flashed across the room at her but he waited until the two women sat down before answering. "Amaru told me to come here. Truth is, I was in the middle of a really great geological analysis that I wanted to finish but she said it's important so I came."

Amaru's hands disappeared into the voluminous arms of her gown. Her eyes and cheeks glowed with suppressed energy but she remained silent. Sam turned to her with a perplexed frown on her face. "Well Amaru? We're here. What is it?"

Amaru's only concession to telling them what to expect was a short, curt, *There are others we must wait for first.* Then she closed her eyes.

Sam and James gave each other a puzzled look, knowing Amaru's habit of meditating during times of stress. She closed out everything and everybody. They also knew it would do no good to question her further. James went to a disguised refrigerator unit and opened it to retrieve two cold drinks. Placing one in front of Sam, he murmured, "I wonder how long we'll have to wait."

The sound of the air-driven doors leading into the room drew their attention. Within seconds, James and Sam were on their feet, rushing across the floor toward the four people who had entered.

"Spence! Oh my God, it's Spence, Ratana, Nathan and Ernie." Sam rushed to the visitors with her arms opened wide in greeting. She reached the group standing in the middle of the room and grasped Ratana in her arms, hugging her with enthusiasm. "Ratana! I've missed you so much."

James clasped hands with Spence, his old Maori friend and colleague. They pressed foreheads and noses together in a traditional welcome. "*Haere Mai*, old friend," James murmured to Spence. Spence hugged him then turned to grin at Sam.

James greeted Nathan, an Aboriginal man who had been more son than student to him when they'd lived in Queensland. "G'day, Nate," he smiled into Nathan's serious brown eyes.

Nathan nodded, smiled in spite of the gravity of his thoughts and replied, "G'day Uncle. It's good to see you again."

Spence eyed James and asked, "Whatcha been up to mate? I haven't seen much of you since your 'disappearance'."

James looked Spence up and down and replied, "Oh, they've kept me pretty busy. Educating Gaia's a full time occupation; for all that Sam does most of that."

"Actually, I do very little," Sam called across to them. "Cindy...I mean, Rima, does most of that. She's better than any babysitter." Sam, still clinging to Ratana's muscled and ebony arm, pulled Ratana along with her as she clasped Nathan in a brief hug. "How are you, Nate? What have you been up to? Why are you here?"

Nathan bowed his head and small smile crept over his lips as he answered, "I'm fine, Sam. Ratana and I are married now. We are learning the old ways from Ernie, and a lot more besides. But, this..." he swept his arm around the room. "...called us away."

Ratana took up where he left off. "A messenger came and told us we were being summoned by the Old Ones. Then Ernie came to get us. We went with him to the Atherton Tableland base and took the portal here." She glanced at Ernie standing quietly aside, smiling indulgently, his clay-stained and faded shorts and headband almost allowing him to blend into the painted mural on the wall behind him.

Spence moved quickly to Sam's side and offered his thin arms up for a hug with a lopsided grin. "What about me, m' lady? Don't I warrant a hug too?"

As Sam smiled at the old man and gave him a press of her forehead and nose then a fierce hug, James glanced over his shoulder at Amaru, wondering why she didn't join them. Amaru sat sedately at the table watching them as they greeted each other again. She sent a question privately to James. *What is this pressing of head and nose she does with Spence?*

James answered her with an amused tone to his mind talk. *It is called 'hongi'. It is literally the sharing and intermingling of breath with a beloved friend or family member. Once performed, the person becomes 'tangata whenua' or 'one of the people of the land'. Spence does not do it lightly.*

Amaru smiled. *A good custom.* Then she nodded at James, sending a silent message to all at the same time. *Welcome, old friends. Please, be seated. It is time to speak of grave things. There will be time enough later for reunions.*

As a group, with the exception of Ernie, who remained standing against the wall, they all filed around the table and seated themselves. Ratana sat quietly, looking at Amaru with curiosity while Spence grinned and looked around the huge room. Nathan steepled his hands before him on the table and adopted a solemn look. James and Sam took the seats they'd vacated moments before. Each still had large smiles on their faces as they beamed at their friends.

After several minutes of silence, Spence leaned over toward Amaru and placed a wrinkled hand on her hairy arm. "What's this all about, Amaru?"

At that moment, a squat, wild-haired man with a full wind-blown beard of reddish hair shambled into the room on bare, callused feet. He wore nothing but a pair of blue, baggy shorts that appeared to have been made from a pair of oversized jeans. The rest of his body was covered in long reddish hair like his beard and his heavy brow ridges and prognathous face gave him an appearance of bestiality completely belied by the warmth and intelligence that shone from his deep-set brown eyes. He held a primitive spear clutched in his right hand and a large hunting knife strapped to his waist with string. Amaru's face didn't change but the other's reactions were a mixture of stunned surprise, shock and amusement. When the man finally made it to the head of the table, he eased his thick, muscular body down into a chair and lovingly placed his spear upon the table. Then he nodded in Amaru's direction but his gaze scanned the faces of the group while he spoke in mind voice. *Hello all, it has been a long time. Do you remember me?*

"Garagh, of course we remember you," James stated in a calm, unhurried voice.

"What's with the spear and the hunting knife, mate?" Spence asked. "You look as if you are kitted out to hunt bear."

Bear? No, I think not--or at least not by myself. Not that there are any bears in this southern land. Garagh sighed. *Sometimes the years weigh heavily upon my shoulders and I seek to lose myself in memories of my youth.*

Amaru smiled. *Do not fear that my great-grandfather is getting senile. He is as fit now, mentally and physically, as he ever was. The black rock protects him.*

Garagh winked and drew out a black quartz crystal that hung on a leather cord around his neck. It had been covered by his thick chest hairs. *I've carried this so long the rubbing against my chest has worn it down.*

Spence laughed politely. "I see that hyperbole is alive and well among your people."

We are as conversant with forms of humour as humans, Spencer Tuhua, Amaru said. *But Grandfather Garagh does not exaggerate. Have you forgotten how old he is?*

Spence frowned. "Well, I remember he said he was thirty thousand years old, but hell, that must be just a figure of speech. Is 'Garagh' a title, perhaps? Nobody lives that long."

"He does," Ernie said, from his position near the wall of the chamber. "I met Garagh when he first arrived in Australia and he has not changed much over the millennia." A gentle smile crinkled the corners of the old Aboriginal's eyes. "A bit fatter, maybe. Once upon a time he had to hunt for his own food."

Garagh stuck out his tongue at Ernie and then laughed. *Unlike you, Wandjina, I must eat to stay alive.*

"If Wandjina says it is so, I believe it," Nathan said. Ratana nodded her agreement.

"That's all very well," Spence said obstinately. "But how? What stops the ageing process?"

There I cannot help you. All I know is that the 'Others' gave me the black crystal and told me never to take it off. Perhaps there is some magic in it from the 'Others'.

Spence slapped the table with the palm of his right hand. "You're invoking magic now? I thought you Neanderthals professed to be scientists."

James stirred. "Clarke's Third Law," he said.

"What?"

"Arthur C. Clarke stated that any sufficiently advanced technology is indistinguishable from magic. Perhaps that's what we have here. These 'Others' are pretty obviously aliens with a technology sufficiently advanced to get here from another star system or dimension. Instead of worrying about how something is done, perhaps we should just accept we don't know everything and get on with what needs to be done. I take it we have been brought here for a reason," James added.

Garagh held up a gnarled hand. *Thank you, James. Yes, I have brought you here for a reason. We have much to discuss and little time before we must leave.*

"Leave?" Sam asked. "To go where--and why?"

Garagh looked at Amaru, who nodded and sat back in her chair, observing the humans carefully. Garagh grunted and continued his mind-speech. *We have told you before of our history and the purpose that we have been called to fulfill--namely, to guard the earth and its inhabitants, to watch humans and try to ameliorate the worst of their excesses, and to watch for and select the specific human genetic structure that will save the planet.*

James nodded. "We remember. How could we forget? It was your meddling that led to the conception of Gaia."

We have apologised for those actions and explained our reasoning already, Amaru said softly. *Are we to be castigated afresh every time the topic is raised?*

James grimaced. "No, of course, you are right. I apologise."

Then to continue, Garagh went on. *You must understand that for all our technology and command of human and Neanderthal genetics, we do not fully understand many things. We are content to be guided by the 'Others' and wait until things become clearer. They have told us that a crisis in the fabric of the earth's history is approaching, and ordered us to find a specific human genotype that could heal the wound. They have not explained how this is to be accomplished, just that your infant daughter Gaia is the one.*

"That's an awfully heavy load to be shouldered by a baby," Sam said. "I will not let her be harmed, by human or Neanderthal--or 'Other'."

No harm will come to her, Amaru said. *She is precious to us all and we will protect her.*

Careful, Amaru, Garagh said in the intimate mode. *Do not promise what you know you cannot perform.*

I will protect her, Garagh.

You do not have that option. The path has been laid out and you will not interfere.

There must be another way.

There is not.

"Do not forget we agreed that Gaia would not be coerced into this role," James said. "When she reaches eighteen she can make her own mind up."

We thought, Garagh continued, *That we had many years ahead of us--years for Gaia to attain her majority, to decide for herself, but events are moving faster than we planned. The time for action is nearly upon us.*

"No," Sam cried. "You can't expect her to do anything now. She's only a baby; she's six months old, for Christ's sake."

It is not we who ask it of her, Samantha, Amaru said gently.

"I know," James replied, "But I'm with Sam a hundred per cent. Gaia's only a baby. If these 'Others' of yours want her to do anything, you tell them to come and see me about it. I'll tell them to go...well; I'll tell them what they can do with their plans."

"Attaboy, Jimmy," Spence murmured. "We're right behind you."

"Us too, Uncle," Nathan said quietly, though he shot a sideways glance at Ernie.

"Please believe that I love Gaia," Ratana said, "But I am certain that neither Wandjina nor Garagh would countenance anything that was even remotely harmful to her. Is that not so, Wandjina?"

"It is so, daughter," Ernie stated. "There are few absolutes in life, but Gaia is loved and appreciated by us all. She will always be protected."

James nodded. "Thank you. I needed to hear it said."

"What has happened that makes you say the time is nearly here?" Spence asked.

The shadow beings, Garagh replied.

"The Quinkan?" James stirred in his seat and put out his hand to squeeze Sam's reassuringly. "Those are not exactly new things, are they?"

"They are not Quinkan," Ernie said. "These things have nothing to do with the Dreamtime or Aboriginal legend. They are called Winambuu and are not of this world."

"Aliens!" Spence exclaimed. "Damn it, could they be these 'Others'?"

No. Though there are coincidences in time, Garagh said. *We have reason to believe that the 'Others' came to earth in response to or in anticipation of, these shadows. From what we can piece together, the Shadow people are inhabitants of another dimension, a parallel universe, which lies alongside ours.*

"How did they get here?"

We don't know. Our scientists hypothesise a weakening in the space-time fabric. Garagh shrugged. *To me, that is just so many words for 'I don't know'.*

Spence nodded sagely. "If all else fails, resort to jargon."

"But are they really dangerous?" Sam asked. "I know they have attacked us a few times, but they were driven off by Ernie each time."

"That is true," Ernie nodded, "But each time was more difficult. They have almost no substance and they learn fast. There may come a time when even my powers are insufficient."

"What can we do then?" James asked. "How can we defeat them if even Wandjina admits himself beaten?"

"We must track them to their source, to the place where they come through from their own world, and seal it off."

"And where is that?"

Ernie shrugged. "I do not know."

"Jeez Louise," Sam exclaimed. "You're not making this easy for us, are you?"

If it was easy, we would have done it already, Garagh said. *That is why we need your help.*

Spence laughed. "Why do a Dreamtime Spirit and a bunch of long-lived technological geniuses led by aliens need the help of a bunch of humans?"

A reasonable question, Amaru said. *We should be able to handle them, yet we cannot. For some reason, they are attracted to you humans, so we think you might hold the key to their defeat. You represent a danger to them.*

"So you want us as bait?" James asked sourly.

You make it sound terrible. We will give you as much protection as possible, but the more we can learn about their purpose, the closer we will come to knowing how to get rid of them.

"Gaia is my only concern," Sam said quietly. "I'm sorry if that seems selfish, Amaru, but I cannot put my daughter...our daughter..." she squeezed her husband's hand, "...in danger. I will not come with you on your quest, nor will I allow Gaia to go with you."

And if it is Gaia they are after? Garagh asked. *What then? While we are off tracking down the enemy, they could strike here against an undefended child.*

"Then don't go," James said bluntly. "If they want Gaia, then you must give her proper protection."

"We must go," Ernie said. "The Shadow People are gathering elsewhere, and we must stop them. The safest place for Gaia--if she is indeed their target--is to come with us."

"Shit," James muttered. "I don't like this one little bit. Where are we going?"

Northern California, Garagh said. *A place called Medicine Lake to be precise. The Shadow People have captured the minds of powerful and influential people, including scientists and the military. A machine has been created, ostensibly to take over men's minds, but it will have another effect--it will weaken the barriers between the worlds, allowing the shadows unlimited access to our own world.*

"My God," Spence breathed. "More of the buggers. Can they be stopped?"

Only by destroying the machine.

James shook his head. "They'll just build another."

Then we must make sure they cannot build another, Garagh said calmly. *We must kill the creators of the machine.*

"Uh-uh, no way Jose," Sam said, vigorously shaking her head. "I'm not going to get mixed up in murder." She stared at Amaru, then at Garagh, and lastly at Ernie. "I'm appalled you'd even consider it."

Garagh sighed. *We have considered other options, Samantha, but nothing else will guarantee another machine is not built. Besides, and please do not take this the wrong way*, he added, *But we are not strictly human and therefore the killing of humans is not really murder.*

"That is a fucking ridiculous answer and you know it." James pushed back his chair and stood up. "Humans and Neanderthals and whatever the hell Ernie is, are all sentient creatures and to kill one is murder. I will not be part of this scheme and neither will Sam. We are taking Gaia and leaving here right now."

"Please sit down, James." Ernie ambled over to the table and stood behind Garagh with one hand on his shoulder. "I have known this man for thirty thousand years and after such a time you get to know someone very well. I will not make excuses for Garagh, for he is mistaken in his views. Firstly, Neanderthals are brothers and sisters of humans, so killing one really would be murder. He knows this, for he has told me it many times. Secondly, killing anyone is not our policy except as a very last resort, and never in cold blood."

"What are you saying? Garagh was just speaking for himself, not the rest of you?"

It is true, James, Garagh agreed. *I spoke what was in my mind, for truly I can see no other way out of this dilemma. If you can see another solution, I will submit willingly.*

"You honestly see us as being so different from you?" Sam asked, her face anguished. "I've always regarded Amaru as a sister."

No, Samantha. We are both human, but I get frustrated by the intransigence of so many humans. They are greedy and selfish and hurtful and sometimes I wish they would all die and leave the world in peace. I spoke from my hurt and frustration. Please forgive me.

James looked at Sam and spoke on the intimate mode. *You think he's telling the truth?*

I don't know, but if he's not and we leave now, he might just go ahead and kill those scientists. I'd feel guilty then that I did not at least try to stop him.

What about you, Spence? Nathan? Ratana?

I think he's telling the truth, said Ratana.

Possibly, added Nathan, *but we should give him the benefit of the doubt anyway.*

Stick with them, Jimmy, and keep an eye on him.

James nodded and sat down. "Very well, Garagh. If we have your word that there will be no murder, we will stay and help you. We must find another solution."

Thank you all, Garagh said. *Not least of all for reminding me of my own humanity. Now, we must move quickly on this as events are unfolding rapidly in California.*

"What exactly is happening there?" Spence asked.

They are building a modified laser that is so powerful; it could weaken the fabric of the universe, allowing the shadows across.

"Yes, you said that before, but lasers are old news. Why now? Why this one?"

It is an unusual concept. It uses magnetism to alter people's perceptions at a distance. They can convince people that they are seeing things that are not really there, convince them to do things they would not normally do. It is as if the Voice of God spoke to them...

"Persinger!" Sam exclaimed. "My sister Andi told me about experiments he'd done in Canada. They were along those lines."

"What was your sister doing that she knew that?" Nathan asked.

"She's a physicist. A damn good one too."

Amaru nodded. *So good that she was hired for this project. She is one of the builders of the machine.*

"Andi? And...and you were going to kill her?"

Garagh looked down at the table and said nothing.

That will not happen now, Amaru said softly. *You have my word on that. We will find another way.*

"Damn right you will," Sam growled. "And I'm coming along to make sure you do."

"So how are we going to do this?" Spence asked. "You said the US military are involved. We won't be able to just walk in and demolish it with sledgehammers, will we?"

"No," Ernie said, "But we have a strong ally in the form of Moon Wolf. He looks like an old native North American, but he is actually a spirit being." The old Aboriginal man smiled. "Think of him as the equivalent of a Wandjina."

"Bloody hell," Nathan murmured. "Two wandjinas. We can't lose."

12

General Thaddeus Spader was at his desk in his cramped quarters, writing up his preliminary report on the first testing of the Vox Dei machine. His typing was slow, the fore-finger of his right hand for the keyboard and the fore-finger of his left for the 'shift' key. It worked well enough, if a little slowly, and he did not want one of the army secretaries privy to what had happened.

The fewer people who know about it the better. General Spader sat back and thought about the witnesses to the demonstration. His aide and Lieutenant Evans were beneath consideration--they would do as they were told. The soldiers who had experienced the incident were confused and likewise would not be saying anything.

The scientists were brilliant but very obviously unstable. He shrugged. There was little they could do as long as he controlled the installation and if worst came to worst, he could eliminate them. *Except Travis Parker.* He was an obnoxious little shit but he fitted quite snugly in the general's pocket. There were uses for men like him.

Morgan Turner was another matter. Theoretically, Turner controlled the purse-strings of the project, but Spader knew that ultimately the Army funded the work and the businessman could be easily side-lined if need be. The man troubled the General, but he could not pinpoint the reason for his distrust. *Maybe I should eliminate him too. It would not be hard--an accident is easy to arrange.*

And what of the other, Turner's whore? A bright enough young woman but an unknown security problem, someone from Turner's past, possibly a lover. The unknown could be dangerous. Better that she meet with some accident. *Maybe the same one as Turner?*

Spader finished the report and read through it twice, making minor corrections before attaching it to an email and sending it to an address committed to memory. He deleted the message from his computer and activated a program designed to wipe all traces of the connection from his hard drive. Briefly, he wondered who was on the other end of the cyberspace connection, but knew curiosity into the matter would be both fruitless and dangerous. The general had few ranks above him in the army and they would get their own reports in due course, but first priority was to his other masters. They were the ones controlling this project and while Spader could see marvelous military applications for the Vox Dei, he suspected that his masters had other ideas, ones that would not sit too well with the US Army. It mattered little to the General as he was being extremely well paid and he looked forward to an early retirement to enjoy his wealth. As long as he did not find himself working openly for his country's enemies, he could justify his actions.

A soft tap sounded on the solid wood of his door.

"Come."

The door opened and a soldier leaned into the room. "Sir, there is a Mr Mannheim asking to see you."

Spader frowned. "Mannheim?" *I don't know any Mannheim...ah, Turner's butler.* "Send him in."

The soldier withdrew and a few minutes later, the thin body of Ehrich Mannheim slid around the door and glided across the bare concrete floor to Spader's desk. Behind him, the door to the room clicked shut.

"What do you want, Mannheim? I'm busy. You have a message from Turner?"

Deep-set, hooded eyes regarded the general. "Ankh-a, sesen-a nifu," Mannheim said softly.

Spader's jaw dropped and he stared at the old man. "Wh...what did you say?" Mannheim just waited, saying nothing further, and Spader's right hand hesitated and then crept upward, touching three fingertips to his forehead.

He is of the Nine, Spader thought, apprehension gripping his heart. *Which response will he give--the high or low?*

"A Nut, tat-ek na em mu nifu amet."

Spader automatically translated the butler's words to himself even as he cringed to hear the low response. *Hail Nut, grant to me the water and air that dwell within you.* He swallowed and cleared his throat. *He outranks me, but by how much?*

"A Atum, tat-ek nanifu pui netem ami sert-ek," Spader responded, his tongue stumbling over the seldom-used syllables of the high response. *Hail Atum, grant to me the sweet breath from your nostrils.* "What do you want?"

"You recognise my authority?"

"Of course!" Spader lumbered to his feet and brought a chair over for his visitor, holding it while Ehrich Mannheim sat down. He returned to his own seat. "How may I be of service to you?"

"The machine is ready?"

Spader nodded. "Yes, today. I have just finished the special report."

"I have seen it."

"You? The message went to you? That is impossible. There would not be time. You knocked on my door only minutes after I sent it and your rooms are..."

"You doubt me?"

"N...no, of course not, but..."

"I read it as you wrote it."

"But that would mean..."

"Exactly. It is a simple matter. Now, enough of this. I have been sent your instructions."

"You've been sent them? Then you are not..."

"One of the Nine?" Ehrich smiled sardonically. "No, we are both servants though I outrank you."

"What would you have me do?"

"Who among the scientists knows the most about the machine?"

Spader considered for a few moments. "They are all expert in their own fields--Newman in computing, Spindler in electronics, Braun in crystal arrays."

"What of Parker?"

"An excellent technician. He has little in the way of original thought, but he is a good backup for every field. Furthermore, he is easily manipulated."

"And Jones?"

"Very capable. I have reason to believe it was her insights that led to the successful completion of the Voice."

"Yes, I agree with your assessment," Ehrich said. "You will make electronic copies of all the research and data associated with the machine. You will take Parker and Jones into protective custody and transport them to this address." The old man took a plain white business card out of his pocket and handed it to the General.

Spader examined it briefly and passed it back. "Why do you say protective custody?"

"Because in an unfortunate tragedy, terrorists will destroy the machine and kill the scientific personnel. You will act immediately to save the survivors."

Spader stared at Mannheim. "You want my men to destroy the machine?"

"No, I said terrorists would do it. I will arrange that and bring them into the base. Your men will just look the other way."

"It would mean the end of my career," Spader objected. "I'd be judged a traitor."

Ehrich laughed, the sound harsh and humourless, as if foreign to his lips. "Hardly that. More likely incompetent, but why should you mind? You will be very well rewarded."

Spader scowled. "When do you want it done?"

"Tomorrow night, but first you will arrange another demonstration. I want the beam to bathe the eastern peak of a mountain called Tunbubudla."

"Where the hell is that? Tunboo-buddy?"

"It's a small mountain in Australia."

"Why do you want it targeted?"

"That is not for you to know, just do it."

Spader shrugged. "If you say so. Will they know where the mountain is? I've never heard of it."

Ehrich passed over another card. "Here are the latitude and longitude. The specifications of the beam are also there. Make sure those instructions are followed to the letter."

"Of course." Spader scanned the figures on the card and whistled. "That's a hell of a lot of energy. I doubt if the generators can cope with that."

"We are connected to the West Coast power grid. Draw on that as necessary."

"Okay. Do you want me to tell you when it's been done?"

"No. Tell me when you are ready to do it. I want to be there when it happens."

* * *

In another part of the Glass Mountain complex, another hand knocked on another door. Andi poked her head around the door jamb and peered into Morgan's opulent living room.

"Morgan? Are you there?"

An empty silence greeted her. She shivered slightly and stepped into the room, closing the door behind her. *It's funny how a place feels completely different when there's nobody home--I think.* Andi moved across a rich Persian carpet toward a fireplace and the single high-backed armchair with its back to her, half-convinced she would find Morgan sitting in it. *But why wouldn't he answer when I entered?* Her mind briefly entertained some possibilities, becoming less likely but more frightening by the moment--he was asleep, he had died, he was possessed by one of those shadow things, he wasn't there at all but a shadow was, waiting for her...

"Morgan?" she called softly, and put her hand on the back of the chair, steeling herself to look around the arm wing. The chair was empty and Andi let out breath she hadn't realised she was holding.

She looked around the room at the sparse furniture, good quality but not much of it for a room this size. A tall bookcase, packed with old books, stood to one side of the fireplace, and a glass-topped mahogany drinks cabinet occupied the other. Across the room, near a door cracked ajar, stood a pair of antique desks. One was a roll top writing desk, the other a heavy stained wooden affair with an inlaid leather top. Incongruously, a computer screen, mouse and keyboard were the only things on its immaculate surface.

Andi walked across and stared at the blank screen for a moment before nudging the mouse. The monitor leapt into life, revealing a background picture of the Lodge seen from Medicine Lake and a double column of icons down the left-hand side of the screen. She scanned the columns and her breath caught at the sight of one labeled with her name. Licking her lips nervously, she glanced around the room once more, and then guided the cursor to the folder.

What am I doing? I'm not here to spy on him. Do I really want to know what he thinks of me? She remembered reading her sister Samantha's diary when they were kids and how angry she'd been. Andi clicked the mouse button twice and the folder opened. *Password required--damn.* She closed the folder and turned away from the desk feeling guilty.

The dark line of the slightly open bedroom door beckoned and she stepped over to it, pulling it open slightly. Her nose wrinkled as she caught a faintly musty odour exuded from the darkness beyond. *Do I want to go in there? No, but I'm going anyway.* She reached into the darkness, her hand feeling along the wall for the light switch. An unwelcome thought drifted unbidden into her mind. *What if something grabs me?* Andi found the switch and flipped it up, a light beside the large bed coming on and filling the large room with a soft yellow glow fading into shades of grey and black around the edges.

She stood in the doorway and looked cautiously around the room. Mirrored sliding doors to one side spoke of closet space, and a chest of drawers and an armchair, together with a king sized bed completed the furnishings. A door, closed, in the far wall, probably led to an en-suite, she decided. *Morgan's obviously not here, so why am I? I should leave.* Andi stepped into the bedroom and ran one hand along the quilted bed cover. She looked into the mirrored doors and saw a thin, dark-haired woman looking back at her.

"What are you doing here, girl?" Andi whispered. "You should get the hell out of Dodge." Her eyes widened as she saw a movement behind the image in the mirror. A door seemed to open in the wall behind her image and a black person step through into the room behind her. Andi whirled and half fell onto the bed, expecting to be attacked by..."What the hell?" The wall behind her was unblemished and nobody, coloured or otherwise, stood behind her. She stared, looking around at the deserted bedroom. Andi got up from the bed and glanced toward the mirror, uttering a cry of surprise as she saw the dark person again, standing just behind her image.

Again she whirled, and again she found herself alone in the room. She looked back at the mirror, which held her now agitated image and that of the dark person. Andi stared, seeing for the first time that it was not a person that stood behind her image but only the sooty outline of a person, a shadow without...*A shadow person.* She felt the hairs on the back of her neck stir.

The shadow moved forward, through her image, and Andi gasped, clutching at her midriff as if the thing was passing through her. She saw nothing in the room though, only the two images in the mirror face of the closet, with her own image now obscured behind the shadow being. *This isn't real. I'm in the beam of the Vox Dei, that's what it is. Someone's feeding me an illusion.* A gust of relief swept through her, even as the shadow being stepped through the glass interface into the room. The creature's eyes opened, revealing the mirror surface of the door through them, glowing yellow in the subdued light of the bedroom.

"You are not real," Andi stated. "You are just an illusion and I will not be afraid of an illusion."

Laughter rippled around the room--thin, dry expellations of air that made Andi think of gases escaping from a bloated corpse. She felt a loathsome touch of dead fingers on her inner being and cringed.

"No," she gasped, "You don't exist. Someone is playing with my mind."

Who are you? The words slithered into Andi's mind.

"J...Jones. And...Andi Jones," she stuttered, as the information was plucked from her.

Come here. I will make you mine.

Andi took a step forward as the yellow glow of the lamp reflecting off the mirror made the creature's eyes blaze. She felt emotions blast through her mind--triumph, hunger, hatred--and a sob was wrung from her throat. "Please," she whispered.

Another step, then another and a dark arm reached out to Andi, as the shadow flowed off the mirror surface and into the space between the closet door and the young woman.

"Stay back." Morgan's crisp command halted the creature. It hung in the air, reminiscent of a dense cloud of gnats and turned toward the man standing in the doorway to the bedroom.

Who are you to command one of the Winambuu?

"I am Morgan Turner and I have entered into a pact with your people. You shall not have her."

She is your mate?

Morgan hesitated and glanced at Andi, willing her to be silent. "Yes, she is my mate. Be gone from here. You intrude on our bedchamber."

Laughter, dry and mocking. *We have left such things behind us, having no need for companionship and love.* The shadow flowed past Morgan and rose toward one of the small air-conditioning vents. Drifting like smoke, it hovered at ceiling level. *When our pact is fulfilled, I will return for your mate. You are willing?*

Morgan shrugged. "Sure, why not? I will have no need of her then." He ignored Andi's moan of outrage and held her wrist tightly until the shadow had flowed through the grating and disappeared. "Sorry about that," he murmured, "But what the hell were you doing in here anyway?"

"Has it gone?" she whispered.

"Perhaps," Morgan muttered softly. "Don't say anything my mate wouldn't say. What are you doing here? It's dangerous."

Andi shuddered. "My God, that thing is...is horrible." She shook herself and leaned against Morgan, thrusting back her fear. "I...I just came to talk about where we go next with the machine. You weren't in the living room so I thought you might be asleep in here."

Morgan nodded and raised a finger to his lips, his eyes moving toward the air-conditioning grate. "Well, I'm tired, so I'm going to sleep for a bit. Did you write to your aunt and uncle yet?"

Andi frowned. "No, not yet. I was going to do that this afternoon, so I can catch the morning mail."

"Tell your Uncle Dave hello from me, and say I look forward to talking with him some time soon."

"Okay. I'll leave you to get some sleep then." With a glance at the grating, Andi reached up and kissed Morgan lightly, then grinned and left the apartment, already formulating the phrases for the letter that would bring the FBI running.

*   *   *

"I've really got to hand it to you, Parker. You're one hell of an actor. If I hadn't known better, I'd have believed you really were an obnoxious asshole."

"Why thank you, Braun, but to tell you the truth, you made it easy."

Braun looked around Parker's tiny room with an expression of distaste. The air-conditioning struggled to cope with the rancid odours from the rumpled sheets and the pile of jumbled clothes at the end of the bed. Piles of papers and half a dozen empty coffee cups littered the floor and the small desk in the corner. Braun steered clear of the bed and swept some papers from an upright chair, sitting down and facing the younger man.

"What's the plan? Have you thought of a way to get the machine out?"

Parker grinned. "Of course. Didn't I tell you I would? Is the buyer ready to take delivery?"

Braun nodded. "When?"

"Day after tomorrow. There's a final test tomorrow afternoon, after which the machine is to be dismantled and packed up for shipment. We'll be able to move it out under the noses of the army."

"How? It's going to take more than the two of us to shift it."

"That's where Captain Hurst comes in. He's organised a squad of soldiers to take it out through the back door. If anyone sees us, they'll just assume we're moving stores."

"Which one is Captain Hurst? There are so many soldiers around it's hard to keep track of them."

"Precisely. A bit of rank and the right papers and even someone unfamiliar will command instant obedience from the rank and file. So don't you worry about Hurst, he'll be here when he's needed."

"What if General Spader sees him? He'll know he's not under his orders."

"Then you'll just have to make sure he doesn't see him," Parker said with a touch of exasperation. "Try earning some of that ten million we're getting for this."

"I've done my part," Braun snapped. "Who the hell found the buyer in the first place? Who solved the problem of the crystal arrays? Who worked out..."

"Okay, okay. Don't get your panties in a twist, Braun. You've done good work, okay? Just don't let anything screw this deal up at the last minute."

Braun allowed himself to be mollified. "What about the others?"

"What about them? They're not part of this deal and I'm not sharing any of my money with them."

"That's not quite what I meant. I mean, Spader's going to go ape-shit when he finds his precious machine's missing. As will Turner, for that matter, and Spindler and Newman are going to catch it."

"Tough." Parker shrugged. "What do you want me to do about it, warn them? A hint of this getting out and we're up shit creek." He looked at Braun suspiciously. "You and that Newman broad were screwing. Does she mean something to you?"

"Hell no. She was just a choice piece of ass when I needed it. We had an understanding that neither of us would be exclusive."

Parker brayed a laugh. "Just as well, Braun. She's been screwing just about every male on the base anyway." He stared at Braun's flushed face. "She did mean something to you, you poor sap."

"Not any longer," Braun grunted. "So when do we move?"

"As I said, tomorrow afternoon there's another test run of the machine. I'm going to suggest to Turner that we all have some sort of celebration at the Lodge, which will get all the major players out of the road. You will stay behind, pleading sickness or something--nobody'll miss you--and rendezvous with Hurst and his men. Supervise the packing and moving of the machine to the northern tunnel. Then in the early hours of the morning, around three, we'll exit through the north entrance. Just make sure your contact has trucks ready."

Braun nodded and got up. "I'll send a message..." He broke off and stared at the air-conditioning grating above Parker's bed. "There's something in there," he murmured. "I saw something move."

Parker peered up. "I don't see anything. Are you sure? I don't know what it could be."

"It's some fucking surveillance camera and it's heard everything we said." Braun edged toward the door. "We've got to get out of here."

"Stay where you are," Parker snapped. He jumped up onto his bed and ripped the grating away, revealing a small oblong air shaft. "There's..." He peered into the black depths of the shaft, frowning. "There's nothing here. No cameras, no microphones, no little spy with a pad and pen." Parker turned with a grin. "You're jumpy. You'd better go and get a drink or better yet, get laid...no wait, you can't do that, your girlfriend's screwing the US Army." He brayed with laughter again, redoubling the volume as Braun hurried red-faced from the room.

13

The twelve of them gathered in a small, deep cavern in the Glass House Mountains complex in Queensland, ready for the journey to northern California. They had debated the use of firearms in the struggle against the shadow creatures but after long discussions, had decided to rely solely on the spiritual powers of their own Wandjina, Ernie, and the Olelbis of the Wintun tribe, Moon Wolf. Although guns would be effective against men controlled by the shadows, three factors mitigated their use. Firstly, they did not want to kill men who, through no fault of their own, were in the clutches of the shadow beings; and secondly, as the US Army was involved, they would be vastly outgunned. Lastly--and this ranked most importantly for Sam and James--they saw the use of guns against humans as being uncivilised. Thus, the backpacks that they wore when they congregated in the cavern were filled with food, water and clothing, but no weapons.

Sam, carrying Gaia, and James, met with Ratana, Nathan and Spence for a cup of coffee in the refectory before heading down to the cavern. Very little was said, and even Gaia was subdued, spending her time locked in a mental conversation with one of the Neanderthal children on the base.

Ready for this, love? James asked.

No. I'm still not convinced we should be taking Gaia into harm's way.

We've been over that. I don't like it either, but if the shadows do attack, I'd rather she was with us than thousands of kilometres away.

Sam shrugged mentally. *I still don't like it.*

Two mountains of hair padded quietly into the refectory. *Are you ready? It is time.*

James nodded. *Ready as we'll ever be, Wulgu.* "Okay guys, let's do it."

Amaru and Garagh were waiting beside the large portal outline on the back wall of the cavern. They greeted the travelers as they arrived.

Welcome all, Amaru said. *Please take your positions; we will start the translation in just a few moments. Garagh, would you run over the instructions once more just to be sure there are no mistakes?*

The old Neanderthal nodded. He had exchanged his old blue jean cutaway shorts for a more traditional animal-hide loincloth for the occasion, and armed himself with a long flint-tipped spear. Garagh looked the quintessential caveman except for the carved black crystal hanging against his chest hairs, and a silver Rolex watch on his left wrist.

There are eleven of us, so we have tuned one of our larger transporter portals to the Mount Shasta site in northern California. The other end of this particular transporter in is an old abandoned mine shaft on that mountain. We will be met by a Native North American called Moon Wolf. Please treat him with all the deference you would pay to our own Wandjina, as he is an equivalent power in that part of the world.

We will move through in six groups, for safety. Wandjina and Wulgu will go through first, followed by Spence three minutes later. Wandjina will contact Moon Wolf while Wulgu will act as security for the group. Nathan and Ratana follow, then Sam and James with Rima and Gaia three minutes behind them. Lastly, Amaru and I will come through, having made sure the portal is ready for a retreat, should it be needed.

"Why three minutes?" Sam asked. "Wouldn't it be safer if we all went through together or one immediately after the other? I don't want to be separated from Gaia longer than I have to be."

It is necessary, Garagh replied. *This is not like the short distance translations across degrees of latitude within Australia's east coast. We are crossing half a world and because of the earth's rotation, there is a short delay before the transporter fields can be reconstituted. The three minutes cannot be shortened.*

"Then let me take Gaia."

I'd like you to cross with your husband, Garagh said. *I have made the calculations based on this arrangement.*

She will be safe with me, Samantha, Rima projected.

I'll be okay, mummy. Rima will look after me.

Sam hesitated, desperately wanting to stay close to her baby daughter, but also recognising the logic of the yowie's statement. *All right, darling, and it'll only be for a few minutes. Rima, keep her safe.*

I will die before I let anything happen to her, but nothing can happen. These portals are safe. I have never heard of a malfunction. Rima took the infant from her mother and cradled her in a special padded harness that allowed her hands to remain free.

Garagh consulted his digital watch. *Are we ready? Then Ernie and Wulgu, would you lead off please?*

The old Aboriginal man smiled and stepped into the rock face with the huge yowie half a pace behind. The rock swallowed them both and shimmered for a moment.

Very good, Garagh said. *Counting down...two minutes, thirty seconds...Spence into position please.*

Bloody hell, Spence thought as he stepped up to the wall, *I'm scared to buggery going through these things. What if it fails and I get stuck in the rock?*

It cannot happen, Garagh replied, *but if it will make you feel better, close your eyes.*

"Nathan and Ratana, you are next."

The first of the husband and wife teams prepared themselves. Ratana wore a happy smile of anticipation, but Nathan frowned, rubbing his temple.

"Are you all right, husband?"

"Yeah, I'm okay. Bit of a headache, that's all."

"Have you taken anything for it?"

"Yeah. Doesn't seem to work though."

"You're having a lot of them. Will you ask Wandjina about them?"

"What the hell can he do? He's a magic man, not a doctor."

Ratana's smile vanished and she looked worriedly at her husband. "Do not hold him in disrespect..."

Go, Garagh said.

Nathan stepped forward and Ratana hurried after him, disappearing into the stone portal a few seconds later.

Everything is going well, Garagh said. *James and Sam, you are next.*

'Bye, mummy, daddy, Gaia said. *See you soon.*

Three minutes, darling. Take care of her, Rima.

With my life.

As the three minutes cycled by, James and Sam, looking back over their shoulders, walked into the portal and vanished.

You are next, Rima, Garagh said. *Keep Gaia safe. We are all depending on you.*

I'm only going to be gone three minutes, Rima thought, puzzlement tingeing her mind.

Of course you are, Amaru added. The Neanderthal woman, her head reaching no higher than the yowie's waist, gave the shaggy being a hug before reaching up to stroke the child's head. *Goodbye, my dears.* Behind their backs, his mind carefully blank, Garagh pressed a button that set off a chain of pre-programmed routines. The lights dimmed momentarily as the whole power structure of the Glass House Mountain base was diverted into the transporter circuits.

Gaia looked across at the Neanderthal woman. *What is wrong? There is something in your mind, Amaru. Rima, what is...*

Three minutes, Garagh said. *Go now, Rima, quickly.*

Wait, Rima, Gaia wailed. *There is something wrong with the...*

Rima stepped into the portal, there was a sudden flash of light and the transporter system shut down.

Amaru looked at Garagh in the dim light, her eyes glistening with unshed tears. *What have we done?* she whispered.

Garagh controlled a tremor in his own voice. *We have discussed this, Amaru. We did what must be done.*

Will she be all right? Will either of them survive?

The mathematics came from the 'Others', you know that. Our scientists confirm the theory, so we must trust to the plan.

What will we tell Samantha and James?

You'll think of something, now help me get this portal working again. We have to be in North America.

* * *

The scientists gathered again around the gleaming Vox Dei machine in the great cavern under Glass Mountain. Morgan Turner was there, together with General Spader and his aide, Captain Anders, and to the surprise of almost everyone, so was Ehrich Mannheim.

"What the fuck is Turner's butler doing here?" Parker asked, loudly enough to be heard by everyone. Nobody replied, and Parker asked again, addressing Turner. "Why is the hired help here, Turner? If he's here to serve drinks, I'll have a brandy."

"Just get on with your work, Parker," Spader replied. "Who I have here is none of your business."

"This is a highly sensitive project," Morgan said. "Surely for security reasons only essential personnel should be present."

Spader glanced at Mannheim's impassive face, and then at Andi before he replied. "Ehrich Mannheim is here at my invitation. He is no security risk."

Morgan shook his head and turned back to his place. Parker shrugged and started preparing the device, officiously interfering with the other scientists as they performed their checks and adjustments. Ehrich watched them closely, his dark eyes missing little, and while he was engaged, Morgan edged over to Andi.

"Did you write to your uncle Dave?" he murmured, not looking at her.

"Yes, but I don't know when the letter's going to go out."

"It went at noon. I saw it in the censor's out basket." He saw April Newman looking at them curiously and pointed to a piece of equipment on the bench and in a louder voice asked Andi what it was for.

"Jesus, Morgan," Andi muttered. "It's a gauss meter. It's written on the damn thing."

Morgan nodded as if she had said something interesting. "How long before they get here?"

"How the hell should I know? I tried to make it sound urgent."

"I hope so. Spader's having it packed up tomorrow and shipped out in a couple of days' time."

"What was all that about with your butler?"

"No idea, but if Spader wants him here, who am I to object?"

"All set," Spindler called. "We are ready to go."

Morgan sighed and moved back to the viewing stand, where he sat down next to Spader. "What's so important about this target in Australia? And should we even be doing this? They are our allies, you know."

"I have my orders," Spader said without expression.

Morgan shrugged. "Okay, whatever you say. You're in charge."

Spader glanced toward the impassive Ehrich, but said nothing, merely lifting his hand as a signal to Parker. The young man turned on the power and the Vox Dei machine cycled up, a deep humming filling the cavern.

"How are we going to know if this test is successful?" Braun asked. "There are no cameras at the test site are there?"

"And what's the program we are sending?" Newman added. "All I was given was a disc to load into the computer. It won't let me see the content."

"That is because the content is classified," Spader said. "As for knowing whether it's working, we have a satellite link coming on line in..." he looked at his watch, "...three minutes."

Captain Anders worked the controls attached to the television monitor and shortly, the static on the screen turned to a high shot of a cloudless coastline and an ocean sparkling in bright sunlight.

"I thought it would be nighttime in Australia," Newman said.

"It's about ten in the morning," Anders explained. "They're seventeen hours ahead of us in California." He fiddled with the controlled and the image rapidly expanded, sliding inland from the coast. "Those rocky outcrops are the Glass House Mountains of Australia's State of Queensland, and that one..." he centered the view on a double peak and zoomed in closer "...is our target Tunbubudla."

Andi stared in fascination at the view. These were the Glass House Mountains where her sister Samantha had gone adventuring a year ago, chasing down some far-fetched story about mysterious black rocks and forest monsters. As far as she knew, the expedition had been a failure, but maybe not a total loss as Sam had married the expedition leader, Professor James Hay. Then she had disappeared, along with her husband, while on their honeymoon. Presumed dead by the authorities, Andi had never lost hope that they would one day be found. She leaned closer to the screen, though she realised that the resolution was insufficient to make out individuals, let alone recognise them.

"Feed the coordinates into the machine," Spader instructed.

That was a simple procedure as all April had to do was punch a single key. The Vox Dei swung slowly on its gimbals and the long barrel swung downward as the central column housing the energy conversion machinery rose, lifting the whole device high off the floor.

"What's wrong?" Spader asked. "It shouldn't be doing that."

"Yes it should," Spindler said. "This is not a conventional weapon that fires through the open air, but one that requires a straight line access to the target. Southern Queensland is over eleven thousand kilometres away and the shortest way there is through the planetary crust and upper mantle."

"And it will reach that far through solid rock?"

"It's not all solid, but yes, it will."

"It won't affect what it passes through?"

"No, not as a modulated magnetic beam. In theory, it is possible to change the magnetaser back into a laser at the far end, but what would be the point of that? The energy demands would be far greater than anything we could produce and anyway, a thought control machine has much greater possibilities than a plain old laser."

"Well, thank you for that lesson in military hardware, Dr Spindler," General Spader said. "I think I will leave it up to my superiors to decide on such things. Perhaps you would demonstrate the machine now?"

"Of course, General." Spindler sighted the long barrel at a mark on the floor and flipped a switch. Energies surged and a whisker-thick beam of light stabbed out for an instant, searing the mark from the concrete floor before winking out of existence. "There, the magnetic beam is in place."

Spader looked at the satellite picture of Tunbubudla on the monitor. "How long before it gets there?"

"It's there now. Over these distances, the transmission is almost instantaneous."

Spader grunted. "I don't see anything happening."

"Well, you wouldn't, would you?" Braun said. "There's nobody there to have an effect on. What's the program being sent anyway?"

Newman shrugged. "Don't ask me, I just uploaded the disc I was given."

"What is the program, General?" Spindler asked. "You must know."

"There is something happening," Ehrich said quietly.

The easternmost peak of Tunbubudla glowed and smoke gushed from the flanks of the small mountain. Within the grey and white billows, spurts of orange fire could be discerned as the bush and surrounding forest burst into flame.

"My God," Morgan breathed. "What's happening? Is...is that real or is it an illusion we're being fed?"

Andi quickly checked the settings on the guidance system. "The beam is centered there, not on us, so that's real...holy cow!"

The top of Tunbubudla blew off in a silent paroxysm, the extinct volcano whose eroded throat plug the rocky mountain comprised, erupted violently, sending billows of ash and lava bombs into the sky.

"Are...are we making that happen?" Newman asked. "Should we shut it off?"

"Leave it," Spader rasped. "We have no proof of that. It could just be coincidence." He leaned forward, studying the screen intently.

"That's fucking unlikely," Parker said. "We just happen to aim our beam at an extinct volcano and it erupts. Jeez, it would make a bloody good weapon if that was the case."

"If there's any doubt, we've got to shut it off." Andi took two paces to the side of the machine and flipped the power switch off. Nothing happened. The hum of an operating laser generator continued, and Tunbubudla kept erupting. "It won't switch off," Andi cried, toggling the switch on and off.

"Leave that machine alone, Dr Jones," Ehrich snapped. "Come away from there."

"It's moving!" Braun yelled. "Look!"

The guidance motors whirred and the long barrel moved infinitesimally. On the television monitor, it looked as if a new vent had opened on the north side of the volcano, as fresh eruptions of glowing rock and ash blasted upward. As they watched in horror, the vent lengthened into an oval, and then into a line of fire and smoke that raced northward, cutting through forest and roads, everything in its path being obliterated in an instant.

"There's a town in its path," Morgan yelled in horror, and turned away with tears in his eyes as the houses and streets flashed into oblivion. "It's the machine, it must be. We have to stop it."

"Leave it, Mr Turner," Ehrich snarled. "General, stop them."

Spader drew his pistol and covered Morgan, who was halfway to the control panel. "Turner, you will stop right there. Captain Anders, you will take charge of the control panel and prevent anyone tampering with it, or switching it off."

Anders hesitated, then drew his own pistol and blocked the controls. "Sorry, Mr Turner, but I must ask you to return to your seat."

"But people out there are dying," Morgan roared, "And we're responsible. That's not some enemy village in Afghanistan or somewhere, that's Australia. They are our allies." He strode forward but stopped as Anders raised his pistol in a two-handed grip and cocked it, holding it rock steady against Turner's chest.

The television monitor flared with light and heads that had turned toward the drama being enacted in the cavern turned back toward what was happening half a world away. The beam had reached Mount Beerwah and the ancient rocks were melting and blasting skyward as another extinct volcano roared back into destructive life.

*   *   *

The cavern in the Glass House Mountains base lurched, the rocks screaming in agony as a blast of energy tore through the mountain.

What's happening? Amaru cried.

We're under attack, Garagh yelled back. He continued to program the portal controls, ignoring the rubble falling from the high ceiling. *Nearly there.*

Amaru screamed again, wordlessly. She gripped Garagh's arm fiercely and turned her tear-streaked face to his. *Our people are dying. I can hear their minds screaming at me.*

So can I, daughter, the old Neanderthal man said. *Do not distract me. I must finish this or we could all die.*

Amaru nodded and concentrated, talking with her mind to the personnel of the base, finding out what she could, gasping in horror at the news. *Tunbubudla and Beerwah are destroyed; the fire is turning toward Coonowrin and Ngungun. I fear Tibrogargan will follow shortly.*

All the more reason for me to do this, then, Garagh growled. His fingers flew and he nodded. *Now we must wait for the energies to coalesce.* He looked at his watch. *Two minutes, with luck.*

Do we have two minutes? Amaru muttered. She winced as a wave of agony flooded her mind. *Our people die.*

I hear them, Garagh confirmed. *Who is doing this, and how?*

Xanatuo says the source is northern California. Somehow they are stimulating the ancient magma chambers beneath these mountains. He says we must shut the beam off or we will all be destroyed.

Garagh grunted. *Did he say how?*

No.

The rock groaned and a wave of heat washed into the cavern. *The fire is here,* Amaru said. *Only the fact that the magma chamber lies deeper beneath Tibrogargan has saved us so far. Is the portal ready? We must use it.*

If the fire is here, then our energy sources may be compromised. It is too dangerous to use the portal.

Then we are lost, together with our people.

Not if we can stop it. There is one person in the enemy camp who might do this, could we but contact her?

Samantha's sister? We do not know her mental signature.

That is true, but Sam knows her sister well. That knowledge may be enough. I will contact Wandjina. Garagh turned away, concentrating.

And I will try to reach Sam, Amaru said quietly.

The two Neanderthals stood in silence, concentrating on the mental patterns of two beings half a world away.

Wandjina?

Garagh? I hear you. What is the matter? Why are you not with us?

*We are under attack. The beam from the Californian machine...*Garagh imparted a mental picture of the problem and what he thought might be the solution.

Amaru was also busy. *Sam? Sam? Answer me.*

What? I can only just hear you. What has happened? Is Gaia all right?

Yes. We are being attacked. You must contact your sister and have her shut down the machine.

What? How? I don't know how to talk to her. Baby, are you there? Mummy loves you. Gaia?

She loves you too, Sam. Wandjina can help. Ernie. Talk to him.

Ernie's rich thoughts enveloped them all. *Sam, we must move quickly if we are to save lives. You must talk to your sister Andi.*

But I don't know how. I've never spoken mentally to her.

I will guide you and strengthen your thoughts. Think of her. Show me a picture of who you know her to be.

Several minutes of silence passed, during which the earth tremors in Mount Tibrogargan increased and the stench of burning rock grew stronger.

I have her, Ernie said at last. *I will hold the line open. Speak to her, Sam.*

What do I say?

She must close the beam down. Tell her we are all in danger.

All right...Andi? Andi, are you there?

* * *

Andi?

Andi's head jerked around. "What?"

Morgan looked up and frowned. "What did you say, Andi?"

"Didn't you just...?" She shook her head and scanned the other people in the cavern.

Andi, are you there?

"Of course, I'm bloody well here. Who's talking?"

Spader stared at the young woman. "Who are you talking to, Dr Jones?"

Andi shook her head again. "Sorry, I thought somebody said something."

Andi. Don't talk, just listen. This is Sam.

Involuntarily, Andi exclaimed "Sam!" causing Spader, and then Ehrich to look round at her.

"What are you saying, and to whom, Dr Jones?" Ehrich asked.

"No one, sorry." Andi waved a hand at the television monitor with its continuing views of destruction. "M...my sister Samantha was in that area last year. I was just thinking how terrible this would be for her."

"If the scenes trouble you, perhaps you should return to your quarters."

"I'm all right." Inside her head, the voice came again. *Andi, it's Sam. Don't say anything. If you formulate a thought, I can hear you.*

Sam? Is that really you?

Yes, now listen, this is very...

Where have you been? I've been worried sick.

Andi. Shut up and listen. That machine of yours is killing people in Australia. You have to stop it.

You're in Australia?

No, but my daughter Gaia is--your niece, and your machine is endangering her. Switch it off. Now.

I...I'll try. It's under guard. Andi stared at Captain Anders, then at the rest of the people in the cavern, watching the unfolding drama on the monitor. She moved casually across to Morgan.

"Are you okay?" he asked, concern in his eyes.

"We have to stop this," Andi murmured. "People are getting killed."

"Agreed, but how? Anders will shoot anyone who tries to stop it."

Andi looked around carefully. "If I started a diversion, it might distract Anders. You could stop the machine."

"Okay, but how do I stop it? Is there an 'off' switch?"

"Yes, but I tried that, it doesn't work. You'll have to pull the plug on the power inlet over on the far wall."

Andi. Hurry!

"Here goes nothing," Andi muttered. She turned and walked across the front of the monitor, drawing people's attention as she went. Marching up to

April Newman, she pushed the smaller woman hard, sending her staggering backward. "It's you, Newman. You're the one who knows all about programming. You always supply the programs for this machine so all this destruction is down to you." Andi pushed the woman again. "Murderer!" she screamed.

Newman stepped backward, then sideways, trying to avoid Andi. "What the hell are you talking about? I had nothing to do with this. Spader gave me the disc with the program already installed."

"Liar. Murderer." Andi slapped April Newman and the smaller woman gasped with shock and tried to bat Andi's arm away.

"Tell her, Spader," Newman demanded. When the General said nothing, she rounded on the other men who were watching the proceedings with varying degrees of concern or amusement. "Ow, stop that you bitch."

Andi gave Newman's blond curls a yank, pulling her forward. She responded with a roundhouse punch that sent Andi reeling back. "You're a liar," she gasped, advancing on the smaller woman again. They grappled, and Andi forced Newman back, knocking into the barrel of the Vox Dei.

"Hey, careful!" Braun yelled. "You'll damage something. Stop them someone--Parker, you're closest."

"Do it yourself," Parker replied. His eyes followed the struggling women with a great smirk plastered over his face.

Spindler tried to interfere, but Andi slapped him away and redoubled her efforts against Newman.

"Turner," Spader called out. "Control your damn employees before I have to get Captain Anders to shoot them. Turner?"

Ehrich turned away from his avid scrutiny of the monitor and saw Morgan edging around the far end of the machine. "There is Turner," he said, pointing. "He is going for the power. Shoot him, Anders. Quickly."

Anders turned, swinging his pistol from where he had been covering the fighting women. He raised it and hesitated, glancing toward Spader. "General?"

"Do it, Anders. That is an order," Spader rapped.

Morgan threw himself behind the generator as Anders pulled the trigger and the bullet whined off the generator housing. He struggled with the giant ceramic plug but could not shift it in his crouching position. As Anders ran toward him, Morgan emptied a toolbox onto the concrete floor and grabbed a large hammer. Another shot ricocheted off the floor and Morgan dodged and swung the hammer at the ceramic connection. It shattered in a sputtering explosion of light, throwing Morgan backward, the machine immediately falling silent as the power died.

Andi ran over to the prostrate, unmoving body of her employer, and fell to her knees beside him. "He's not breathing. I...I think his heart's stopped."

Spader pushed Parker toward the doorway. "Get the medics--hurry."

Anders meanwhile, holstered his pistol and pushed Andi to one side. "I know CPR." He knelt beside Morgan and applied the heel of one hand to the basal part of the unconscious man's sternum, pushing down hard in a short, sharp rhythm, counting out the thrusts aloud. Andi nodded and positioned herself near Morgan's head and tilted it back, clearing the air passages. When Anders reached the end of his counted thrusts, she blew, filling his lungs twice before allowing the captain to resume.

Several minutes later, with Morgan still unconscious, the medics arrived and took charge, hurrying him off to the infirmary.

The scientists left, after looking with curiosity at Andi who remained sitting on the floor. Ehrich walked out without a backward glance and Spader followed. Anders remained for a moment. "Sorry I tried shooting him, Dr Jones. I was only following orders you know."

Andi scowled. "That old excuse."

Anders pursed his lips and offered a hand to the sitting woman, but she shook her head. "Okay," he said, and left her alone in the silent chamber.

After a few moments, Andi struggled to her feet. *Samantha? Are you there? Are you all right?*

Her mind, like the chamber under Glass Mountain, remained silent.

14

"How the hell was I to know that stupid bastard would lose it like that?" Parker said. He paced up and down in his room, almost hopping with nervous energy and worrying at a torn fingernail with his crooked yellow teeth. "We were on the point of success, being able to blow this miserable place with a fortune, and what happens? That fucking Morgan Turner blows a cog and screws things up."

Braun lounged in the only easy chair in the room. He scratched his head and looked quizzically at the younger man. "You could say it was Turner that screwed everything up, but only because the Jones bitch helped. She was the diversion that almost worked."

Parker stared at the other scientist. "What? You believe she deliberately picked on Newman enabling Turner to go mad and try and wreck things?"

"Is that so incredible? We know they're buddies already, and she had tried to shut the machine off earlier. When that doesn't work, she creates a diversion while he shuts it down." Braun shrugged. "It seems obvious to me."

"What fucking nonsense this whole thing is." Parker sat down on his unmade bed and stared across the room at the far wall, thinking. "Why would they want to wreck the machine?" he muttered. "It's a fucking marvelous invention."

"I thought that was obvious," Braun said. "The beam was killing people in Australia."

Parker shrugged. "Yeah, okay, but to try to wreck the damn thing? Just shutting it off would have achieved that. There was no reason to destroy it."

"Perhaps she felt a bit more strongly about it. After all, her sister had been in that part of Australia. Hell, perhaps her sister is still there. I don't know why I'm telling you all this--you were there too. And I must admit I thought you'd be a little more concerned about the destruction."

"Why? I don't know anyone in Australia. Are you that concerned?"

Braun shifted uncomfortably in his chair. "If they ever find out it was us..."

"Even if they did, this is an army project and we were under orders." Parker shrugged again. "It's not our fault."

Braun grimaced. "If you say so, but I don't like it."

"I can see why Jones might be upset but what's Turner's motive? Why would he go berserk?"

"Perhaps he saw it as a chance to score points with Jones. Get into her pants."

"Shit, you guys who are ruled by your dicks," Parker sneered. "You're telling me he damn near got himself killed for a piece of ass? Is that what you'd do?"

Braun flushed angrily. "No way, I'm just saying it's possible. We know they have a history of some sort but she's not sleeping with him." He shrugged again. "What the hell does it matter? I'm just looking for a reason for his behaviour."

Parker grinned. "Makes you think though."

"About what? Whether they're sleeping together?"

"No, you sad dick. Get your mind out of the gutter. About the Vox Dei. I never knew it had those capabilities, did you?"

Braun hesitated. As scientist in charge of the crystal arrays and the transmogrification of the laser into the magnetaser, he should have been most aware of the possibilities of a beam reversal. Reluctantly, he decided the other man would not believe him, so he told the truth. "No, I had no idea. In fact, I would have said it was impossible. I don't see how you can possible reverse the beam change at a distance without another battery of crystals."

"I didn't think you knew."

"Oh, and you do, I suppose?"

"No, but I have no difficulty admitting it." Parker laughed. "Do you at least see what this means?"

Braun stared resentfully at the other man. "What?" he said sulkily.

"It means your buyer is going to be coughing up a lot more than a paltry ten million dollars. This machine has suddenly become an unstoppable weapon of mass destruction. Hell, imagine if that power was unleashed on a city."

"You wouldn't do that, would you?"

Parker snorted. "I wouldn't--and I doubt anyone actually would. The mere threat would be enough. Imagine a demonstration on some uninhabited island and then an ultimatum--cough up or burn. Shit!"

Braun thought hard. "He would, wouldn't he? Twenty million, you think? Ten each?"

"How the hell did I ever get mixed up with such a small mind? If you're satisfied with ten million, let me tell you I'm not. A hundred million would be closer to the mark, maybe more."

"He'd never go for it. That's a hell of a lot of money and what have we got to show him? A bunch of programs and some footage that could have been digitally created."

"Then we'll have to show him more. Contact the buyer and tell him what happened this time and to be ready for the next demonstration."

"What next one? The damn thing's broken."

"The ceramic connector's broken. That can be fixed in a few hours. I'll suggest to Spader that the machine will have to be tested again. This time, though, I'll find out where the demonstration will be, in advance."

Braun nodded grudgingly. "It could work."

"Damn straight," Parker crowed. "Contact the buyer. I'll con Spader."

*　　*　　*

"Turner and Jones are loose cannons," Ehrich said. "They must be neutralised."

"I hope you are not suggesting we kill them," Spader growled. "This is still the US Army and we don't go around killing civilians, no matter how inconvenient they are. Besides, Turner's in hospital and won't be going anywhere soon. If you think Jones is still a threat I can have her locked up."

"Have you forgotten who is in charge?" Ehrich asked softly.

"No, I haven't, but why risk awkward questions when we can achieve the same results by behaving calmly?"

Ehrich considered for a few moments before nodding. "Have Dr Jones locked up somewhere dark."

Spader frowned at the suggestion, but could think of no good reason to refuse his superior. "What was that all about with the machine?"

Ehrich raised an eyebrow quizzically.

"We committed an act of war on a friendly country."

"I did not see aggression, just a formerly dormant volcano field spring back into life." Ehrich shrugged. "The loss of life and property is to be regretted, of course, but I daresay they will all be fully compensated by the insurance companies."

"But the Vox Dei caused it."

Ehrich stared coolly at the General. "It was my understanding that the laser became a magnetaser to carry information. Supposedly, the beam cannot change back. How then is our machine to blame for what happened?"

"What about the fact that we were aiming right at the mountain when it blew up?"

"Coincidence, General. What possible reason could I have to want to commit this supposed crime?"

"I don't know," Spader admitted. "But would you tell me if you had a reason?"

"You are used to giving and taking orders, are you not, General?" Ehrich did not wait for a reply to what was a rhetorical question. "Well, as you rise through the ranks of the Brotherhood of Nine, you will do likewise. I am far above you, but I too take my orders from my superiors. I have learned not to question my orders but to carry them out quickly and completely, to the best of my ability. You would do well to follow my example."

"I am loyal to the Nine," Spader said in a low voice.

"Good, then let us have no more talk of petty moralities. We do what must be done."

Spader nodded. "What are your orders?"

"Have the machine repaired. It must be tested once more."

"Where? Australia again?"

Ehrich grinned mirthlessly. "No, that purpose has been served. Somewhere closer this time."

"Where?"

"I will prepare the program for the machine and let you know in due course."

"I don't wish to appear to doubt your orders, Mannheim, but can you..." Spader was interrupted by a knock on the door. "Who the hell is...Come!"

The door opened and Parker sauntered in, grinning at the General. His smile slipped when he saw Ehrich but he nodded at the man.

"Hello Ehrich. What are you doing here? How's your boss?"

"Dr Parker." Ehrich inclined his head slightly, his gaze boring into the other man's eyes. "Mr Turner is recovering in the infirmary. It will be a day or two before he rejoins us."

Parker fidgeted under Ehrich's unrelenting stare. "Any idea why he blew a gasket like that? We were lucky he didn't do more damage."

"Precisely how much damage was done, doctor? And how long will it take to fix?"

"Not much. The ceramic power plug and one of the crystal blocks. A few hours should do it." Parker hesitated before asking again, "Do you know why Turner lost it?"

"Stress, I would imagine. Mr Turner has been under a lot of pressure."

"I think Jones had something to do with it. They've been together a lot recently."

"An interesting supposition. Perhaps General Spader will investigate. I have no authority here."

"No, of course not. Well, what about it, General? Are you going to investigate her?"

"I have a number of other things vying for my attention, Parker," Spader rasped, "But I will make sure the matter is looked into. Why are you here?"

"I wanted to ask you about the machine." Parker jerked his head toward Ehrich. "Can I talk freely in front of him? He's just Turner's butler after all. No offence," he added.

Ehrich inclined his head minimally, but said nothing.

"You may. Mr Mannheim represents Mr Turner's interests until such time as Mr Turner recovers completely."

"Okay then. What I wanted to say was that the damage to the machine is minimal and can easily be repaired."

Spader nodded. "That was my understanding."

"Then as soon as it is repaired, we should institute another test."

"Really? Why? The machine functioned perfectly satisfactorily."

"It did?" Parker looked surprised. "You knew it was going to do that? To convert back into a laser?"

"I remind you that this project is classified."

"Yeah, and I'm one of the scientists working on the damn classified machine. Hell, even we didn't know it was going to do that. Did you?"

Spader decided he was not going to admit his ignorance, so he remained silent, giving the scientist what he considered to be an enigmatic stare.

"You didn't, huh? Well, I'd sure as hell like to see the specifications for that modification." He waited for the General's response, looking hopeful. "No? So when are you going to run another test?"

"I told you. I don't think we need to do one."

"What if that laser reconversion was just a fluke? What if, after the repairs, you can't duplicate those results? Your bosses are going to be mightily pissed off."

"Dr Parker does have a point, General," Ehrich said softly. "I think we should run another test."

"Now you're talking," Parker crowed. "When and where?"

"As soon as the repairs are done, I would say." Ehrich shrugged. "It is not for me to decide where. I'm only Mr Turner's assistant."

"That's okay with you, General?" Parker asked.

Spader glanced at Ehrich but received no further help. "Sure. You let me know when it's fixed."

"And where will the test take place?"

"I'll let you know."

"May I suggest somewhere close by? So we can see the results first-hand."

"I'll let you know."

"Jeez, the fucking military mind. Don't you ever make a decision on your own?"

"Dr Parker, please remember that you are no longer essential to this project. You have been useful, but I'm sure we can make the repairs without recourse to your expertise. I have said I will let you know. If that is not satisfactory, I can have you removed from the team forthwith. Do I make myself clear?"

"Yeah, don't get your panties in a twist," Parker muttered. Louder, he said, "Okay, okay, you made your point. I'll shut up and let you get on with it, but tell me as soon as you make up your mind." He turned on his heel and, ignoring Ehrich, stalked from the room, slamming the door behind him.

"Damn the man," Spader said as the reverberations died away. "As if I haven't got better things to do."

"Ignore his desires. Focus on what needs to be done."

Spader nodded and picked up the telephone receiver. He spoke to his aide, Captain Anders, and outlined exactly what he expected to happen within the next twenty-four hours, and who he expected to accomplish it. When he finished, he listened to Anders repeat back his instructions and told him to carry on.

"One thing worries me," Spader said to Ehrich as he hung up the phone. "Why was Parker so insistent on knowing where the test is to take place? It shouldn't matter to him at all."

Ehrich nodded. "Yes, it was curious."

"Perhaps he was just being self-important, wanting to know something none of his colleagues know."

"Or he can see a benefit in knowing."

Spader frowned. "Such as?"

"Money and ideology are the two most common reasons for betrayal. I cannot see ideology as the governing force behind Dr Travis Parker, so I would guess he hopes to make money with the knowledge."

"How?"

"That is indeed the question," Ehrich said. "I shall see what I can find out."

Spader raised an eyebrow. "You have spies in here? Who is it? I have a right to know."

"On the contrary, General, you do not need to know and for the sake of your own health, you do not want to know."

"I need to know if you have suborned my men for your own purposes. There are no civilians on this base except the scientists, Turner and yourself." Spader thought hard for a moment. "Wait, you were responsible for April Newman being hired. She's your spy."

Ehrich bared his teeth in what he took to be an expression of merriment. "Not even close." He held up a hand as Spader opened his mouth to speak again. "I forbid you to question me further on this. To ease your mind though, none of your soldiers work for me."

Spader shrugged and yawned. "Okay, I'll leave it to you then though I'll be damned if I can figure out how you'll do it."

"The other question is what we do with the scientists after this is all over."

"I thought you'd decided that already. You said you were going to have terrorists strike and destroy the machine and the scientists--tonight in fact. Is that not now going to happen?"

"Not tonight," Ehrich said. "It is imperative we complete one more test, destroy one more site before I terminate the project."

"But you are still determined to do this?"

"Of course. The Nine cannot afford to leave the machine, or knowledge of its construction, in the hands of the US Army. They would make another, and the edge we had would be eroded." Ehrich moved toward the door. "I will get things moving and supply you with the program and target later tonight." He nodded a dismissive farewell to General Spader and left the room.

The guard outside flicked a curious gaze at the thin, stiff man as he left, but said nothing. He had learned early that while the general might control his life in the army, the man known as Turner's butler had his hand on the throat of every man on the base. The guard watched him go with some relief. His buddies reckoned Ehrich was a hypnotist, capable of planting a suggestion in a man's disbelieving mind. Twice, a soldier had been dismissive of the quiet butler and each time, the only thing he had said in retaliation was 'beware the night', and each time horrific nightmares had followed.

Ehrich refused to hurry--haste made mistakes--and deliberately walked slowly back to his own quarters. While his body appeared relaxed however, his mind was working furiously. He did not spare a thought for the guard outside the general's door, nor for the other soldiers in the corridors. It did not even register with him that they stepped aside, assiduously avoiding his touch. The outside world did not concern him at all--only what was to come.

I'll have to call the shadows, he thought. *That's the only way to find out what Parker's up to.*

When he reached the suite of rooms that housed Morgan Turner and him, he stopped to check that his employer had not returned unexpectedly from the infirmary. The living room lay dim and silent and though he listened, nothing disturbed the emptiness of the suite. He closed the door and walked down the corridor to his own small apartment.

Ehrich's own space was Spartan in the extreme. He had embraced a life of service to the Nine at an early age and had eschewed comforts and personal gain in his drive to climb the rungs of the organisation toward power and knowledge. The arrival of the shadow beings, the Winambuu, had given him a long sought boost, an ability to impress the Nine themselves, now so close above him in the hierarchy. It was a dangerous game, and had Ehrich been a religious man, he would have suspected allying himself with the shadows had put his mortal soul in peril. He had long been an atheist, however, and knew that all he had to lose was his mind and his life. The gains were incalculable though, and he reckoned the stakes worthwhile.

He stood in the middle of his room--ignoring the bare walls, the narrow cot bed, the plain table and upright chair, and the laptop computer which was his only luxury item--and addressed the gaping black ventilation duct high up on one wall, just below the ceiling. "Winambuu, come to me."

Silence greeted him, and a gentle curl of cold air that slipped into the room, welcome in itself, but bearing with it a faint unidentifiable odour. Ehrich found himself thinking of country churchyards from a distant youth, snow crunching under foot as he walked beneath skeletal trees and past hoar-frosted granite headstones, the moon bathing the cemetery in dark shadow rather than silvery light. The tomb yawned before him and he heard a dry, scaly slithering within its depths, but he could not move, frozen like the surrounding grave markers as he waited for...

Ehrich shivered despite himself. He knew what the shadows were trying to do and he resisted it. "Winambuu, cease your games and come to me."

The sound of a grave cloth rasping over a frozen corpse whispered from the vent. *What do you want, human?*

"Show yourself."

Dark smoke poured from the opening, but unlike smoke it did not dissipate but hung in the air, vaguely human in shape, with yellow, unblinking eyeholes turned toward Ehrich. *Do you like what you see, human?* it whispered mockingly.

"Are you the one I spoke with before?"

Amusement. *I am Winambuu.*

"There is little point talking to you unless you know what I seek. Fetch the one I spoke with before."

Anger. *You do not command the Winambuu.*

"Nevertheless, you will do as I say."

With a hiss of fury, the shadow swept back into the duct as if sucked by a giant vacuum. There was silence in the room for the space of time it takes to remember a half-forgotten thought, then abruptly, another shadow appeared in the room.

I am Winambuu. The smoke form appeared more cohesive, more solid than the first one, but in all other respects it was identical.

Ehrich knew that he had no way of knowing for sure that this was the being he had dealt with before--they did not seem to have individual names or even true identities. "I have done what you asked. The machine has laid waste the Australian mountains."

The work was not complete. Why was it stopped before destruction was total?

Ehrich explained what had happened. "The machine is being repaired. Tomorrow we test it again. We can complete the destruction of the Glass House Mountains if you like."

The enemy has gone from there. You will destroy another place.

"Whatever you like. Where?"

The information is on your computer. Create a disc and feed it to the machine.

Ehrich nodded, glancing at his laptop. Somehow, the shadow beings could interact with the electronic components and create complex programs ready to be downloaded onto a disc. "There is something I need, Winambuu."

Ask.

"One of the scientists, Travis Parker, is very curious about where the machine will be tested next time. I would like to know why."

You know the price. Are you willing?

Ehrich nodded, though reluctantly. "I need to know very soon."

I know now. Nothing that goes on in your base escapes our notice. We overheard this Travis Parker of yours talking to a Kenneth Braun.

"What did they say?"

They desire to take the machine. They spoke of a Captain Hurst who will help them.

"But why does he want to know where the next test is? If he just wanted to steal it, it would not matter."

He wishes an exhibition of power. He thinks to trade the machine for wealth.

"We cannot allow this."

No. They must be stopped.

"Why did you not stop them immediately?"

A feeling of contempt flowed over Ehrich. *Why should I? It amuses me to watch their futile efforts. Every man in this place will die soon anyway. We shall destroy our enemies and then you shall carry the machine to a place of our choosing, there to use it to destroy the fabric of space-time so that our kind cannot be kept out of this world.*

The words chilled Ehrich, though he knew that the aims of the Brotherhood of Nine were no less sanguine. In part it was the lack of any human emotion in the dry whispers, in part the utter disregard for life. He would willingly kill for the Nine, as he had in Australia, but only as much as was needed to accomplish any given purpose. Wanton killing was wasteful of resources.

"When will I take the machine away?"

After the test in which you destroy our enemies in North America. You will use the machine to destroy this base and every human within, and then carry the machine away.

"I will need help."

You shall have it. We will possess all we need.

Ehrich shivered, knowing from experience what possession meant. "Who will you..."

Enough. Anger flowed, almost palpably. *It is time for you to pay the price.*

Ehrich opened his mouth to speak, in a vain attempt to put the moment off. *Now I know how a man feels who is made to dig his own grave. If co-operation will buy a few more instants of life...*"Aaah." The black shadow flowed, pouring into his mouth and through his nostrils, filling every cavity of his body before oozing out to occupy his tissues with the tenuous substance of Winambuu being. Ehrich felt as if he was drowning, helpless to prevent his occupation. After a few moments of panic, during which he could not move a muscle, the shadow relaxed and Ehrich found he could breathe again.

A thought that was not his own skittered along his neurons. *You humans have an interesting biology. I will experience the sex act. Choose a partner.*

"I...I do not have a...a partner," Ehrich gasped, forcing his tongue and lips to form the words.

Then I will choose one.

An image formed in Ehrich's mind and his rising unease dissipated slightly. "What if he does not want to?"

My brethren can be quite persuasive. Ehrich started walking jerkily toward the door of his apartment, feelings of lust that were not totally due to the possession of the Winambuu, starting to surge within him.

15

"Where's my baby? Where's Gaia?" Concern but not yet panic tinged Sam's voice as she confronted Amaru.

The Neanderthal man and woman had just stepped out of the rock wall of the tunnel into the small group of people who had preceded them. They clustered around, anxiously asking about the attack on the Glass House Mountain base.

Everything is all right, Garagh said, holding up his hands to sooth the turmoil of his listeners. *We don't know how precisely, but the shadow people engineered an attack on us using this machine we have come to destroy. It has done great damage, but nothing that cannot be repaired.*

Except over a hundred of our people, Amaru mourned. *Let us not forget their loss.*

I am not forgetting them, Garagh chided, *But they would be the first to encourage us to do the job we came to do.*

"What about Gaia?" James pushed his way forward and confronted Garagh, looking down at the thickset but diminutive man. "Where is she? I thought she was coming through ahead of you."

For a moment, Garagh refused to meet James' eyes. *What do you mean? Is she not here?*

"Do you think we'd be asking if she was?" Sam's voice rose as she confronted Garagh too. "What happened? Where's my baby?"

Amaru came to stand alongside her great-grandfather, gazing up at the tall human woman with a depth of sorrow showing. *Samantha, she is safe.*

"Thank God." James sighed deeply. "But where is she? Did you decide to leave her behind?"

"You don't sound too sure," Sam said, eyeing Amaru askance. "And what if there is another attack? I want to go back. I should be with her."

Remember Rima is with her.

"I know, and I'm grateful, but it's not the same thing." Sam looked beyond Amaru to the featureless tunnel wall. "Where's the portal? Set it so I can go back to be with her."

I am sorry, Samantha, Amaru said. *The portal is inoperable at the moment. No one can go back just yet.*

"Why is it inoperable?" Spence asked, staring at the two Neanderthals. "I've grown used to your body language and you're hiding something."

"Are you?" James asked. "What is it?"

Garagh nodded. *We did not want to alarm you...*

"My baby!" Sam cried.

...as we cannot be certain, but...well, we were under attack when we came through the portal. I fear it malfunctioned.

Ratana cried out in anguish and put her arms around Sam. Nathan looked troubled. "How did it malfunction? With what effect?"

We don't know, Amaru said calmly, *But we are not worried. There are many safeguards written into these devices.*

"Where is Gaia?" James said flatly, stepping close to Garagh in his anger. "Stop beating about the bush and tell us. Is she back at Glass House Mountain base?"

Garagh retreated a step and glared at James. *No, she is not. I believe that the attack caused something to fail in the portal as Rima and Gaia stepped through it-- something in the direction finder, not in the actual teleport mechanism itself.*

"Then where is she?"

I don't know. She could have gone to any one of a hundred destinations.

"Or nowhere," Nathan murmured, his eyes gleaming with fascination. He looked at Spence, noting the shock and horror on the older man's face, and shrugged. "Hey, I don't know the mechanism by which these things work. Isn't that a possibility?"

"Nathan," Ratana hissed. "Shhh!" She hugged Sam closer to her.

I do not know the mechanism either, Garagh replied. *You must talk to our scientists if you are interested, but they assure me they are completely safe.*

"Nothing's completely safe," Nathan said.

We have been using portals for half a thousand years, Amaru said softly. *In all that time, I can only recall two malfunctions. In both cases, the person was found alive and well a few days later.*

"What had happened to them?" James asked.

They went to a portal destination other than the one they intended. Spence thought about this for a moment. "And it took them a few days to figure that out and return?

No, Spencer. Not all our portals, not all our chambers are in constant use. We have shut many of them down but they can still take one-way traffic. When this happens, a technician must go through the portal to reset it.

"So this means exactly what?" James asked. "You know where they are but there will be a delay getting them back? Or you don't know where they are?"

We don't know where they are at present.

Please do not be concerned, Amaru said soothingly. *Rima is with her and she has sworn to protect Gaia with her life. Wherever they are, no harm will come to her.*

"Then find her," Sam snapped. "Find her and bring her here, or send me to her."

It is not that simple, Samantha. The portal is inoperable for the moment, and the means by which we can search the many caverns worldwide is back at the base.

"Then what are you going to do?" James asked grimly. "And I should warn you, do not say you will do nothing."

You are unnecessarily harsh with us, Garagh said. *None of this was our fault, and we feel your loss--your temporary loss--keenly.* He looked beyond James for a moment, into the darkness of the tunnel and a faint blue light that bobbed and weaved as it came closer. *Amaru will stay behind and conduct a search through the communications channel of this portal. While it will not transport matter, it does have a limited communications function. She can contact home base and set up a search. It will be slow, but it will be done.*

"Then I'm staying to help her," Sam said.

"And I." Ratana held Sam tightly and stared at the little group as if daring any of them to challenge her right to stay.

James nodded. "Thank you, Ratana." He hugged Sam and kissed her. "Do you want me to stay too?"

"No, you go and do your boy's things. Ratana and I will be fine. Just look after yourself and come back to me quickly."

Here is Wandjina, Garagh said, gesturing toward the tunnel. *And others are with him.*

A blue light illuminated the tunnel, the steady light issuing from Ernie's cupped hand held aloft. The old Aboriginal man was clothed in a red loincloth and headband and was daubed in white wood ash in the patterns pertinent to the tribe to which he purported to belong. He looked younger, his muscles tight and rounded and the grey was gone from his hair.

"Crikey, mate," Spence said. "You look different. You been working out or something?"

Wandjina grinned. "The appearance of age is useful when one is asked for counsel. When action is required, I adopt a younger body."

"And the designs?"

"I need all the help I can get from the ancestors."

"I know what you mean. I have my own back-up." Spence took out a heavy greenstone tiki from under his shirt. The carving twirled on its leather cord, the smooth limbs of the squat carved figurine scintillating in the blue fire. "It's been in my tribe for many generations, passed down from father to son."

"Who's your friend, Ernie?" James asked quietly.

Standing slightly behind the Aboriginal man, half-concealed in the shadows cast by the blue light, stood a tall, grey-haired Native American. Unlike Wandjina, this man was dressed simply in a modern shirt and jeans with heavy hiking boots on his feet. He smiled gently but did not say a word.

"This is Olelbis, otherwise known as Moon Wolf. He has come to help us in our fight against the shadow people. Olelbis, this is Dr James Hay, his wife Samantha, Spencer Tuhua..."

Moon Wolf held up his hands, palms toward Spence. "You are a holy one, Spencer Tuhua. I can feel your being."

Spencer bowed. "And I yours, old one. I am in your service."

"This is Nathan Wambiri and his wife Ratana," Wandjina went on, "And these are representatives of the ancient men, Amaru and Garagh."

"I am honoured," Moon Wolf said simply. "But Wandjina, so few? What can we accomplish?"

"Few, but worthy," Wandjina said. "And there is Wulgu, who waits outside to guard the entrance."

"Wulgu? Ah, you mean the Shupchet, the Sasquatch? I saw him dimly in the forest. Is he reliable? I have found them prone to wandering off when they lose interest."

Wandjina grinned. "You haven't met Wulgu. He's as intelligent as any man."

"And there's no one I'd rather have guard my back in a tight situation," Spence added.

Wulgu is not a Sasquatch, Garagh said. *He is an Australian yowie. We created the yowie using our own and gorilla genes and gave them high intelligence and loyalty. Sasquatch, on the other hand, is descended from the ancient* Gigantopithecus *and while physically similar to the yowie, is mentally very different.*

Moon Wolf looked troubled. "You tamper with the genetic material? You seek to make yourselves gods?"

Garagh bridled. *Not gods. We follow the leadership of ones who call themselves the 'Others' and have taught us these techniques.*

"Who are these 'Others' you speak of?"

Wandjina slipped an image of a spacecraft in planetary orbit into Moon Wolf's mind.

"Aliens? You trust beings from elsewhere to advise you on the governance of your own People, of the planet?"

They have guided us for thirty thousand years and they have not betrayed our trust. When they first contacted me, I was suspicious, but they have always been truthful.

"You have lived for thirty thousand years?" Moon Wolf exclaimed. "Are you sure you are not a Great One like Wandjina and me?" He stared at the stocky Neanderthal for a few moments. "No, you are human, after your fashion, though artificially strengthened."

Garagh nodded. *I know of this. We should be going. The females will stay here and contact our home base. There has been an accident and we must correct it.*

The old Native American frowned. "There is something in your mind concerning this accident which I do not understand. You have..."

Wandjina interrupted mentally. *Please say nothing, Olelbis. I will explain this matter to you as we journey, and show you why Garagh has acted as he has.*

Moon Wolf shrugged and looked away. "It is none of my concern. Come then, we should get moving if we are to be in place by tomorrow's nightfall."

"Where are we going?" James asked.

"And where are we now, for that matter," Nathan added.

"We are in the depths of the mountain Bulyum-pui-yuk that you call Shasta. We are going to a small hillock called Glass Mountain some fifty miles away."

"What an odd coincidence," Spence remarked.

"Er, how are we going to go fifty miles across mountainous country in less than a day?" Nathan asked. "I only ask because I really don't feel much like hiking."

Moon Wolf smiled, his teeth glittering in the blue light still shining steadily from the upraised hand of Wandjina. "I do not know how you do it in Australia, but we have our own ways." He turned and set off up the gently sloping adit, seemingly not needing illumination to make his way over the roughened stone floor.

As Wandjina increased the strength of the blue spectral light, Nathan hurried off after Moon Wolf and engaged him in conversation. "I'm very interested in your local North American ways of travel across great distances," he said. "My people have holy men called Karadji, who can, with preparation, travel like an emu--do you know the emu? It's a large flightless bird that can run at great speed. My grandfather Mick is a Karadji-man and he can run very fast for hours on end, but he cannot transfer the ability to anyone else. I take it you can? I can't see of any other way to get where we're going so fast. Can you transfer the ability?"

"Nathan Wambiri, you talk as much as the young men of the Wintun people. I will tell you what I tell them--exercise the tongue less and the mind more. But as you are new to our ways, I will reassure you. I can transfer the ability to travel quickly to all of you. Have no fear; you will be there by nightfall." The tall Native American strode ahead, leaving an abashed Nathan to follow with the others.

They walked for half an hour before they caught sight of a faint glimmering of grey ahead of them. The light from outside grew slowly until the mine adit debouched onto a small flattish area bounded by tall pine trees. Waiting for them under the trees were Moon Wolf and three young men dressed in a similar fashion. Aside from their youth and their black hair tied back in ponytails, they all strongly resembled Moon Wolf, so much so, in fact, that Spence remarked on it before any introductions could be made.

"Are these your kin, Moon Wolf?" Spence asked. "There is a strong family resemblance."

The old Native American looked nonplussed for a moment. "Oh, sorry, I tend to identify with my people and forget it can be confusing to outsiders." His features rippled and flowed slightly, his eyes deepening in their sockets and his nose strengthening into a hawk's beak. "Now let me introduce my loyal assistants. This is Robert Walking Bear, this is John Tall Tree, and this is Ed Sun-on-Still-Waters. They are all of the Wintun tribe and have agreed to help us counter the dark ones."

The three young Native Americans greeted them all but stared askance at Garagh. Shorter than any of them, but bulking as much as any two, his thick pelt and oddly misshapen skull obviously made them nervous.

After a quick mental conference with Moon Wolf, Wandjina washed their minds with relaxing thoughts and explained that Garagh was in fact the leader of the Neanderthal race, come to honour them by joining in their fight. They visibly relaxed under his ministrations.

"We thank you for your offer of help," Wandjina went on, out loud. He introduced himself, and then the other humans. "There is one other you should know about. His name is Wulgu and he has stood close behind you for the last hour."

"With respect, old one," John Tall Tree said. "We are trained in the ways of the mountain and forest, and no one has come close to us. We would have heard him, for we can hear the cougar as it stalks its prey."

Ed Sun-on-Still-Waters nodded. "We hear the butterfly as it sips nectar from a flower."

"And we can watch the dance of the winged Wokwuk on a still summer's night," Robert Walking Bear added.

"Very poetic," Moon Wolf said with a smile. "Have I not warned you young men against boasting?"

"Indeed you have, Great One," Ed said, "But we are not boasting, merely stating the truth. I don't know where this Wulgu is, but he has not been close to us."

"John, Wulgu says you asked Ed twenty minutes ago whether you should ask Peggy to the Community dance next month," Wandjina stated.

John paled. "That is not possible. I leaned close to his ear and whispered. No one could have overheard me."

"Wulgu was only an arm's length from you at the time." Wandjina said. "See, here he is." He gestured toward a stand of birch saplings only ten feet away.

The trunks of the saplings and their branches moved slightly, as if a heat haze disturbed the air, and a tall, broad brown shape took form. Involuntarily, the three young Native Americans took a step backward, their eyes widening.

"Shupchet," Ed breathed.

"Sasquatch," John said.

"Bigfoot," Robert confirmed.

"No, a yowie from Australia," Wandjina corrected. "His name is Wulgu, and he says he approves of your bushcraft."

The three Native Americans looked sheepish but couldn't keep their eyes off the yowie. "Sorry," Ed said, "We don't mean to stare, but Shupchet are very rare and hard to see. Is he...er, safe?"

"Ask him," James said with a smile. "Think his name and ask a question in your mind."

"You're kidding?" Robert cocked his head to one side and thought, *Wulgu? Can you hear me?*

Yes I can, Robert Walking Bear. I am pleased to meet you.

Robert beamed with pleasure and immediately launched into a blizzard of questions which Moon Wolf tersely interrupted.

"Time is passing, we must leave immediately." He looked round at the mixed company. "John, you will travel with Wandjina and me. Robert, seeing as you have an affinity for Wulgu, you will travel with him and Spencer. Ed, accompany James, Garagh and Nathan."

"You're going to show us how to travel like the emu?" Nathan asked eagerly. "American style?"

Moon Wolf grinned and nodded. "First, we must leave this place and find a strip of open land. The vibrations are not right here."

The Native American companions hid smiles, but Wulgu caught a stray thought from Robert and rumbled, sending it on to James and Spence.

This is a human joke?

Wulgu, Spence replied, hiding a smile. *Does Moon Wolf look like a human? Deep inside?*

No. then why?

Wait and see.

Moon Wolf waved the party to follow and set off down a steep trail into the foothills of Mt Shasta. The track was rough and overgrown and it took them twenty minutes to emerge onto a narrow rutted road where three battered four-wheel drive vehicles stood in a line.

Moon Wolf gestured to them. "They may be old but they are well maintained. Ed runs a small automobile workshop. When we reach the highway, Nathan, we shall truly run as fast as your emu--maybe faster."

Nathan looked crestfallen and a little bit angry. "Very funny. I thought you were being serious when you said you could travel like the emu."

Moon Wolf regarded the young Aboriginal man calmly. "I am serious, Nathan Wambiri. I, Wandjina here, and your grandfather can travel as the wind does, but we cannot enable others to do so. I'm sorry if I have upset you with my humour."

Nathan grumbled a bit and refused to meet anyone's eyes for a few minutes, but he said, "Yeah, well, that's okay, I guess. I should have been less trusting."

"Not less trusting, Nathan," Wandjina said. "Only be more discerning and always be ready to laugh at yourself."

What I want to know, Wulgu broadcast, neatly taking the attention from his human friend, *is how I'm going to fit in one of these cars. These seats are very small.*

"That's okay, Wulgu," Robert said. "The seats fold down and it's a hatchback. If you don't mind crawling in the back, there should be plenty of room."

If I must, Wulgu sighed, *but it does not seem dignified.* He went to the indicated vehicle and examined the opening at the rear. Tentatively, he crawled inside, the springs groaning in protest as the yowie's great weight pushed it down. Wulgu's massive feet protruded from the back as the inside of the vehicle was just too small to accommodate him.

"We'll have to throw a tarpaulin or a blanket over him," Ed said. "Otherwise he'll be noticed. There's bound to be traffic on the roads."

No. I will not be bundled up like rubbish...

"Trash," James murmured at Robert's questioning look.

...I can disguise myself sufficiently for the short time any other human is near.

"As you wish it, Old One of the Forests," Moon Wolf murmured, "But we must be going."

I like it, Wulgu remarked to Spence, *Old One of the Forest. It bestows great dignity upon me.*

Old Stink of the Forest, if you ask me, Spence replied as he climbed into the front passenger seat of the same vehicle. *You're a little bit whiffy in confined spaces, Wulgu old chum.*

Wulgu told him what he thought of human odours and Spence subsided into an embarrassed silence.

The journey out of the foothills of Mount Shasta took nearly three hours, as the roads they chose to negotiate were rutted and overgrown, far from the roads in use by people using the mountain for recreational purposes. Once they reached the sealed roads, they picked up speed, heading roughly north-east but with many diversions resulting from the vagaries of topography.

Traffic was light and rather than being a cause for concern, the people traveling behind the heavily laden vehicle carrying Wulgu, enjoyed the disguises he employed. Being large and hairy, he usually took the form of a large dog in the back of the vehicle, one of his massive feet becoming the head hanging out in the slipstream. On other occasions he opted for invisibility, the rear of the vehicle slipping and sliding out of vision as the yowie wrestled with rapidly changing backgrounds. Interestingly, at least three times, small children saw him and screamed to their parents to look at the huge monkey. None of the adults could see what their offspring saw, however, so no harm was done.

"How is it that the children can see the yowie?" John Tall Tree asked after the first time.

"What we see if often conditioned by our expectations," Wandjina explained. "The children have few preconceptions of what reality is supposed to be, but their parents 'know' beyond doubt that there can be no large monkey here, so they cannot see it."

I am not a monkey, Wulgu said from car ahead. He sounded aggrieved.

No, you are not, Wandjina agreed. *You are a noble Old One of the Forest.*

Just after midday, they reached the shores of Medicine Lake and John guided the vehicles up a side road that led to a small rise overlooking the sparkling water and the wooded island with its dock and fenced lodge.

"We wait here until it is nearly dark," Moon Wolf said. "Then we have a hike of about two miles, away from the lake to the north side of Glass Mountain." He pointed out the barren landscape and strangely rounded hill they would be climbing.

I will be glad of the exercise, Wulgu said, stretching and baring his huge fangs. *Riding in cars is only for weak humans.*

James had a pair of binoculars out of his pack and was studying the island dock intently. "There's something going on down there. I can't quite make it out, but those men that have just arrived look official." He passed the binoculars to Wandjina, who waved them away.

The old Aboriginal stared across the miles. "They are FBI, or so their jackets proclaim, and facing them are soldiers."

"Shit," Nathan exclaimed. "What the hell are we getting into?"

"I'd say a bit of an adventure," Spence replied with a grin. He slapped Nathan on the shoulder. "Things were getting a bit dull."

Ed Sun-on-Still-Waters looked worried. "Moon Wolf, we should have brought our rifles. I can drive back to town and get them."

Moon Wolf shook his head. "A man who carries a gun comes to rely on it, and a gun has only one use. I do not want any of those people down there to die by our hands. Besides, we will not need them. While the FBI faces the US Army at the front door, we shall quietly enter through the back door and be finished before they even know we are there."

16

S ergeant Otway, in charge of the detail guarding the landing area hesitated when he saw a small flotilla of motor launches heading for the dock on the island of Medicine Lake. A loudhailer identified the fleet as FBI and ordered the soldiers to move away from the dock. The sergeant immediately called in a report to his superior and told his men to stand their ground but to offer no resistance. By the time the first of the FBI agents stepped ashore, Lieutenant Evans was hurrying out of the lodge with reinforcements. The men formed a cordon around the building and Evans ordered Otway and his men to fall back on his position.

"Rifles at the ready, Sergeant," Evans said. "But safeties on. I want no accidents." He walked out to meet the FBI agents who had now all landed. One of them stepped forward to meet the Lieutenant, who introduced himself.

"Good afternoon, Lieutenant Evans," said the agent. "I am Agent Collins." He handed over his identification to Evans who examined it carefully. "I also have a Federal Court Order and Warrant to remove the persons listed." Collins took back his identification folder and handed over a thin sheaf of papers.

Evans gave the papers a cursory glance. "They look to be in order, but I do not have the authority to let you in."

"That is a Federal Warrant, Lieutenant. I suggest that gives you all the authority you need."

"I'm sorry, Agent Collins," Evans said. "But this is technically a US Army base and I cannot recognise any outside authority without the permission of my superior officers."

"Then get permission," Collins said crisply. He waited until Lieutenant Evans disappeared inside the lodge before returning to the other agents on the landing dock. "They're stalling," he growled to Agent Kowalski and Marc Lachlan.

"I told you we should have come in force the first time," Kowalski said. "Now we give them time to hide the evidence."

"Can't we just go in and get Andi?" Marc asked. "You're FBI, for God's sake and you have a warrant. What more do you need?"

Collins regarded Marc calmly. "You are right, Mr Lachlan. We don't need anything more, but those soldiers are youngsters and if they've been told to stop us, they'll attempt to do so, and I don't want people getting hurt on either side."

"So what do we do?"

"We wait."

Inside the lodge, Lieutenant Evans was on the telephone to Captain Anders, General Spader's aide. He read out the Court Order and Warrant, repeating some of the more complicated parts.

"Who are the warrants made out for?"

"Turner, Jones, Spindler, Braun, Newman and Parker," Evans read out.

"Does it say why?"

"Suspicion of terrorist activities."

"Jesus! The General will need some damned high up backing to..." Anders caught himself and swore under his breath. "Never mind that. Just hold the lodge, Evans. That's an order. I'll be up there to sort this out as soon as I can." He hung up and sat back, thinking. He knew the General's thinking on the security of the base and the importance of the project, and knew there were some actions he should take immediately. He lifted the telephone receiver again and paged Captain Hurst.

"Hurst, get twenty men together and get them up to the lodge. Take over from Evans and hold the place."

"Sure, Captain," Hurst replied. "What's up?"

"The FBI has arrived with warrants for the scientists."

"Shitfire! Are you going to tell the General?"

"Yes, now get going. Deny them entry to the lodge but keep it low-key and peaceable if you can. I don't want to try and stop them if they decide to force the issue." Anders got up and left his office, running over in his mind what needed to be done as he walked towards the General's suite.

Hurst, meanwhile, left his room at the run, briefly stopping to relay Anders' instructions to another sergeant. "Baker, get up there on the double and support Lieutenant Evans. I'll be along in a few minutes. I expect to see everything in order when I get there."

"Yes sir." The sergeant saluted and hurried off, calling to his men.

Hurst raced for the laboratory, where he found Parker and Braun going over some data with Spindler. "General wants to see you Parker. You too Braun," he snapped.

"What the hell for?" Parker grumbled. "Tell him I'm busy."

Hurst ostentatiously unclipped the guard on his holster. "I am instructed to make sure you obey, no matter what."

Parker glared at Hurst but got up and, followed by Braun, trooped out into the corridor. "You've got a fucking nerve," Parker snarled. "Have you forgotten I'm the boss around here?"

"Then start acting like it. The FBI has arrived with arrest warrants for you lot."

"Oh, shit, they're onto us," Braun moaned. "We've got to get out of here."

"So the General wanting to see us was just a story?"

"You got it," Hurst confirmed. "Now, I have to get up to the lodge. There is no way the Army is relinquishing you to the Feds, so keep calm and keep your heads down. We'll sort this out."

Parker scowled as Hurst hurried off and grabbed Braun by the arm, dragging him along the corridors toward his room.

"What's the rush now?" Braun whined, pulling his arm free from Parker's grip. "You heard Hurst; the army's going to protect us."

"Yeah, but for how long? We can't afford to wait. If the FBI have got a whiff of our plans we'll be so far up shit creek you'll need a lifetime to get back out--and life is exactly what we'd get."

"But we can't get out now, by ourselves. Without Hurst and his men, we'll have to leave the machine and without that we have nothing. I mean, forget about the hundred million, I never seriously thought we'd get that, but we wouldn't even have the original ten million."

"That's a fuck sight better than going to jail for the rest of our lives. But it's not all bad news," Parker gloated. "We can download the specifications and the programs onto disks and take them with us. I reckon if there is nothing else available, we'll get our money for those disks. We could even make copies and sell them to whoever would buy them."

Captain Anders knocked on General Spader's door and walked in. He was surprised to see Ehrich Mannheim standing behind the General, but wasted no time wondering what he was doing there. "We have a problem, sir. The FBI have arrived on the island and are demanding access."

Spader frowned. "What do they want?"

"They have search and arrest warrants--for Turner and the scientists."

"No!" Ehrich barked. "They cannot have them. Not yet."

Anders looked mildly astonished at Ehrich's outburst, but said nothing, waiting for Spader to admonish the man. When he did not, Anders felt chilled, wondering just who this man was.

"What should I tell them, sir?" he asked the General.

Spader considered for a few moments, fiddling with his pen. "What dispositions have you made?"

"Lieutenant Evans was on duty with Otway and about twenty men when the FBI arrived. He has thrown a cordon around the lodge and is guarding it. I sent Captain Hurst up there with twenty more with orders to hold but attempt nothing provocative, sir."

"Do you think that's enough?" Spader asked. "I believe you should present an enemy with overwhelming force right from the start. It discourages him."

"Sir, there are only a dozen agents up there, with hand guns. All our men are armed with automatics."

"Take another..." The telephone on Spader's desk rang and the General answered it. "Yes? Where are you?...When was this?...Okay, thank you." He hung up and scowled. "That was Spindler in the lab. He says Hurst came by a few minutes ago and removed Parker and Braun from the lab--at gunpoint. I thought you said you'd sent him up to the lodge? What the hell's he doing?"

"I don't know, sir. I'll find out."

"Do that. Double the force up there. On no account is the FBI to be allowed inside the base. This is US Army property and they have no jurisdiction."

Anders saluted and left.

When he was safely out of the room, the General turned to Ehrich with an uneasy look on his face. "What the hell's going on?" he asked.

"Plainly, our enemies have manipulated the system for their own ends. Either that or those men up there are not genuine FBI agents," Ehrich said. "You will not surrender the scientists or the machine, Spader. Remember who you work for." He made a sign with his right hand and Spader nodded vigorously.

"I have not forgotten, chosen of the Nine, but the situation is complex." Spader glanced at Ehrich's scowling face and hurried on. "This base is technically US Army soil, as I said, but the FBI could get my superiors to countermand any orders I give. If that happened, I would have no choice but to surrender."

"No choice?" Ehrich asked coldly. "Think again, General."

"I can't disobey a direct order from my superior. I'd be relieved of my command and court-martialled."

"Would you rather disobey a direct order from the Nine?"

Spader paled. "Of course not, but..."

"There is no choice, Spader. Obey the Nine as a faithful servant and you will be looked after. Disobey..." Ehrich left the threat hanging.

"I...I will obey."

"Good. You have men you can trust in your command? Really trust?"

Spader nodded.

"Then have them transport the Baby Vox to the access tunnels. We can use it to throw any FBI attack into confusion. Also, have them prepare the Vox Dei machine. There is one more test to be carried out and then it will not matter what happens."

"The test is that important?" Spader asked.

"It is more important than our lives, individually or collectively."

"Then I will do my utmost, but if my superiors are brought in and I am removed from command, all resistance will collapse."

"Hold out long enough and it will not matter." Ehrich looked at his watch. "It is nearly two o'clock now. Assume the FBI has called for backup. It cannot be very near else they would have brought it in the first place. So if they have to fly them in from Portland or San Francisco, or even Las Vegas, it will take time. Imagine they arrive at nightfall--not the best time to be storming a redoubt. Delay them with talk, promises, whatever you need to, but give me until midnight and you then can abjectly apologise and let them in."

"What about the scientists?"

"I will need Spindler, Braun, Parker and Newman to set up the machine. Once it is in operation, you can use them as bargaining tools if you wish. Jones and Turner will remain locked up though." Ehrich smiled chillingly. "I have plans for them."

Spader shook his head. "I don't want to know." He got up and straightened his jacket. "I'm going up top to see what's happening."

Captain Hurst had, meanwhile, arrived at the lodge, having disdained the slow ride available on the electric cars through the long access tunnel, and had jogged the distance, arriving slightly sweaty, breathing hard, but pleased with himself. He found that Lieutenant Evans had laid out his defence well, giving his men plenty of cover, and allowing overlapping fields of fire. Hurst walked around the defenses and made a few minor changes, based more on being seen to be in command, than being really necessary. He stood with

Evans and looked down toward the dock where a dozen men in blue flak jackets emblazoned with the letters 'FBI' on the back, stood around watching the soldiers.

"Who's the civilian?" Hurst asked, jerking his head in the direction of the dock.

"No idea, sir. He doesn't appear to be in charge, he's not using any particular equipment. In fact, I don't even think he's armed."

"Then he's not important."

Evans nodded dubiously. "What's the plan, sir? Those agents have got court orders and warrants."

"Let's go take a look." He set off down the slope of the lawn toward the water's edge, strolling rather than striding, with Evans hurrying to catch up. The agents saw them coming and three men, the civilian among them, walked out to intercept the army officers. Hurst greeted them affably and introduced himself. "You've met Lieutenant Evans already."

"Agent Collins, Agent Kowalski." The speaker did not introduce the civilian and Hurst examined him with some curiosity, but said nothing.

"We have duly signed court orders allowing us access to this property and arrest warrants for six people," Agent Collins said.

"Yes, I have them here," Hurst said, pulling them out of his pocket. "I'm sorry you've had a wasted trip, Agent Collins, but your court order is, as we speak, being appealed by Army attorneys. I expect it will be voided any time now. As for the people on your warrants--well, they are not here. You've been given false information."

"That's a lie," Marc snapped. "Dr Andromeda Jones is here. I know because..."

"That's enough," Collins said, quietly but firmly.

"Who is this?" Hurst asked. "I don't believe you introduced him."

"Marc Lachlan," Collins said. "He's a physicist who worked with Jones and some of the other scientists. He's here to make sure they are correctly identified."

"How fascinating." Hurst yawned. "I thought you had modern techniques like DNA testing to prove identity."

"A witness is quite sufficient. Now I suggest you let us in to check your statement."

"Sorry, Agent Collins--no can do. I'm sure you understand my dilemma. I want to help you but I cannot go against the orders of my superior officer who gave me specific instructions to preserve the integrity of the base."

"Who is your superior?"

"Captain Anders," Hurst said with a smile.

Collins sighed. "You cannot tell me a mere Captain is in charge of this project. Who is the commanding officer on this base?"

"That would be General Thaddeus Spader."

"Then let me talk to him."

"I'd be delighted--if he gives permission."

"Ask him."

Hurst examined his watch. "Fourteen-fifty hours. I'm afraid the general had rather a busy night last night--the exigencies of command, you understand. He is presently having a siesta with firm orders he is only to be awoken in an emergency."

"And you don't think that FBI landing on his island with court orders is an emergency?"

"Why, no." Hurst smiled. "We are just having a pleasant talk. I see no emergency."

Kowalski swore and whipped out his automatic, jabbing it into the side of the Captain's throat. "What about now? Do you see an emergency yet?"

"Agent Kowalski," Hurst murmured calmly, "Before you do anything you'd regret, please look beyond me to the lodge. There should be about twenty trained men up there with their weapons aimed and ready. Your force will be massacred."

"You'd be the first," Kowalski growled, but the pressure of his automatic on the captain's throat eased a fraction.

"I'm a soldier," Hurst said calmly. "I'm prepared to die doing my duty."

"So am I."

"Very commendable, Agent Kowalski, but my death would mean I had successfully carried out my orders, whereas yours would signal your failure." Hurst raised his arm and gently pushed the FBI agent's hand aside. "Let us be civilised about this."

"Put your gun away," Agent Collins said. "This achieves nothing."

With a snarl of frustration, Kowalski holstered his gun and turned away.

"Captain Hurst," Collins said. "Please wake your commanding officer."

"I'm sorry; I thought I had made myself clear on that point. I will only wake him in case of an emergency."

"Then you will have your emergency. I have radioed my own superiors and we will have backup here by nightfall--enough to take this base by force if necessary. Furthermore, General Baxter, who is Spader's direct superior will be here also. If your general is still asleep or refuses to allow us in, he will be relieved of his command and the same goes for any officers under his command who refuse to obey lawful authority."

Hurst frowned and Evans looked troubled. "Do what you have to do," the captain said. "Be assured, I will do my duty." He turned on his heel and walked back to the lodge, Lieutenant Evans at his heels.

"Were you serious?" Marc asked. "You're going to go in with guns blazing if they don't surrender?"

"If we have to. I'm hoping his officers come to their senses first, particularly when Baxter arrives."

"Shit, we could have another Waco. That's the army in there, Collins, with a hell of a lot more weapons than any cultists, in case you hadn't noticed."

"You worry too much. We know what we're doing."

"And what about Andi and the other civilians? Are they going to be acceptable losses when this thing's over?

"Nothing will happen to them," Agent Collins soothed. "The backup will be here by nightfall. It'll all be over by midnight." He nodded to Kowalski and headed back down to the dock area where his colleagues were dug in.

Marc watched him walk away, and then turned to scan the soldiers in and around the lodge. "All be over?" he muttered. "That's just what I'm afraid of."

17

Just before nightfall, the watchers on the hill saw a small fleet of helicopters beat its way out of the cloudy skies to the south and descend onto an open patch of ground at one end of the Medicine Lake island, about two hundred metres from the lodge.

James, his binoculars glued to his face, kept up a commentary to his friends. "FBI by the looks of it...At least another...oh, fifty, I'd say, maybe more. Plenty of equipment being unloaded...Can't see what type of...Hello, there's an army big-wig. I can't see his rank but he looks important. He's just standing off to one side talking to the FBI agents...Damn, the light's fading fast. I can't see...They're not moving up to the lodge, just setting up a camp or something."

"Leave it, James," Wandjina said. "What is happening there is none of our concern. Moon Wolf says it is time to go."

Moon Wolf sent Robert Walking Bear and John Tall Tree ahead to scout the way and make sure there were no unexpected obstacles or surprises awaiting them between the lake and the northern flank of Glass Mountain. The old Native American would lead the expedition, with Ed Sun-on-Still-Waters bringing up the rear. Wulgu, who could travel much faster than the humans, elected to go separately, moving parallel to the trails and investigating anything untoward, meeting them on the mountain.

"He can't get lost," Wandjina explained. "Although he's never been here before, he'll be in mental contact with me at all times."

They set off as the sun dipped below the horizon and the shadow of the land swept over them. The pine forests darkened and the gravel trails that led off to the northeast became indistinct.

"How are we going to see?" Nathan queried. "Us poor humans don't have your supernatural abilities."

"Wandjina and I will create light to guide your steps. The path is not hard except the last few hundred paces. I will call up Wokwuk to aid us over those parts."

"What the hell are Wokwuk?" Spence asked. "Or don't I want to know?"

Ed laughed softly. "Wokwuk is the son of Olelbis and Mem Loimis. Bits of him fell to earth from the heavenly realm and turned into different plants and animals, even rocks. Moon Wolf is saying creation will come to help us."

Spence halted and let the others get ahead a little before whispering to Ed. "Who is Moon Wolf--really? Our old guy calls himself Wandjina, one of the Aboriginal creator spirits, but that's a bit far-fetched. I mean, he has powers for sure but I'd hesitate to say we were in the company of gods."

Ed shrugged. "I do not know about your Wandjina, but Moon Wolf defers to him and I cannot imagine him doing so to a lesser being. Moon Wolf is Olelbis himself...or if not Olelbis, then one of the lesser Olelbis. He, or another, made this land and everything in it. Certainly, he guards and protects creation."

Spence looked skeptical. "You know this for an empirical fact, or are these stories you have heard?"

"You are a New Zealand Maori, aren't you? A shaman, I've been told..."

"Tohunga," Spence said.

"Right. So tell me, Spence, as a tohunga of your people and a scientist, do you believe the stories of your gods and heroes as told around the campfires. Are they myth or real?"

Spence chuckled and started up the trail again, hurrying to catch sight of the others in the dusk. "When I wear my scientist's hat they are myths," he said over his shoulder, "But in my heart I know they are real."

"You have experienced what cannot be logically explained?" Ed asked, walking behind him.

Spence nodded and slowed, keeping sufficiently far behind Nathan that he could not be heard. "I have seen the nature god Tane walk the forests of my childhood, up in the Urewera mountains, I have seen the taniwha of my tribe swimming the deep rivers and lakes, I have watched the black cats vanish before my eyes and I have conversed with the spirits of my ancestors."

Ed nodded with satisfaction. "Then you know."

Spence sighed. "Yes, and it scares me every time."

"Mortal flesh does not coexist easily with the gods. I have known Moon Wolf for several years and although he is at pains to appear as a gentle old man, he still scares the crap out of me at times."

"Yeah, Wandjina's a bit like that too. His favourite form is as an old Aboriginal tracker called Ernie. Sweet and gentle, but when he takes up his power, sparks fly."

"Speaking of sparks..." Ed Sun-on-Still-Waters pointed up the trail. From the meadows and woodland beside the track as it wound its way toward the still unseen Glass Mountain, tiny flashing yellow-green points of light converged on the travellers.

"Fireflies," Spence observed, "But there's a hell of a lot of them."

"Fragments of Wokwuk," Ed said. "Did I not say creation would come to help us?"

The fireflies poured out of the surrounding countryside and formed up in a band of light along the trail. So bright was their combined light that every irregularity of the trail was apparent, and Moon Wolf called on the travellers to move faster, hurrying them onward. As they passed, the fireflies whirled away like a snowstorm and their lights went out, plunging the track behind them back into darkness.

The bioluminescence fell away as they entered the pine plantations surrounding the Glass Mountain, and the trail grew indistinct again, though the way appeared as a pale glimmer of gravel in the moonlight.

Moonlight? We're in a forest. Spence looked up and was astounded to see the tips of the pines bending to each side of the track, allowing a gentle shaft of silvery light to bathe the path in front of them. Garagh lifted up his arms and called out to the moon in an unknown tongue, harsh and guttural.

"The pines. More Wokwuk?" Spence asked softly.

Ed nodded. "Who is this Garagh that greets the moon?" he whispered. "He looks like he is more closely related to your yowie than to humans."

Spence chuckled. "That's a good guess. He's a Neanderthal, a caveman, supposedly extinct these last thirty thousand years, but he's actually a scientist. I know, I find it hard to believe myself, but I've seen him at work. His speciality is genetics and the yowie is actually one of his genetically engineered creations."

Ed whistled softly. "Tell me more."

"Sure, but it's a long story, so it'll have to be later."

The path wound upward, gradually steepening, and passed out of the pine forest and into a region of bare earth, scrubby bushes and grass. Shadows slipped and slid around them, causing them all to look up, startled. The moon, or what they had thought was the moon, raced silently across the cloudless sky and vanished into the south.

"Was that a UFO?" James asked. "Garagh, was that your doing?"

Garagh inclined his head but would not admit to it, even mentally.

"Bloody hell," Spence muttered. "Now I can add flying saucers to my list of strange experiences."

Starlight was now the only source of light but it was sufficient as they scrambled further up the mountain. As they wound around to the north side, the trail dipped and passed by a small patch of thick vegetation. A figure detached itself from the darkness and stepped into the trail in front of them.

"We thought something must have happened," Robert Walking Bear said.

Moon Wolf patted the young man on the shoulder. "Is the way open?" he asked, and then, without waiting for an answer, disappeared into the bushes.

"No, it's padlocked," Robert said to the darkness. He beckoned to the others and led the way into the thicket. Twenty paces in, the shrubs thinned, revealing a small patch of grass in front of an old mine shaft. The entrance was blocked with thick iron bars and a doorway chained and padlocked prevented entry. A battered and faded painted sign proclaimed the inky shaft leading into the rock of the hillside was a shaft closed by the Department of Mines and that no one was to enter on pain of prosecution. Figures stood waiting for them, one huge, two small.

"Have you scouted the area, Wulgu?" Wandjina asked.

Of course. There are no humans on the mountain, though the tunnel stinks of them-- and other things.

?

The shadow things.

Wandjina nodded and conferred with Moon Wolf. "The yowie cannot enter the tunnel, his size precludes it. I will leave him on guard, but I will need at least one other to stay with him."

"Ed," Moon Wolf stated.

"Great One, please no. Let me enter with the rest of you."

"This is not a position of safety, Ed. There are other things abroad on the mountain and you will need to be vigilant. It will do us little good to succeed within the mountain only to find ourselves outflanked and cut off."

Ed and I will do our duty, Wulgu said.

"If...if you command it, Great One. I will stay with the yowie."

I am Wulgu. I have a name, or should I just call you 'human'?

"Very well," Wandjina said. "Now I do not know what we will find within the tunnel, but I expect it to lead us into the heart of the underground base. We have two objectives--the first is to find and destroy the machine they have built. I don't know exactly what it looks like but when Samantha and her sister were in communication, there was this image in their minds..." He broadcast an image of a long-barrelled machine connected to a huge power source. "Something this large will be in a large room or cavern, so don't waste time searching small places. If you find it, call out mentally and start destroying it, any way you can."

"How do we call out mentally?" John Tall Tree asked. "I can hear some of you sometimes, just bits and pieces, but I've no idea how to talk like that."

"Me either," Robert Walking Bear said.

I will teach them. Garagh grunted. *Come, we have little time.* He led them to one side and they stood in silence, their eyes fixed on one another.

"Okay," Wandjina went on. "Our second goal is to find Samantha's sister Andi and bring her out. This is her image and mental signature..."

"What about the shadows?" Nathan asked. He looked into the dark tunnel behind its padlocked gate and shivered. "Those things scare me."

"That is why Olelbis and I are here," Wandjina said. "I cannot promise you invincibility, but we can keep them busy while you others fulfil our purpose."

"And the padlock?" Spence asked. "I don't suppose you have a key or boltcutters."

Moon Wolf smiled and the rusty lock snapped open, the wound chain unravelling and slithering off into the darkness of the shrubbery like an iron snake.

"Impressive," James murmured. He gripped the iron bars and pulled. The door swung wide with a loud creak. "After you, Ernie, I think...hello, don't look now but we've got company."

Everybody immediately responded by swinging round to look into the shrubbery where James was looking.

"I don't see anyone," Robert said. He and John stepped forward to join Ed in the open, their eyes casting about as they sought the intruder.

There is no one here, Wulgu rumbled softly. *I would have heard them.*

"No one you can see or hear, Wulgu, nor any of you others except one I think," Wandjina murmured. "Spencer Tuhua, do you recognise the man with the moku, the facial tattoos?"

Spence stared at the dimly seen figure and paled. "It is my father, who was tohunga before me."

"Why is he here?" James murmured, "And how is it that I can see him, even if only dimly?"

"You are my brother," Spence said simply. "In spirit if not in flesh. See, he beckons me...father, is it time?"

"Time?" Nathan asked. "Time for what? Who the hell are you talking to, mate?"

Tears crept down Spence's face, glinting in the starlight. "He is calling me to my ancestors. It is our way, but I grieve that I cannot be there for my friends when they need me. Father, wait an hour, I beg you. Let me fight alongside my friends one last time."

"He nods," James said softly.

"I see." Spence nodded fiercely and brushed the tears away. "So, I have one last opportunity to make a difference." He took out a stained handkerchief from the pocket of his khaki shorts and blew his nose, a loud honk. "Okay, let's get to it, Wandjina. I haven't got all night."

The old Aboriginal man clapped his Maori friend on the shoulder without a word and led the way past the iron gate. As he stepped into shadow, he cupped his left hand and a pure blue-white light blazed out, lighting their way.

"Bloody hell," James said. "You couldn't have done that earlier? On the path up here?"

"It would have been wrong to deny the fireflies their contribution," Wandjina said, "but we cannot ask them to plunge deep into the earth to light our way. Come, we are wasting time."

*   *   *

Tensions were rising on the island in Medicine Lake. A large contingent of FBI and a handful of high-ranking army officers had debarked from the helicopters and had gathered behind makeshift defensive walls within sight of the soldiers guarding the lodge.

General James Thompson, designate of the Chief of Staff of the United States Army, under the Director of Intelligence, interrupted Agent Collins' outline of procedures.

"I'm sorry, Agent Collins, and with due deference to Deputy Assistant Director Knowles, but I will not stand by while you plan the armed invasion of an army base. I insist we open with negotiations."

Collins stopped in mid-flow and glared at General Thompson. "We've tried that already, General, and we just got the run-around. I gave them until nightfall to cooperate and they've ignored me. Now we do it the hard way."

"Then be prepared for heavy casualties, these are professional soldiers you're up against, not drug pushers."

"We know how to do our job. Now, if you'll excuse me..."

"I'd like to talk to the commanding officer, this General Spader."

"Go ahead, but if you're not back by..." Collins glanced at his watch, "...eight, we're coming in anyway."

General Thompson nodded and, beckoning to his aide, left the crowded tent and started up the grassy slope toward the front steps of the lodge. They were challenged by guards as they approached, and passed through a succession of increasingly senior officers before ending up in a small office in the lodge.

"General Thaddeus Spader?" Thompson asked. He glanced at Captain Anders before introducing himself and the Colonel acting as his aide. "What is going on here? I have examined the court orders and warrants and they are all in order. I don't normally approve of civilian agencies acting on army territory, but in this case I have no choice. What I don't understand is why you have not even tried to get instructions from your superiors. I should never have had to come all the way out here to give you your orders."

"No sir," Spader said, still seated behind his desk.

"No sir? That's all you have to say? General Spader, I am removing you from command of this base and this project, effective immediately. Colonel Pickins, you will take over. Please arrange for General Spader's confinement until he can be shipped out. Captain Anders, place yourself and the men in this base under Colonel Pickins' command."

Colonel Pickins saluted crisply. "Yes sir." Anders shifted uncomfortably and looked at Spader for instructions.

"Just a moment," Spader said. He picked up the telephone receiver punched a number in. "Yes, they are here with me now...in the lodge...what?" He stared up at Thompson and his aide. "You are sure?" Spader hung up, stood, and pulled his revolver from its holster. He cocked it and pointed it at Thompson. "Very clever, but not quite clever enough. Consider yourselves under arrest."

"What the blue blazes are you talking about?" Thompson exploded. "Pickens, Anders, arrest that man."

"Stand back!" Spader shouted. "You are not General Thompson but an Al-Qaida operative bent on sabotage. I warn you, I will shoot if I have to."

"My God, you're right," Anders said. "How could I not have seen it before?" He pulled his revolver and stepping forward, relieved the other men of their weapons. "Get your hands up, you bloody rag-heads."

Thompson flushed strongly and stared at his aide. "How the hell did you sneak through the system, Pickins, or whatever your name is?"

"You're the traitor, General, and now you're trying to pin the blame on me." Pickins leapt at Thompson and grappled with him, roaring with rage.

"Stop them, Anders," Spader yelled.

"How sir?" Anders hesitated, and then shouted to them to stop. When nothing happened, he aimed at the two struggling men and pulled the trigger.

General Thompson cried out and jerked and Pickins slumped to the floor. Anders moved swiftly and brought the barrel of his revolver down hard on Thompson's head.

"Good man," Spader said. He sat down again and sat staring into space for a minute, his face moving strangely as he battled with conflicting thoughts. Then he nodded and reached across the desk, switching on the intercom system and clearing his throat. "Now hear this. This is General Spader and I have something of great importance to say to you. Many of you will be wondering why men calling themselves federal agents are camped outside our base. Well, I have just been officially informed that these men are not federal agents but are instead a cadre of Al-Qaida terrorists, disguised to infiltrate and sabotage our project. These men will stop at nothing to achieve their evil ends, so I am giving you a direct order now. You will resist any attempt by these Al-Qaida operatives to enter the lodge and the base beyond, by any means at your disposal. Make no mistake; these men will kill you if they get the chance. If you must, use deadly force, but they must not succeed. That is all. God be with you."

Spader snapped off the intercom and sat in silence for a moment before standing and brandishing his revolver. "Time to kick some Arab ass, Anders," he said with a grin.

* * *

Down in the depths of the base, in the large cavern that housed both the Vox Dei and the prototype Baby Vox, Ehrich hovered over the computer keyboard connected to the machine, feeding in the data needed to operate and guide the giant laser. He whistled tunelessly as he worked, looking across at the gently humming Baby Vox from time to time, breaking into a grin every time he did so. The beam of the smaller machine was focussed on the lodge and the upper part of the connecting corridors, bathing the rooms and the men within them in a flood of radiation. Harmless in itself, the radiation made men highly susceptible to suggestion. All that was needed was the suggestion that Middle Eastern terrorists were invading the base and the army and federal agents would battle to the death. While everyone had their hands full, Ehrich would be able to carry out the final test required by the Winambuu.

Spindler, Braun, Parker and Newman had helped him set up the machines, but when everything was in readiness, he had dismissed them. They had not wanted to go, being jealous of their creation and the uses to which it was being put, but Ehrich was prepared and showed them written authorisation from General Spader and a document with a forged signature of Morgan Turner granting his full access to the personnel and equipment of the base. Where the scientists went, he did not care, and made the suggestion that they might like to avail themselves of the amenities of the lodge. With luck, they would get caught up in the hostilities.

There. Ehrich fed in the last line of data and pressed 'Enter'. The screen flowed with complex equations and the mechanism operating the guidance system hummed and whirred, slowly swinging the long barrel of the Vox Dei round. *Where is it pointing? What direction is that?* Ehrich frowned and peered at the screen, trying to decipher sense from the columns of figures. *Two fifty-eight point three seven? Is that a compass reading?* He racks his brains to remember what lay approximately to the west-southwest and came up a blank. *Never mind, ours is not to reason why.* Ehrich pressed the firing button.

18

"Morgan! Did you hear that?" Andi pressed up against the iron door and called through the small grating that let in a dim shaft of light from the corridor outside the cell. "It sounded like an explosion."

Morgan's answer came faintly from further down the corridor. "It was, and there was small arms fire before it. I think the cavalry is here."

Andi sat down on the rough stone floor with her back to the door and contemplated the dim outlines of her cell. Her only light filtered in through the door grating but she could just make out the cot bed and a plastic portable toilet in the far corner. Nothing else disturbed the clean lines of walls or floor, and nothing moved upon them. *That's one advantage of being locked up in a new facility*, she thought. *No vermin*. An air duct high on the back wall let in a cool breeze of recirculated air. She knew Morgan was in what she guessed was a similar cell further down the corridor, but how they were going to get out of there was beyond her. *Maybe if the FBI takes over the base. But what if it doesn't? I don't like our chances if we are left to Ehrich Mannheim's tender mercies.*

"Andi."

She struggled upright again and peered sideways through the grating, though she knew she would not be able to see her fellow prisoner. "What?"

"The FBI isn't going to be able to find us easily. We're in the passages that lie behind the false door in my apartment. It was an emergency bolt hole. No one knows about it."

Andi thought about this for a minute. "You're telling me this to cheer me up?"

"Something like that." Andi could hear the humour in his voice. "No, listen, when we tried to shut down the machine it was because you got a...telepathic message from your sister, right? Well, could you do that again? Talk to her and tell her where we are?"

"I don't know how. She contacted me. Damn it Morgan, you know enough science to know telepathy isn't theoretically possible."

"Sure. Like she didn't talk to you, and we never saw those shadow things either. Try, Andi. What have we got to lose?"

"What do I do?"

"How the hell should I know? Concentrate on her name, call out mentally, make ring-ring noises or something."

"Okay." There was complete silence for the next few minutes except for the distant popping sound that had made them think of gunfire, and the faint sighing of the air conditioner. "Nothing's happening. I feel like a fool."

"Who can see you? Keep trying."

"How is it going to help anyway? Samantha isn't with the FBI."

"True, but have you got a better idea?"

"No." Andi went back to yelling inside her head. The sound of gunfire became more insistent and then the air conditioning fell silent, to be replaced by a soft susurration as if a pile of dead leaves was falling gently into an open grave.

"We're in trouble," Morgan called out urgently.

*   *   *

As soon as the soldiers within the lodge believed that the crowd of men behind the makeshift barricades was made up of Middle Eastern terrorists, they opened fire. Several agents fell in that first ragged volley and the rest dived for cover.

"What the fuck did Thompson say to them?" Kowalski screamed, making himself as small a target as possible behind cases of ammunition.

Collins swore incoherently and ordered everyone back into the trees; assigned medics to care for the fallen and swiftly started organising a counter-attack. Flak jackets, gas masks and helmets were issued to everyone, together with automatic weapons, tasers, stun and gas grenades, turning the agents into walking armories. He looked over his men with a critical eye and nodded, then quickly outlined the plan of attack.

"Okay, we're going in and we're going in hard." Collins opened up a plan of the lodge and proceeded to draw on it with a marker as the squad leaders gathered round. "Shoot out the side windows first, followed by stun grenades, then tear gas. We give them a minute and we hit the front entrance. Unfortunately, the place is set into the side of a hill so there isn't a back entrance, but if we go in hard and fast, I believe we can roll them up quickly. Taser anyone you see who isn't wearing an FBI jacket and leave them for the follow-up crews. I'd rather not have unnecessary bloodshed, so incapacitate if you can, but if it comes down to a choice between your life and his, shoot to kill."

Collins looked around at the grim faces of his men. "I know some of you don't like the idea of going up against the army. After all, they're supposed to be on our side. But remember this, they are defying the law, both federal and state, by denying us access, and at this point are no better than organised criminals. We have the full backing of the judiciary and the armed forces Chiefs. Okay, take your positions. Windows first, then grenades on my signal. Again, wait for me before going in." He nodded, pleased with the looks of determination on their faces. "Good luck."

The side windows of the lodge splintered and shattered under a burst of automatic fire, followed by the hissing arcs of grenades. Shouts were drowned out by concussions that shook free any remaining glass and then swirls of grey smoke filled the rooms and eddied out onto the verandahs. The lights inside the lodge went out, leaving the building bathed in darkness. Searchlights stabbed inward, blinding the defenders and lighting the front entrance and windows in a misty glare. A confused cacophony issued from the building, shouts and groans and tearing coughs, mingled with sporadic gunfire still that ripped into the trees, sending splinters of bark and showers of pine needles flying.

Collins counted down the seconds, but in reality he was judging the effect their attack had had on the defenders. "Near enough," he growled, after about ninety seconds. He pulled his mask down over his face and waved his men forward, charging over the grass, bent double with his taser shotgun at the ready. Kowalski was on his heels and a dozen more behind him, others vaulting onto the wide verandahs with a clatter of boots and in through the shattered windows. Immediately, fresh gunfire broke out, together with the electric arcing of the tasers, mingling with screams of pain, shock and outrage.

Collins yelled with surprise as he and Kowalski burst in through the front door and saw the scene of devastation and confusion that filled the lobby. Bodies lay everywhere in a litter of overturned furniture. Most of the men were curled up or on their knees struggling to breathe rather than fight, and Collins was amazed to see that they were not in army uniform but looked like nothing more than petty hoodlums. *Hoodlums carrying automatic weapons*, he corrected as he dived for cover, muzzle flashes winking out of the roiling smoke and fumes. He fired back with his taser shotgun and the shooter collapsed screaming.

Agents poured into the lodge and Collins led the charge to the rear of the building and the ramps to the lower tunnels. Neither the stun grenades nor the riot gas had had much effect here and the resistance was fierce. A hail of gunfire poured out of the tunnels, pinning the agents down and preventing further progress.

"Where the hell did all these mobsters come from?" Collins complained. "And what have they done with the soldiers?"

"Fucked if I know," Kowalski muttered, "But they're bloody well-armed."

"Any thoughts on how we get into the tunnel?"

Kowalski waited for a lull in the firing and peered quickly round the edge of the tunnel, ducking back as marksmen pinpointed him, sending splinters of concrete flying. "There look to be service alcoves about fifty yards away on both sides." He called up men with grenades and a series of stun grenades filled the tunnel with a deafening explosion in the confined space. The gunfire ceased abruptly and, after tossing a gas grenade, Kowalski led a charge into the tunnel, securing the service alcoves without incident. Gunfire started up again and the FBI prepared to repeat their attack.

*   *   *

The Vox Dei rapidly cycled up to full power, drawing immense amounts of energy from the power grid, dimming the lights throughout the underground complex. In a blinding instant, the laser leader beam leapt across the cavern and ripped into the far wall, exploding rock into vapour that swirled and condensed into drifting hot dust. The brilliant bar of light died but the machine continued to operate and over seventy kilometres away and several kilometres underground the magnetic beam, in response to the coded commands within the Vox Dei's computer, flashed back into heat energy. Tremendous forces are needed to rip the cap of rock that we call solid ground asunder, but those energies lie beneath us everywhere. In places, along weakened zones where dormant volcanoes sit like quiescent boils, the energy lies closer below the surface. In times past--recent geologic past-- molten rock from the earth's hot interior blasted upward through these weakened zones to create the distinctive cones called volcanoes. Eruptions may cease, and the volcano become dormant or extinct, but the weakness within its bowels remain.

The Glass House Mountains of Australia were ancient volcanoes, lying dead and cold until a burst of energy along a forgotten weakness brought them back to violent life. Mount Shasta in California is also a dormant volcano. It last erupted only two hundred years ago, so the fires of its creation are easily re-awakened. The magma chamber deep below the mountain roared back into life under the hammer blows from Vox Dei and superheated gases expanded, blowing upward through choked vents. The mountain shook.

*   *   *

Sam sat watching Amaru with increasing impatience as the old Neanderthal woman laboriously sent through another coded transmission on the portal's communication link. Amaru had explained that there were some hundred or so possible destinations to which someone could be sent by a malfunctioning portal, and that it would be necessary to check them one at a time by contacting the Greys on duty at each site. In the several hours since the others had left, she had checked thirty-seven of them.

Come on, come on, damn you, Sam thought, not for the first time. *Why does it take so long?*

Easy, Sam. Ratana reached out and squeezed the tall American woman's arm. *We'll find her.*

Sam's mind radiated warmth and appreciation toward the Torres Strait Islander woman, but she voiced her frustration. "You'd think that a race as technologically advanced as Neanderthals would have come up with a faster form of communication," she muttered.

Amaru did not look around from her study of what looked like a smooth circle of rock on the wall of the mine adit. *Communication speed is not the problem, Samantha*, she said gently. *We just could not foresee a situation where we would need a more sophisticated means of talking to someone at the other end of a portal. It has always been quicker just to pass through it.*

"These things never go wrong?" Ratana asked.

Not in this way. Occasionally they shut down, but even then they can only do so once they have delivered their cargo. That is why I am not concerned for the safety of Rima and Gaia. They have been delivered somewhere. It is just a matter of finding out where.

"So why does it take so long to search?" Sam asked, "If you say communication speed is not the problem."

Just a moment. Amaru's fingertips rested delicately on another part of the smooth rock circle for a few moments before she sighed and leaned her head against the rock wall of the tunnel. *They are not there either.* She turned to face the two human women. *We never installed a true communication device into the portals--what need have we ever had? What I am doing here is monitoring the extremely small vibrations that are produced by the electronic components of the portal. I can use my mind to create minute currents that can be picked up at the other end and deciphered. That is what takes so long. It took me over three hours to attract the attention of someone at the other end and nearly as long to agree on a code for the measured pulses. Now they are going through the possible destinations of this portal one at a time, looking for our loved ones. Never fear, Samantha, Ratana; we will find them. I promise you.*

"And when we do? Can we get to them?"

That will depend on where they are, but I promise you, Samantha, you will be reunited with your baby daughter.

Sam nodded and her shoulders slumped, but Ratana, who was still looking at the Neanderthal woman, caught a glimpse of something in her eye, a stray thought that was rapidly tucked back into her mental shield.

"What is it, Amaru?" the Islander woman asked. "You were thinking 'further than you think, further than you could possibly think'. What do you mean by that?"

Amaru did not reply at once but held up one hand and cocked her head as if listening. *I can hear it again,* she whispered.

"Hear what?" Sam asked. "I can't hear..." She stopped as the rock floor beneath her vibrated. "What is it? An earthquake?"

*This is what I felt when the Winambuu attacked. I fear they are...*The rocks of the mountain groaned and trembled and the floor of the tunnel was showered with fine rock from the roof. The three women scrambled to their feet and held each other as the rock around them squealed and split.

"We should get out of here," Ratana said. "Will the portal take us anywhere?"

Amaru shook her head. *It has been shut down while we communicated and anyway, we could not be sure where it would deliver us.*

"Then we need to get out up the tunnel," Sam cried out, tugging on the other women's hands. "Come on."

They ran, Sam holding their single battery lantern. The floor of the adit was smooth, but enough rock had fallen from the roof to make the footing treacherous in the swinging light and shadow. They stumbled and almost fell, pulled one another up, and ran on. Abruptly, the mountain shook so violently that they were thrown off their feet amidst the roar of falling rock all about them. Ratana screamed and Sam dragged her toward the walls of the adit, sheltering her with her own body as the rocks fell all about them. Dimly, she heard Amaru calling out.

Garagh, father...Samantha, forgive me, it is for the best...Garagh, I cannot...

The rock still trembled and distantly, Sam heard rumbling explosions, but all she could see was Ratana's body beneath her and the dim wedge of light cast by the fallen torch. She shook herself and stood up, the Islander woman looking up as she did so.

"Are we alive?" Ratana asked, coughing from the billows of rock dust.

"Yeah, we made it," Sam confirmed. She picked up the torch and swept the space around them with its weak beam. "Where's Amaru?" She stared at the tons of fallen rock that blocked the tunnel ahead of and behind them.

"Amaru? Amaru? Where are...Oh God, Ratana, I heard her dying. She's under that somewhere. She cried out mentally and I...I heard her die." Sam broke down into racking sobs that turned into paroxysms of coughing. "We're going to die too."

"Nonsense," Ratana said, though doubt coloured her voice. "The others will find us."

"How? They don't know this has happened and they're miles away. They'll never get here in time."

Ratana stared at her, a grey ghost sitting on a great boulder. "What do you mean 'in time'? Are...are we going to...to run out of air?"

"We might last that long," Sam said with a wry smile, "But can't you feel the mountain? Those damn shadows have set off another volcanic eruption with their damn machine and we're going to get caught up in it."

"What can we do?"

"Not a damn thing--just hope that James and Nathan and the rest of them get there in time to shut down the machine. Of course, then they have to get back here and dig us out provided half the mountain hasn't fallen on us."

Oh Nathan, my love. Ratana looked up suddenly with hope in her eyes. "We can call them mentally and tell them what has happened."

Sam groaned and slapped her thigh, a cloud of rock dust billowing up and making her cough afresh. "Why didn't I think of that? You try Nathan, I'll call James." She concentrated, imaging James sitting beside her, fashioning his physical and mental attributes in her mind. *James. Nothing. James?*

Hi honey, what's up? Have you found Gaia?

Sam screamed and started babbling out loud. "James, thank God. There's been a rockfall, we're trapped and Amaru's dead and the shadows..." She took a deep breath and looked at Ratana. "Have you found Nathan?"

Ratana shook her head. "I can feel him but he's fuzzy. You and James have had more practice. Talk to him, quickly."

*James. We are trapped by a rockfall. Mount Shasta is erupting. Amaru says...*She broke off and sobbed.

Sam! You've got to get out of there. What does Amaru say?

We can't get out, we're trapped and Amaru is dead. She said the shadows are using the machine again to make Mount Shasta erupt. You've got to stop them, quickly.

We don't know where the machine is. We are halfway into the base, we think, but once there we don't know where...

Andi. She'll know.

Yes, but where's Andi?

Sam did not reply for several moments, feeling the weight of the mountain crushing them. *What do we do then?*

You talked to Andi before. Contact her and get her to stop the machine again, or guide us to it so we can stop it. I'm sorry, love. I can't think of anything else. Chin up. As soon as we can we'll be back to dig you out.

Okay. I had Ernie's help last time--can he help?

I asked him; he said no, but that you had the closest bond with her. He says to remember her flavour, her signature, and call...I gotta go, love, we're coming up to the base and...James mental voice ceased.

Sam sat very still and thought about Andi, what she looked like, the way her voice sounded and the way she thought. She remembered the time, only hours ago, when she had talked to her across the miles--what it had felt like to talk to her that way--*Andi?*

*   *   *

Andi heard the dry slithering sounds coming from the air duct and bit her lip to stop herself crying out. Morgan was babbling with fear and that sound made her skin crawl too. Her employer was a strong, intelligent man but he had a lot more experience of these creatures and if their approach was enough to fill him with terror, they must really be bad.

Keep quiet. I must keep quiet. Maybe they are not coming here--after all, those air ducts connect the whole base. Maybe they are going someplace else. Andi stared at the dark oblong of the duct almost lost in the gloom of the cell in fascination, much as she imagined a rabbit would stare at an approaching rattlesnake.

"Nooo..." The sound was forced out of her as the darkness of the duct flowed and dripped, shadows sliding over the walls and ceiling of her cell. From Morgan's cell she heard a cry of agony.

Yessss, Morgan-mate. As agreed, we have returned to claim you.

"I...I did not agree."

Amusement. *The Winambuu take what they will.* The shadows flowed down the walls, coalescing into smoky figures in the air in front of her. Andi scrambled away, pressing herself back in a frenzy of loathing and fear as if she could push herself through the rock walls to escape. She screamed when they first touched her, the light, dry whispers of the grave cloth across her skin making her cringe and filling her mind with images of decay and leprosy.

"Help me!" she cried out in agony.

Andi.

"Wh...who? Help me please!"

Andi. It's Sam. Can you hear me?

"Sam?" *Sam!* "Where are you? Hurry, please."

Andi, think at me, like last time. Don't vocalise. Andi, have you got the machine on again? It's making a mountain erupt and I'm trapped.

Concern for her sister swept her own fears aside and Andi concentrated, her mind remembering how she had talked with her sister before. *Sam, I'm locked up. I don't know what's happening with the machine.* The shadow touch became more insistent, more pervasive, and she shuddered. *Sam, the shadows are here. What do I do?*

Resist, Andi. They have limited powers unless you give into them, or they take you by surprise. Andi, you've got to get out of there and shut the machine down.

I can't. I'm locked up.

Then describe where you are. I can pass this on to James and he can let you out.

He's here? Where? I thought that was the FBI.

?

Andi quickly described her deal with the FBI and how she had sent word. *I can hear gunfire, but if you say James and his friends are here...*

They do not have guns. It must be the FBI you hear.

Whoever. Andi cried out as the shadows touch became intimate, invasive. *Hurry, Sam.*

Tell me where you are, Andi. Describe how to get to you.

Andi started a long, involved description but quickly got bogged down in ambiguity and lack of detail. *Hang on.* She racked her brain to recall a rough map of the base Morgan had drawn for her, and concentrated on the image.

Got it. Okay, sis. Hang tight. Help is on its way.

Hurry, Sam. I don't know how long..."Oh, God, no." She moaned and writhed, ineffectually tearing at the swirling sooty cloud that surrounded her, wondering how long she could hold out against the shadows.

19

The back door to the Glass Mountain complex was designed as a bolt hole, an exit in case of trouble, and while the existence of the passage was known to a handful, very few knew of its exact whereabouts. The inner passages were an extension of the carved and finished rooms and corridors of the base itself, but the outer, upper part utilized the presence of an old abandoned mine. James knew, therefore, that they were nearing their goal when the floor underfoot smoothed out and the air became less dank. Shortly afterward, the first lights appeared, small bulbs recessed in the walls that acted as guidance rather than shedding light on the surroundings. Wandjina's blue-white spiritual radiance still flooded the passageway, allowing them to move rapidly. They came to the first side passages and paused, looking into the darkness on either side.

"I'd say we still follow the main passage," James whispered. "But I could be wrong. Any of these could lead us to the machine."

Wandjina nodded. "Your instincts are good, I think." He trotted off down the main passage, the others running after him.

More side passages appeared, some of which were lit like the main one, so Robert and Nathan ran off down one of them to explore. They were back a few minutes later to report that there appeared to be an empty storage chamber at the other end.

"What about the other branches?" Spence asked. "Do we have to check them all? I get the idea that we are in a bit of a hurry here."

"It would be a pity if we ran right past the machine in our eagerness to penetrate the base," Moon Wolf observed.

"Could you not ask of the rock itself, Great One?" John Tall Tree asked.

"Ordinarily, yes, but the wrongness lies heavy within the crystal heart of this mountain and the rocks are silent."

James.

Honey! You'd gone silent. Are you okay? Did you find Andi?

"What is it, Aparrerinja?" Wandjina asked. "Is Samantha still all right?"

"Yeah, she's okay. Hang on a moment." *Honey?*

I'm here. Andi's in trouble, love. She's locked up and under attack by the shadows. You have to get to her quickly. Here's a rough map of where she is.

Okay, sweetie, I'll get right onto it. Are you and Ratana all right?

Yes, just hurry.

James pointed down the main corridor. "Down there. Sam sent me a map courtesy of her sister." They ran down the passage, guided by the map in James' head, until they reached a T-junction. "Okay, Andi's locked up to the right and the main complex is to the left." He described the way through Morgan's apartment and the corridors that lay beyond, leading to the main laboratory. "With luck, that's where the machine will be."

"Very good, Aparrerinja," Wandjina said. "You take Spence and free your sister-in-law. The rest of us will proceed to the laboratory and smash the machine."

James shook his head. "Andi's under attack by the shadow beings. Spence and I cannot fight them off. You'll have to come too."

"I can do that," Moon Wolf said. "Take Spence with you, Wandjina, and leave me Robert and John. We will counter these beings."

Wandjina nodded, and the two groups separated. James led his group at a run, winding through a maze of corridors and empty storage chambers until they came upon a dimly lit corridor with half a dozen barred doors.

"This is it, I think. Andi! Are you here?"

"Here, here! Help me, please!"

"There." James pointed at a locked and bolted door. Moon Wolf nodded and gestured and the door swung open. A cloud of dark particles boiled out into the corridor, formed into vaguely humanoid shapes and swept toward the humans. "Watch out!" James yelled, throwing himself back.

Moon Wolf gestured again but the shadows did no more than hesitate before rushing on. "Robert, John," the old Native American said tersely, "Spread your arms--the Coyote song--quickly."

Despite the fact the shadows were already swirling about their heads, their touch making them flinch, both young men broke into a chant in the Wintun language, spreading their arms and stamping rhythmically. Moon Wolf joined in and slowly, the shadows retreated.

"James," Moon Wolf panted. "Get your sister out of the cell. We cannot hold them forever."

James dived into the cell and moments later re-emerged holding up an exhausted and terrified young woman. He helped her past the chanters and into the corridor beyond, where she suddenly struggled to break free.

"No, we must go back for Morgan. He's in the next cell to mine. Please, you must help him."

James lowered her to the ground and ran back, rattling the lock on the next cell door. "It's locked. Moon Wolf, can you open it?"

The old man nodded and broke off the chant once more to gesture. The door flew open and he returned to aid the young men, but the shadows advanced as the men tired. James disappeared into the cell but was out again less than a minute later, shaking his head.

"He's dead."

"No, he can't be. I survived. Check him again," Andi sobbed.

"He's dead, Andi. I checked." James hurried back to her side. "There's nothing we can do." He held her comfortingly. "I think his heart gave out, he looked quite peaceful."

The shadows sought to encircle the trio of singing, dancing men, but were driven back, though with increasing difficulty.

"We need to leave," Moon Wolf called out, exhaustion edging his voice.

Andi wiped away her tears. "Morgan was a good man." She frowned suddenly and looked up at James. "Sam. Is she all right? Did you turn the machine off?"

"She's okay. And the others are using the map you sent to find the lab. They'll be smashing it any moment now."

"The machine's not in the lab. They moved it."

The shadows swirled and struck a double blow, aiming at the weak links in those opposing them. Robert and John staggered, but regained their balance and rhythm with the aid of Moon Wolf.

"Dr James," called Robert Walking Bear. "We must leave, now."

"It is true," Moon Wolf added. "These beings are not of this creation and my powers will not harm them, only hold them. And I cannot do that for much longer."

"Then how can we run if they cannot be held back?"

"All of you must run. I will hold them and prevent them following."

"What about you? We can't just leave you."

Moon Wolf turned his head and smiled tiredly. "Do you have some power you have not told me about, James?" He groaned and was forced back a step. "I thought not. You cannot help me, so at least obey me. Run!"

"We obey, Olelbis," Robert and John said together. They turned and sped down the corridor, pulling James and Andi with them.

James looked back as they turned the corner and he saw Moon Wolf standing tall in a bright white light as the cloud of shadows pressed close about him. A blinding, soundless explosion filled the corridor and when James' eyes had ceased to send formless splashes of bright colour dancing along his optic nerves, he saw that the corridor was empty. "Oh shit," he muttered. Shaking his head, he ran on, catching up with the others at the T-junction.

"What happened?" John Tall Tree asked.

James shook his head, not wanting to answer. "Where's the lab, Andi?"

"The machine's not there, I told you. We need to..."

"We need to find the others first," James interrupted.

Andi nodded. "Of course. This way." She led the way at a run, racing through the corridors and burst into the laboratory, where she skidded to a halt at the sight of a huge shambling caveman apparently clothed in a loincloth and a reddish fur coat.

The caveman turned at their entrance and smiled. *Ah, you must be Andi Jones, Samantha's sister.* He held out a huge paw, which Andi took hesitantly. *My name is Garagh. Your sister thinks of you often and I feel as if I almost know you.*

"Er, okay...thank you."

"Nice to meet you, and all that," Spence said crisply, "But can we leave the conversations to later. The bloody machine isn't here. You wouldn't happen to know where it is, would you, Miss Andi?"

James stabbed fingers toward the men in the room. "Ernie, Garagh you've met, and Spence. This is Nathan. Everyone, this is Sam's sister Andi."

"Gidday," Nathan murmured. Ernie just nodded, looking beyond James to where Robert and John stood in the doorway.

"Where's Moon Wolf?"

"Olelbis keeps the demons at bay while we escape," John declared.

Wandjina looked at James. "I do not feel his energies," he said softly. "What happened, Aparrerinja?"

He...he fell. Or at least he exploded in a great flash of light, taking the shadows with him. I think he's dead.

Ones such as he do not die easily. Aloud, Wandjina continued. "Miss Jones, would you please lead us to the machine?"

Andi led them off again through the deserted rooms and passageways. At one point she stopped at an intersection and stared down a broad avenue that ran into a darkness lit only by a drawn out string of lights. Explosions and gunfire reverberated in the close confines of the tunnel. "That access tunnel is one of two that lead to the lodge," she said. "I suppose that's where the FBI are...and Marc."

"Is the machine up there?" James asked.

"No."

"Then why are we delaying? Every moment longer puts Sam and Ratana in more danger. Have you forgotten?"

Andi flushed and set off again, leading them back into the corridors behind Morgan's apartment, but by a different route. "It's just ahead. You can see the lights..."

A whiplash cracked in front of her and concrete chips stung her cheek as Spence crashed into her and bore her sprawling to the floor. Another shot split the air as the rest of the party dived for what cover they could. Ahead, peering round the doorway of the cavern, a short man aimed an army revolver and fired again at Andi.

Spence grunted and swore, clutching Andi tightly beneath him. He half crawled, half staggered into the doorway of a side room and collapsed, letting Andi fall to one side. "Bugger me," he breathed, looking at a rapidly spreading red stain on his shirt.

James stared across the corridor at his old friend and started across, reeling back as another bullet whined off the wall near his head.

"I see you, Jones you bitch," screamed the thin man in the cavern. "Did I get you, or did that poor sod get in the way? I'll get you next time."

"Parker!" Andi yelled back. "Give it up, that's the FBI coming and you haven't got a chance."

Parker screamed with laughter. "Ehrich set the Baby Vox on them. They all think the others are terrorists. They won't be bothering us." Another bullet whined past Andi.

"Is Ehrich there with you?"

"He's here, and he's using the big machine, but God knows on what. He's doing his thing, and I'm doing mine." He fired down the corridor again.

That's five, said Nathan. *One more and we can rush him.*

Unless he's been reloading between shots, James rejoined. "Dr Parker, could I ask you to help us switch the machine off? It's killing people, my wife included."

"Who the hell are you?"

"Dr Hay, from Australia. Please, Dr Parker, help us switch the machine off."

"Go to hell," Parker screamed. He fired twice more.

"So much for diplomacy and depleted chambers. Has anyone else got any ideas?"

Spence.

Wandjina?

How badly are you hurt? Let me see...ah.

Bad?

Your father is correct.

Spence hid his thoughts while James discussed the situation with Nathan and the Native Americans.

Wandjina, I can do it, Garagh said.

I know, my friend, but with Amaru gone you are our last hope. We cannot risk you.

I'll do it, Spence thought. *Or I would, but I can't exactly make my feet obey me. It's a real bugger.* He grinned, blood trickling from the corner of his mouth.

I can give you strength.

Thanks Wandjina. Can you also...lessen the pain a bit? Spence struggled to his feet, bracing his back against the wall. *That's better.*

James saw Spence swaying on his feet and called out in alarm. "Sit down, Spence, for God's sake, you're hurt. Andi, make him."

Spence pushed Andi gently aside. *James, Nathan, Garagh, it's been a privilege knowing you. You too, young fellahs,* he nodded toward Robert and John. He swayed out into the corridor and started into a shambling run toward the corridor.

"No!" James yelled, leaping forward, only to be pulled back by Garagh.

Parker gaped and fired, missing the blood-soaked figure coming toward him. He fired again, grinning as the impact knocked the old man to one side, but staring as he came on. He fired again, and a fourth time at point blank range just as Spence collided with him, knocking him back into the room.

With a cry of anguish, James wrestled free and sprinted after his friend and into the cavern, falling over the tangled bodies of Spence and Parker in the entrance. "Spence. Oh my God, no." He pulled the blood-drenched man off the slight body of the scientist. Parker's head lay at an odd angle and James knew the man's neck was broken. Spence lay still and unmoving and James wept openly.

Wandjina gently pulled James to his feet. "Mourn later, Aparrerinja. We have work to do."

Across the length of the great cavern lay the gleaming length of the Vox Dei. Although no gleaming bar of energy issued from its crystal lattices and long barrel, it hummed malevolently, pouring its invisible energies to one side, through the cavern wall. Closer at hand lay the smaller version known as Baby Vox, hurling its own energies at a nearer target.

Andi walked across to the Baby Vox, reached over its squat barrel and flicked a switch. The contented hum of its cooling system died and the laser light within its inner workings flicked out. "There, it's harmless."

Behind her, through the open doorway, the distant faint crackle of gunfire stopped as sense returned to army and FBI alike, an awakening from a nightmare of illusion.

"What the hell are you doing, Parker? Oh, it's you." Ehrich looked up from behind the power source of the Vox Dei, goggles and ear protectors masking his features. He ripped them off and threw them carelessly onto a bench. "It's too late, you know, Dr Jones. The Winambuu tell me they have ripped open the barriers and saved themselves. You can't stop them now."

"I have no idea what you're talking about," Andi called down the length of the cavern. "All I know is that you are killing my sister with that machine and we are going to stop you."

Ehrich smiled. "That rag-taggle band?" He stared for a moment. "Is that a real live caveman? They said there were some among the enemy."

"Switch the machine off," James called, "And we'll let you go. We only want to save lives."

"Very commendable," Ehrich said. "You would just let me walk out of here?"

"No!" Andi yelled. "Your creatures killed Morgan."

"Indeed? Well, he was a weak-willed man. They are not my creatures, though they have done my bidding on occasion."

"Enough of this. We will let you go, Ehrich, provided you step away from the machine now."

Ehrich shrugged, turned and picked up a heavy wrench and brought it down sharply on the controls of the machine. There was a spluttering snap and crackle and the monitor went dead, but the machine continued to operate without a pause. "Good luck," he sneered, before running into the depths of the cavern.

"Let him go," James yelled, racing for the machine. "Concentrate on shutting this off. Andi, what do we do?"

Andi looked over the wrecked control panel. "I would have thought this would have been enough." She punched a couple of keys without visible effect. "We'll have to shut off the power. That did it last time."

"Hurry then."

Andi moved to the place where the power cables snaked out of the wall and stared in puzzlement. "It's been changed. There used to be switches and plugs here but now the cables just come out of the wall. Look, you can see the new concrete where they've done it."

"You can't switch it off?" Robert asked. "Can you do something to the machine itself? Break something, maybe?"

"It didn't have much effect smashing the controls," Nathan grinned. "Perhaps it can't be broken."

"Bloody hell, Nate," James said. "Your wife's being threatened by this thing and you joke about it?"

"She's okay. I heard from her earlier. They're in a rock chamber sitting on their bums while we run around doing everything."

James turned away from him in some disgust. "Andi, what can you usefully break?"

"The crystal array," she replied promptly. "If we can get these covers off." She slapped the gleaming plates of stainless steel covering the barrel.

"Someone's coming--or something," John Tall Tree said. He looked into the gloom at the rear of the cavern where Ehrich had run. "Do you think it's that creepy guy coming back?"

Instead, the noise grew louder, a buzzing, rustling roar that culminated in a flood of inky blackness that swept out of the tunnel at the rear of the cavern and crashed over the humans standing around the Vox Dei like a tsunami.

"Fall back!" Wandjina yelled. "Behind me." The old Aboriginal man raised his hands and a crackling, snapping arc of lightning leapt between his hands. The shadows swirled away from the intense light and broke up into shards, driving down at individuals. "Get behind me," Wandjina called again. He now spread his arms wide, lowering them to either side and the arc of lightning spread out into a vivid sheet of light that faded to a pearly glow as it wrapped around the seven of them. The shadows howled impotently outside the five metre diameter hemisphere of light, beating upon its gleaming surface but unable to penetrate it.

What now, Wandjina? Garagh asked. *It is a mighty defence but we are no closer to our objective.*

Wandjina frowned and thought hard.

"Whatever it is you are going to do," Andi murmured, "You'd better do it fast. Sam tells me Mount Shasta is about to blow."

"You are speaking with her?" James asked, agony showing on his face. "Why can't I?" *Sam. Sam.*

"Just briefly. I don't know why you can't hear her."

There is a blood connection, Garagh rumbled. *Wandjina, we must do something.*

"I can defend or I can attack. I cannot do both."

"Anything we can do, Great One?" Robert asked.

"As a matter of fact, there is. Everyone find something shiny, reflective, like those metal panels. I will collapse the shield and use the energy like a spear. If you can orient the plates correctly, I can spill some of the energy over them and you can keep the shadows at bay while I attack the machine."

James and John grabbed metal plates and handed the shinier ones out. Nathan complained about the weight of his but the others said nothing, just waggling them around experimentally.

"Ready?" With a sound akin to wet cardboard ripping, the hemisphere collapsed and a thin spear of light appeared in Wandjina's hands. For a heartbeat, the shadows hung above and around them, and then with a thin cry of triumph, surged inward.

Wandjina swung his spear, carefully, and a thin beam of light shot out of its tip, striking the reflective plates and sending dazzling shards of light dancing around the cavern. James and Nathan staggered back as the light swept over them, blindingly. "Work as a team," Wandjina said. "Choose different areas to control, otherwise we'll have chaos."

Slowly, the old Aborigine spun in the centre of the group and each person in turn wielded their plate, sending coruscations of light into the cloud around them, beating it back. As the shadow cloud withdrew, Wandjina turned his attention and his spear to the machine. His first blast was ineffective as the light beam blasted off the curved steel plates without doing any damage.

"Aim for the base," Andi called, dancing and weaving, the intermittent bolts of energy from Wandjina's wand striking to the heart of the cloud in her sector, throwing it back. "Undermine it, collapse it into the floor."

The spear point dipped and the rocky floor erupted in a blizzard of dust and gravel.

20

The battle raged in the tunnels below Medicine Lake and in the long approaches to the base under Glass Mountain. FBI agents fought against soldiers of the US Army, each totally convinced that the people they were fighting were enemies of the State. After the initial assault on the lodge that left dozens of the soldiers and a few agents dead or wounded, the action had bogged down in a slow and bloody advance that saw the FBI agents slowly but surely gain the upper hand. It was not that the soldiers were less well trained or had less desire to fight, but was an accident of their initial mental programming.

The soldiers had been led to believe, under the mind-altering influence of the Baby Vox, that their opponents were trained and fanatical terrorists and, despite their hatred for their perceived enemy, were a little bit cautious in getting to grips with them. The FBI agents, on the other hand, believed their antagonists to be hoodlums of organised crime, and their attitude was more one of contempt rather than respect. The effect was that the soldiers picked up on the attitude of the agents, and the agents felt the fear growing among their foes, emboldening them.

When the beam of the Baby Vox cut off, each side saw, between one eye blink and the next, the true nature of their foe. Guns and rifles dropped, and in the horrified silence, warriors of both sides looked to their officers for guidance.

General Spader, shocked by the bloodshed yet still driven to resist the FBI incursion by his belief in, and fear of, the Nine, ordered a continuation of the battle but was relieved of his command by Captain Anders, at gunpoint. General Thompson, shaken by the murder of his aide, assumed command of the base and immediately ordered the soldiers to lay down their arms and return to their barracks. Captain Anders then set about finding the persons named in the federal warrants, but was shocked to find that Braun and Newman had been killed in the fighting. No one knew why they were in the passages under the lodge and nobody could be certain which side had fired the fatal shots. Not that it mattered. Everyone was trying to forget the horrific mind-set that had led to the slaughter, though Lieutenant Evans revealed the nature of the research taking place and the possible role of the small machine in the recent events.

Marc Lachlan had entered the base as the firing died away, and picked his way over debris and dead bodies, bypassing the rooms set up to care for the injured. He coughed from the residual tear gas which the ventilation system was rapidly clearing, but persevered as he was now very worried about Andi's safety. When he came to the room where General Thompson was arguing with Agent Collins about the best course of action, he listened for a moment before sneaking past and heading deeper into the base. The corridors were now deserted and the closer he got to the living areas, the fewer disturbances were evident.

Gradually, as he pushed onward, a noise had been intruding on his thoughts, but Marc could not place it. A crackling, snapping noise, it put him in mind of frying bacon, but he quickly decided it was electrical in nature and veered toward it, becoming convinced that it was the machine, and if the machine was still in use, Andi would be somewhere close by. Guided by the crackling, which was now becoming more like a roar of released energies overlain with indistinct shouting, Marc found himself in a vast cavern staring at two dead men lying in a pool of blood and beyond, a sight that had him doubting his sanity.

*   *   *

Wandjina danced, not the ritualised movements of his people, the Australian Aborigine, where every step, every gesture and cry, told part of a story, but a fluid, weaving routine where his gleaming dark body counter pointed the brilliant white flares that blasted from his spear. He ducked and whirled, bolts of light touching the six plates of steel that moved around him in the hands of his fellow dancers, and thence ripping into the swirling black cloud that surrounded them all. Every few moments, the old Aboriginal whirled away and gouts of energy sent another chunk of concrete and stone flying, disintegrating into dust and fine gravel. As the hole at the base of the great machine got deeper, the movements of the black cloud grew more frenetic, and a wail of despair and anger beat at the ears of the listeners.

"It's working," Andi panted, stumbling with exhaustion, a blast from Wandjina's spear nearly searing her fingers. "I saw it move."

"I think you are right, Ms Andi," Robert Walking Bear confirmed. "Listen to the shadow demons. They can feel their defeat."

The howling of the Winambuu reached a crescendo as they hurled themselves on the humans in a last ditch effort to protect the machine. They pressed in close and now, as they neared the source of Wandjina's energy, they started to die, exploding into a blizzard of fine dust that winked out of existence before it fell to the floor. The other shadow beings tore away like a tornado, a cyclonic disturbance that lifted up every moveable object in the cavern and hurled them at their tormenters. Garagh fell when a spanner clipped the side of his head, and John Tall Tree collapsed cursing an injured leg.

"Everybody down," Wandjina roared. His spear disappeared and the lightning blazed between his hands again as the protective shield slammed around his little group. The rush of objects smashed silently into the wall and slid to the floor. "Time to end it?" he asked.

Indeed, Garagh said calmly.

"Bloody their noses," James growled.

"Kick butt, Great One," Robert grinned.

"Whup their ass," John added.

"Hit 'em where the sun doesn't shine," Nathan said fiercely.

"End it," Andi agreed, nodding her head.

The shield collapsed and Wandjina's spear blazed with actinic fury, sending after-images dancing around the cavern walls. The dark cloud was tossed and thrown apart in chaos before gathering itself into a semblance of its former self and rushing to escape down the passages at the far end of the cavern.

Wandjina now swung his spear toward the Vox Dei and his energies roared like the surface of the sun, a great chasm opening up at its base. Slowly, almost reluctantly, the long barrel tilted and dropped, the body of the machine swaying and falling into the huge split in the rock. The power cables snaked across the floor, dragged by the falling machine and tightening, halting its descent. Vox Dei still hummed and flickered within its crystal heart, pouring its malevolent energies no longer at Mount Shasta, but now directly downward into the deep magma chamber far below Glass Mountain.

"Cut through the power cord, Wandjina," James said. "Finish it."

The spear swung downward and sheared through the thick power cables in an eruption of sparks, melting the copper cores in a red-gold puddle at their feet. The machine lurched and fell ten meters, lodging barrel downward in the chasm.

"Well damn," Nathan said in the relative silence. "We did it, boys and girl."

"Yeah," Andi agreed. "Thank God that's over."

Wandjina and John immediately set about tending to the injuries of Garagh and Robert, but thankfully, they were superficial.

James walked over to the chasm and looked down at the wreckage of the Vox Dei. He studied the machine and stared at the severed cable, a frown growing on his face. "Why is the machine still working?" he asked.

"What? It can't be," Andi said, walking over to join him. "It must be just the residual energies shorting out or...shit!" She stared down in open disbelief. "How can it be operating? Where's the energy coming from? It's breaking all the laws of physics."

The cavern shook as a temblor ripped up from the buried magma chamber, and chunks of stone fell from the roof.

"Can you blast it, Wandjina?" James asked.

The old Aborigine sighed. "Even I have my limits, Aparrerinja. It resisted me before and I fear that it will do so again now that I am weaker."

"Then what do we do?" Nathan asked. "We came here to destroy it."

"It will destroy itself when this volcano erupts," John said.

Nathan gaped. "This is a volcano? We're standing around talking in an erupting volcano? Does anyone else see the absurdity of the situation?"

"Perhaps we should withdraw then?" Garagh observed mildly.

"Fuckin'-A," Nathan muttered. "The first sensible suggestion I've heard all night."

Another tremor shook the cavern and they started back toward the cavern entrance and stopped as they caught sight of the young man standing there, eyes wide.

"Marc!" Andi screamed, and raced across, throwing herself into his arms. "You came for me! You didn't just send in the cavalry."

Marc grinned and hugged Andi, kissing her when her head came up. "You think I'd miss this?" He looked beyond her at the others. "Doesn't look like you needed much help."

"Hey, it's the thought that counts, Marc. You risked your life for me."

"Yeah, I did, didn't I?" Marc grinned, pleased. "Who are you other guys?" He frowned, searching for memories that slipped from his grasp like greased pigs. "Some of you look familiar, but I can't quite..."

James stepped up and shook Marc's hand. "James Hay, Marc. We met briefly in Australia. Nathan, Ernie and Garagh you've met too, but not Robert and John."

"How can he not remember?" Nathan asked, sounding faintly injured.

The mind block is in place, Garagh said. *It protects him so do not try to revive his memories.*

The ground shook again and a wash of heat swept over them. "Time we were leaving," Wandjina said. "Aparrerinja, bid farewell to your friend."

"Oh God, yes. How could I have forgotten Spence?" James dropped to his knees beside the sprawled body of his friend, unmindful of the blood that soaked into his clothes. "Spence, old friend, I wish I could tell you how much you meant to me all these years. You were a true mate." Tears coursed down his cheeks as he spoke.

"Glad t...to hear it, mate," Spence breathed, his eyes flickering open, "'Cept you...you owe me a p...pint, and I won't be...able to...collect...it."

"Oh, Jesus, you're alive." James sobbed and cradled his friends head. "We've got to get you out of here, the mountain's about..."

"Not goin' any...where..." Spence coughed, and blood bubbled up on his lips.

"Of course you are. We're going to get you out of here and..."

"Just...shut up...and listen." Spence struggled to sit up in James' arms, his face pale and sunken, the fresh arterial blood glistening on his lips. "My father is...standing over there and...and he always...was an impatient sod." His hand twitched and moved to James'. "Take my tiki and give it to my...son Rahi."

"Son? I didn't know you had a son."

Spence nodded slowly, painfully. His breath came more raggedly. "Gisborne...don't know where...his mother Moana...tell him..."

"I will," James assured him. His tears flowed unashamedly as he wept for his friend.

"Don't cry...you daft bugger. Anyone...would think...this was...was...a sad..." Spence's face lit up and his eyes moved to the doorway. "I'm ready..." His head slumped back and his eyes slowly glazed.

James burst into tears, before fumbling around his dead friend's neck for the thin leather thong holding the blood-covered tiki that was his ward as tohunga of his tribe. He slipped it into his trouser pocket and laid Spence's body down gently.

"Time to go," Wandjina said softly. "He is with his ancestors now. Do not be sad for he smiles at you."

James nodded and got to his feet, brushing away the tears. "Goodbye, mate. We'll meet again." He turned and faced the others, grim-faced as another rumble from the chasm shook the floor. "One further thought. How are we going to get everyone out of this base? We can't just run and leave the soldiers and agents to be blown up."

"What the hell do you suggest?" Nathan asked. "Military types are just as likely to lock us up for spreading malicious rumours. I say we just bugger off and let them worry about it. They must have felt the shocks by now; we don't have to risk..."

"Unacceptable, Nate," James said, staring at his young friend. "We have to warn them."

Marc pointed to a wall telephone. "We could always call them. They might believe me."

"Can you instil enough urgency in your voice?" A blast of heat and ash vented from the chasm and more rock fell from the ceiling. "I don't think we have long."

"Wait." Andi ran over to the Baby Vox and bent over its controls, switching it back on and tapping instructions into the keyboard.

"What are you doing?"

"I'm spreading the beam to cover the whole front part of the base and turning up the volume. Now all you have to do is plant the right idea in their minds."

Marc grinned. "Gotcha." He picked up the telephone and switched on the loudspeaker and punched in 'Broadcast', knowing his voice would be speaking into every room and corridor in the base. "Now hear this. This is Marc Lachlan speaking from the depths of the Glass Mountain army base. Agent Collins, General Thompson, you know who I am--you can recognise my voice. I came in to find Dr Jones but I found much more. The scientists here have rigged up a giant laser which is drilling down into the lava beneath this volcano we are in and the project is now out of control..."

"Speed it up, Marc, we don't have time for long explanations," James said softly.

"...the volcano is erupting. Already lava and ash is pouring into the base. In minutes, we will be overcome and be killed unless we run for it--out onto the island. Quickly! Flee for your lives!" Marc cupped a hand over the mouthpiece. "Will that do?"

"Excellently," James said with a grim smile. "We're only on the outskirts of the beam but even I can feel panic fluttering in my breast."

"Very poetic, Uncle," Nathan grated. "Can we get the fuck out of here now?"

James nodded. "Back the way we came, you too Marc." He led the way, back into the main part of the base to access the living quarters and the bolt hole behind Morgan Turner's apartments. Panic grew rapidly, flooding their minds with an unreasoning terror and threatening to send them stampeding for the nearest exit, despite the fact they knew the reason for their fear. The emanations from the Baby Vox tipped the balance between reason and unreason, tempting them with a simpler, animalistic reaction. They fled, running through the twists and turns of the corridors, with the floor trembling beneath them. As they reached the long straight corridor leading north to the old mine adit, they passed out of the zone of influence of the machine, and automatically slowed in their headlong flight.

"That was one strange feeling," Robert said as he slowed to a walk. "I knew the reason for my panic was artificial but it didn't make it any less real."

"Then perhaps you should replace your artificial fear with a genuine one," James commented as he ran past him. "This volcano is going to blow and we're still inside it."

* * *

The planning session between Agent Collins, General Thompson and Captain Anders was in full swing when the loudspeakers crackled and Marc's voice boomed out. Conversation died as their eyes locked on the speaker, and their minds began to comprehend the words. Images blossomed in their minds, pictures of ruin and devastation and of men screaming in agony as burning lava and hot ash churned through the corridors, trapping them all in an underground tomb.

"We've got to get out," Collins yelled. "Kowalski, Edders, get the men out, immediately." He ran out the door, shouting for his men.

Captain Anders knew what was happening but was unable to control himself. "It's...it's the machine. Someone is using it to cr...create panic."

General Thompson edged around the table, putting himself closer to the door and safety. "Why would Mr Lachlan do that?" He fought down his terror, feeling ashamed that he was on the point of giving in to fear. *I am not afraid*, he told himself and shivered, knowing it was a lie.

"I don't think Lachlan is to blame, sir. I think he's been taken by the same person or persons who made us fight earlier."

"I thought that was Spader. We have him in custody." Thompson edged closer to the door, wishing the others were not present. *I could just run then, but I'll be damned if I let others see it.*

Captain Anders gripped the table to keep himself from fleeing. *Cowardice in the face of the enemy--it would finish me.* "Not Spader, sir. Ehrich Mannheim. I've seen them together, he was definitely in charge."

"Then we have to stop him."

"Yes sir. How?" *Why don't we discuss this back in the lodge? Come on General, you know I can't leave before you.*

"Use your head, Captain. We know what's causing this fear, we can overcome it."

"Wh...what about the lava, sir?"

"There is no damn lava. It's a ruse to give this Mannheim time to...to do something." Thompson strode to the door and looked out. Two soldiers hurried past and the General roared at them to stop. Discipline won out and they halted, looking anxiously back toward the depths of the base. "Come here, Anders. Do you feel any heat? See any ash? No, and you know why? Because there isn't any. It's a trick and I'm not going to let Lachlan and Mannheim get away with it."

As the General spoke, Anders and the two soldiers listened with increasing comprehension. The panic of being burned alive by an erupting volcano faded and was replaced by a growing fear that the instigator of this tragedy would escape.

One of the soldiers asked. "We're not going to let him get away with it are we, General?"

"Not on your life, soldier. Anders, see if you can find another dozen men. We are heading in there to put an end to his murderous scheming."

Anders ran down the corridors and out of sight and after a few minutes, as Thompson started to entertain the notion that perhaps the captain might lack intestinal fortitude, he trotted back at the head of seven men. He saluted. "Sorry sir, this is all I could find...unless you want me to look further afield."

"It'll do." Thompson briefly addressed the men, building on the theme of the deception that was taking place and assuring them that the only thing to fear was the shame of letting the culprit escape. Visibly, the resolve of the soldiers stiffened. "Okay then," General Thompson said. "Follow me." He strode off toward the heart of the base to arrest Lachlan and Mannheim, Captain Anders and nine soldiers following him resolutely.

*   *   *

Ehrich Mannheim stopped in the mine adit about twenty meters from the entrance, close enough that he could see the erratic beam of a torch outside. He cursed inwardly that a guard had been set and thought for a few moments.

"You will have to help me," he said quietly.

Why should we? hissed the darkness around him. *You humans have been less than successful in ridding us of our enemies.*

Ehrich chuckled coldly. "And you were successful back there in the cavern? You were routed by that old Australian man. Another few minutes and Shasta would have blown, tearing the veil between our worlds to shreds. You would have been safe then."

The hissing, rustling cries swelled with anger before dying down again. *We lied. Our desire is not to shatter some barrier but to kill a child and her mother.*

"Why? How could a woman and child be so dangerous?"

We are not sure. The plans of the enemy are hidden, but they think to eliminate us by means of them. That is why we must kill them.

Ehrich laughed softly. "You failed."

We almost succeeded.

"'Almost' is the cry of the failure," Ehrich sneered. "But I can help you." He patted his jacket pocket. "I have the complete specifications of the Vox Dei. I can find other scientists and build it again and this time there will be no pretence. You will determine the targets, whatever they are. If you want this child dead, I will do it for you."

And what do you want in return?

"Get me safely away from here. And then work with me for the benefit of those I represent--the Nine."

It will be done. Follow now, and swiftly.

The Winambuu swept past Ehrich in a fluttering, whispering horde and poured out of the mine entrance into the stand of pine trees like a cloud of bats, enveloping the human and the great yowie.

Wulgu roared and beat at the insubstantial beings without effect, while Ed Sun-on-Still-waters dived for the cover of the bushes, curling into a fetal ball and trying to shut out the horror.

Hard on the heels of the shadows, ran Ehrich. He stepped out of the adit and took in the scene in the tiny clearing at a glance. Edging around the howling yowie, he took off through the trees. When he reached the path, he turned toward the lake and settled into a jog, a thin cloud of shadows hovering over his head.

"I need transport away from here. Can you get me a helicopter and pilot?"

Yesss. The shadows lifted and streaked through the pre-dawn darkness, arrowing down toward the lake and the wooded island where several helicopters waited.

Back at the mine entrance, Wulgu felt himself tiring. The main body of the shadows still assaulted him and though they could do little to harm him physically, their insidious attack on his mind filled him with a horror of being taken over and controlled. He fought back, roaring with rage and beating at the cloud with a branch ripped from a tree. The black cloud surrounded his head, blinding him and filling his mouth and nostrils, and he fell to the ground.

A light penetrated the cloud, gleaming and white and indescribably beautiful. *It can't be dawn*, thought Wulgu. *That's not for two hours yet.* The glow increased, strong and pure and the shadows were peeled away, scattered before the effulgent rays that shone from the old mine. Wulgu rolled to his knees and stared at the glowing figure that emerged. The great yowie had never bowed his head to any creature, not even Garagh his creator or Wandjina who was as close to a deity as could be found in Australia. This figure before him filled him with awe and he had no desire to rise to his feet.

Who are you?

The brilliant light snapped off, leaving behind an old man in a checked shirt and faded jeans, whose skin still glowed softly with an inner light. "Hello Wulgu," Moon Wolf said. "Where are the others?"

Wulgu rose slowly to his feet, eyeing the old Native American warily. *They haven't returned. How were you separated?*

Moon Wolf shrugged and yawned. "They will be along shortly, I'm sure. Meanwhile, we should prepare to get away from here. Can you not feel that the mountain is awakening?" As if to underscore his words the ground shook slightly and scores of birds in the trees started an agitated twittering.

There will be an eruption?

"Possibly. Where is Ed?"

"I am here, Great One." Ed came out of the bushes hanging his head. "I am ashamed, Olelbis, for I fled from the black ones."

"Be easy, Ed. Alone you could do nothing. I would rather you lived than wasted your life in useless heroics. Now, come out to the mountain path, we must see where the enemy has gone."

21

Out on the bare hillside, where the walking track wound down to the distant Medicine Lake, darkness covered the land, though to the southeast the first faint greying of the sky presaged dawn.

Ed Sun-on-Still-Waters searched the darkness for any sign of the shadows or the man who ran with them. "I cannot see them, Olelbis."

Nor I, Wulgu added. *And my eyes are better than a human's.*

"No, nor can even I," Moon Wolf admitted, "But I can sense them. The man runs with them still, down toward the lake, and others of the Black Ones have stolen a helicopter from the island."

The yowie turned suddenly and looked back toward the stand of pine trees and the mine adit. *The others come,* Wulgu cried. *James, Garagh, Wandjina, a woman...and Marc! I did not think to see you again.*

He cannot hear you, Wulgu, Wandjina thought, *for he has shut reality from his mind.*

But he will see me.

Not if he can avoid it.

Marc stood trembling at the back of the group, clutching Andi and looking down at his feet, back the way they had come, up at the sky, anywhere but at the giant yowie.

Andi held him and soothed him, murmuring, but she stared at Wulgu avidly. "What is it?" she whispered to Marc.

"It...it's an Australian yowie. Like a Bigfoot. Don't look at it. Don't think at it. Ignore it and it'll go away."

"It's magnificent."

"It's dangerous, but if you ignore it, it can't hurt you. I know."

Wandjina shook his head and smiled before joining Moon Wolf as he stared toward Medicine Lake. A series of muffled explosions sent rolling tremors through Glass Mountain, and a blast of superheated air erupted from the mine, igniting the pine trees. Another fainter glow could be seen on the island but that died away even as they watched. The tremors lessened in frequency and amplitude.

"I think the machine has finally died," Wandjina observed.

Moon Wolf nodded. "The mountain is calming. I can feel it."

Wulgu hunkered down in front of James. *Where is the old man? Spence? I see grief in your mind.*

"Spence died, saving us all. It would be fair to say we could not have succeeded without his sacrifice."

When this is over, I will grieve for him, for I counted him as a true friend.

James nodded. "This is Andi, Sam's sister. We couldn't have done it without her either."

I am pleased to meet you, Andi. Wulgu lowered his great shaggy head and peered into Andi's eyes.

"I...I heard him," Andi cried nervously.

"No!" Marc pushed her back and stood between her and the yowie, shaking with fear. He stared up at Wulgu. "You will not harm her," he said. "Not while I have life in me."

Amusement flickered across the yowie's mind. *She is his mate?* he asked James.

Not yet, but I think he is hopeful.

Then I must raise his status in her eyes. The great yowie dropped his head and looked away from Marc, slumping his broad shoulders and edging back. *I bow to your will,* he thought, directing it at Andi. With an ease surprising in one of his bulk, Wulgu faded away into the night.

Andi's eyes grew wide and she stared at Marc with respect. "You faced him down. For me?"

James joined Wandjina and Moon Wolf. "What's happening?"

"The Winambuu have taken over a pilot and stolen a helicopter. They plan on flying Ehrich out of here."

"We can't let him escape. It will have been for nothing if he can just do it again."

"He will not escape," Moon Wolf said firmly. "Robert, John, Ed--come to me. We have work to do. We must summon Twe Tjea-adku."

The young Native Americans hung back, reluctant to take part, but at Moon Wolf's urging, they gathered together in a circle, facing out, with Moon Wolf facing the holy mountain Bulyum-pui-yuk. Moon Wolf raised his arms and spread them wide and led a complicated chant, the only phrase of which James could recognise was the one previously spoken--Twe Tjea-adku.

"What are they doing, Uncle?" Nathan asked. "Who or what are they summoning?"

James shook his head but Wandjina answered. "He is calling up an elemental."

Marc and Andi moved up to stand alongside, watching the ceremony taking place as the first hint of dawn lightened the horizon. "I've heard of elementals," Marc said. "What are they?"

Wandjina smiled. "Are you sure you want to know? Wulgu is as a cub to one of those."

"I can handle it," Marc blustered. "I...I made the...the yowie back down, didn't I?"

"So you did. Well, an elemental is a force of nature. Forget about what you read in books about sylphs, gnomes, undines and salamanders. I'm talking about the real heavyweights of the spirit world--the spiritual equivalents of the earthquake, the storm wind, the lightning stroke, the tsunami. Imagine any of these becoming a flesh and blood creature and turning up on your doorstep. I can't think of any power of man that could stand against them."

"Flesh and blood?" James asked. "Truly?"

"Not really, Aparrerinja, but the next best thing. They can interact with the physical world for a time."

"Well, he'd better hurry up and appear," Andi said. "There's the hijacked helicopter. It's taking off."

The chanting ceremony led by Moon Wolf, with his three helpers calling the responses reached a crescendo as the old man let loose a long ululating cry and fell to his knees. Silence fell on the mountain side.

"Well?" Nathan asked. "Were you successful? Where's this Too-gee-add-koo?"

"Twe Tjea-adku," Wandjina corrected gently. "The storm incarnate, the thunderbird. See, he comes, riding the wind."

James followed the line of Wandjina's outstretched hand with his eyes and felt his gut clench. Where the night sky had been cloudless, the velvety black cloth scattered with gleaming diamonds, a storm had gathered unseen in the southwest, around Mt Shasta. Heavy clouds rolled toward them, blotting out the paling stars, and rent with myriad strokes of lightning. In the forefront of the storm, giant wings beat ponderously, their downbeat roiling the cloud, as the thunderbird answered the call of Olelbis.

James' scientific mind worked frantically to cope with the sight. "It must be at least..." Knowing he was poor at estimating size, he halved the number he thought of, hesitated, then halved it again and then again. "...fifty feet across."

Beside him, Andi clutched his arm tightly. "It can't exist," she murmured. "No living thing that large could possibly fly. Even the giant pterosaur Quetzalcoatalus was a fraction of its size. That thing's as big as a jumbo jet."

"The laws of physics do not apply to an elemental," Wandjina said.

The helicopter stayed low, beating its way across the lake toward the onrushing thunderbird, then suddenly the occupants must have seen it, for the craft turned sharply and increased speed.

The thunderbird dipped down over the lake, its wingtips raising whitecaps on the water as it rapidly overhauled the helicopter. The aircraft jinked, side slipping, but the elemental followed, incredibly agile for a thing that size. Great claws reached out and the helicopter swung toward it this time and lifted, the rotor blades ripping an explosion of feathers from the thunderbird's flank. It screamed an ear-shattering expression of rage and beat its way aloft, the pine trees in the forest around the lake's edge bending and snapping in the hurricane downdraft. The helicopter made a run for it at full throttle across the lake.

"They're getting away," Andi shouted in frustration. "Where is it, it's disappeared."

The elemental had vanished into the thick cloud cover that now blanketed the lake and environs. The light, increasing by the minute with the approach of dawn, now retreated back under the cloud. Across the lake, the helicopter rose steeply to lift above the hills and as it rose high in the air, the thunderbird fell to meet it. It plunged from the cloud, wings held in close to its great body and its talons outstretched. Lightning played about the massive bird, lighting it in hues of gold and red and white. At the last moment, before the rotor blades could slice into the outstretched legs, the thunderbird snapped one wing out and toppled sideways through the air, and as it fell past the rising helicopter, lunged upward and gripped the body of the aircraft in claws that sheared through metal in a death grip.

The pilot of the helicopter was evidently skilled but he was fighting a battle that could not be won. He fought to keep his craft aloft, but the weight of the huge bird carried it downward. The shadows boiled out of the shattered craft as it fell, and enveloped the head of the thunderbird, but lightning slashed into them and they scattered. Thunderbird and prey careered downward and just as it seemed both must plunge into the lake, the great bird disengaged and beat its great wings, screaming its defiance of the helpless aircraft as it shattered itself on the rocky shoreline. A pause, during which the elemental clawed its way back into the sky, then the helicopter exploded in a ball of flame that lit the underbelly of the great bird. Moments later, the thunderbird had disappeared into the cloud. A silence fell on the lake, disturbed only by the last rumblings of the storm, and it started to rain.

22

A ndi's cabin in the mountains of Colorado no longer sat in a field of snow as spring, long delayed, had filled the rushing streams with melt water and thrown a tablecloth of delicate green lace over meadow and deciduous forest, though the ancient pines still brooded darkly in the background. The air was chilly, and Andi waited until the sun was well up and casting its butter-yellow mantle over the front porch before venturing out. She sat on the porch steps with a mug of black coffee and sipped at the hot brew while she contemplated the peaceful scene at her doorstep. Within the cabin she could hear faint noises of someone moving around and after a few minutes the door creaked open and Marc walked out, yawning and scratching his stubbled face. He leaned down and kissed Andi on the forehead before sitting down beside her and leaning back on the other porch post.

"Sleep well?" Andi asked.

"Like the proverbial log. Speaking of which, I'd better go chop some more if we're going to have company."

"Wait a while. Enjoy the morning sun."

"What time are they arriving?"

"Who knows? They didn't even say how they were getting here. Sam was totally unconcerned that the road was washed out, so maybe they're flying in."

"Or using more exotic means," Marc muttered.

Andi laughed lazily, closing her eyes and basking in the sun's warmth. "Yeah, my sister has a high level of strangeness about her these days."

"You could too if you got involved with her."

Andi opened one eye and stared at Marc for a moment before closing it again. "Don't worry, sweetheart, I'm not going to go all strange on you and start associating with cavemen, Bigfoot and spirits. You're the only one for me."

Marc reached out and squeezed Andi's hand. "I love you too...oh, shit." His hand spasmed, gripping Andi tightly.

Her eyes flew open and for a moment she stared uncomprehendingly at the two figures standing at the edge of the meadow at the front of the cabin. "Sam?" she said, "Where the hell did you spring from?"

"Hi Sis, have you got the coffee on?" Sam sauntered up to the cabin and hugged first Andi and then Marc. James followed and offered a more subdued greeting to them both.

Marc shook James' hand and looked askance at the older man. "Am I going to regret asking how you got here? I didn't hear a vehicle of any sort."

James grinned. "Ernie lent me his stones." He took a polished black oval out of his jacket pocket and held it up. "The others are back in the field."

"I knew I didn't want to know. Isn't that dangerous, just leaving them lying there? What is someone--or an animal--wanders into the circle by mistake?"

"Safe as houses--safer in fact, houses collapse. Nothing would happen without the control stone, which I have."

"Why do you call him Ernie? I thought his name was Wandjina and he was a god or something?"

James laughed out loud. "Remember when we first met him near Tunbubudla? He was Ernie then, and I guess I'll always think of him that way. He's not really a god, though he is a spirit being, and very humble for all his powers. You should try talking to him sometime."

Marc shuddered. "I'll pass, thanks all the same." He looked round and saw that the women had disappeared into the cabin. "You want some coffee?"

"Sure."

The two men had just started up the steps when the door opened and Andi and Sam emerged, holding mugs and a pot of freshly brewed coffee.

"No milk, I'm afraid," Andi said, "But we have creamer."

It was James' turn to shudder. "How you Yanks can contaminate good coffee with that stuff, I'll never know."

Marc winked. "The secret is not to serve good coffee in the first place. Then you can't spoil it." He tipped a generous spoon of creamer into his own cup and stirred vigorously.

They sat on the edge of the porch and enjoyed their coffee in silence, taking in the cool, crisp mountain air and the warm sunshine, the calling of songbirds in the thickets and the distant staccato rapping of a woodpecker.

"Any news on Gaia?" Andi murmured.

Sam shook her head, not trusting herself to speak.

"They've searched everywhere but there's no trace of her," James said quietly. "The Neanderthal scientists say there was an anomalous power surge with a unique signature at the moment of translation though. The remnants of this surge are still in the circuitry and they are hopeful of being able to track it down."

"Meanwhile my Gaia is all alone," Sam said, wiping away tears.

"They'll find her, Sam, I'm sure of it," Andi said quietly and slipped an arm around her sister's shoulder.

"And she's not alone, love," James added. "Rima is with her and would give her life to protect her."

"Rima?" Marc asked.

"You knew her as Cindy. She's really a female yowie, and a devoted nurse. She dotes on Gaia."

"No kidding?" Marc thought for a moment. "I knew that...I think."

"Don't worry about it. If you need to remember, you will. Otherwise, just get on with your life."

"Good advice, Marc," Sam added. "You too, Andi. Speaking of which, did you hear from the lawyer handling Morgan Turner's estate yet?"

"Yeah. Apparently he's left me something close to a million, after taxes. And don't look at me like that, Sis, I didn't ask him to, and I didn't do anything to encourage him."

"Never said you did, Andi. Still..." Sam let the sentence hang for a moment, enjoying the look of frustrated embarrassment on her sister's face. "What are you going to do with it?"

"I'm going to buy a hunting lodge a few miles further up the valley. The lease on this place is just about up and I can't bear to drag myself away from the mountains."

"Is it big enough for two?" James asked with a twinkle in his eye.

"If you're trying to find out if he's asked me--then yes, he has."

"Andi!" Sam hugged and kissed her kid sister, and then started on Marc. "When's the wedding?"

"Sometime soon. We haven't decided yet but we'll let you know."

"You'd better," James grinned, "Otherwise we'll just have to drop in unannounced."

"Don't you dare," Andi said. "Sis, talk to your man."

"Okay, okay." James held his hands up in surrender. "I promise."

They sat in a companionable silence for a little while longer.

"Did you hear anything about what happened inside the base?" James asked Marc. "Did your FBI friends tell you?"

Glass Trilogy Book 2: A Glass Darkly by Max Overton

"Not much, but General Thompson, the army guy they brought in to take charge, was reported missing in a boating accident at about that time. Putting two and two together, I'd guess he didn't survive the attack."

"There was also an almost unreported accident at an army base in Oregon. Something like forty soldiers killed and wounded." Andi shrugged. "Coincidence? Or cover up?"

"Knowing governments, I'd say certainly a cover up, but I don't think they'll have to try very hard." James chuckled. "Sometimes even I have trouble believing what I see, and I see it almost daily. I can't imagine the general public would believe the truth if you showed them pictures."

"Funny you should say that," Andi commented. "Turns out there was someone with a camera out at dawn near Medicine Lake and he snapped a digital image of a very large bird."

"The thunderbird?" Sam asked. "Wow, I'd like to see that. What are people saying about the photo?"

"That it's been digitally altered. That's the problem with modern digital photography and computer programs. You can make a picture show anything. The cryptozoologist diehards are adamant it's real, everyone else is shouting fake."

"Except we know it was real."

"Was it though?" Marc asked. "I mean, I know we saw it but you said yourself that it was too big to fly. Laws of physics you said."

"That's true, and Ernie said it was a spirit, from elsewhere, where maybe there are different laws."

"Yes, but it came to our universe," Marc said obstinately. "It should then be governed by our laws."

James shrugged. "I don't know the answer to that one. Maybe it brought over some of its own universe when it came."

"Or maybe some of the laws of physics haven't been discovered yet," Andi added.

"The same holds for the Winambuu, the shadow people," Sam said softly. "They acted like intelligent, if malicious, beings, but nothing we find in our world. Where did they come from, and why did they come here in the first place?"

"And where have they gone now?" Marc asked.

James grimaced. "And that bloody Ehrich person. Was he killed in the crash, or did he escape?"

"There was only one person in the wreckage," Andi said. "The army pilot. Whether Ehrich fell into the lake and died, or survived the crash and died later of his injuries, or lived, is something we may never know."

Silence reigned again as they each contemplated recent events.

"You never told us how you got out of the cave, Sis," Andi said. "For a while, I was in mental contact and then I lost you. James said you were okay, so I didn't worry, but I'm curious. You were there with a cavewoman, a Neanderthal, is that right?"

Sam shook her head. "Amaru was killed when the tunnel collapsed. Ratana and I were trapped behind tons of rock. Luckily you stopped Mount Shasta before it could explode, so we just sat there until we were rescued."

"Yes, but how were you rescued? Are you telling me half a dozen men and a yowie shifted all that rock?"

Sam laughed. "Ask my husband. He saw it all. The first thing we knew was daylight streaming in."

"We didn't do anything," James said. "Moon Wolf did it all. It was the damnedest thing. In Wintun mythology, he is the god Olelbis and Wokwuk is his son. Everything on earth--people, animals, plants, rocks, water--are all bits of Wokwuk. Moon Wolf just stood in front of the choked mine and asked the whole mess very politely to come out--and it did. Boulders just rolled out, dust and rocks floated out and away down the slope. Then he thanked them all and we went in to find Sam and Ratana."

"That must have been quite a sight," Marc said pensively. "Do you think it really happened?"

"What do you mean?" Sam asked. "I'm here aren't I?" She punched Marc hard on the arm.

"Ow, yes, but that's not what I meant. What if...oh, I don't know...what if it wasn't really blocked and...and Moon Wolf just made it look that way so that...so that he could impress you?"

"If you don't mind me saying, Marc old son, that's a bloody weak argument. After all we had seen, do you think he still needed to impress us? If you're going to join this family, you're going to have to sharpen up your ideas, mate."

Marc nodded glumly. "Yeah, I guess I'd better just get used to the idea that I'm marrying into a bunch of spooky weirdos...Ow!" Marc threw his arms up to protect himself as the others tossed him off the porch and sat on him.

From the green shade of an aspen on the fringes of the meadow, Andi's semi-feral cat Piwacket sat and watched the humans. There was one among them he trusted as much as he would ever trust a human, but the others were strangers. He was content to sit and wait. Sooner or later they would leave, humans always did, and then he could return to the cabin. In the meantime, there were many things a cat could hunt in the undergrowth.

There were other things too. Piwackit's back hair bristled at the memory, and he growled softly. Dark things that lived in the deepest shadow, within rotting tree trunks and in the cracks between rocks. They came out to watch the cabin when night fell, slipping between the trees with no more than a sibilant whisper, as if a snake was passing. Piwackit hid when they came out, and watched the shadows as they watched the cabin, waiting for something to happen.

Interlude 2

The cabin lights shone brightly in the blackness of a night far removed from the glow of civilisation. The night was almost silent saving the soft soughing of a gentle breeze rustling the new aspen leaves. Every now and then, a muffled burst of laughter or animated conversation emanated from the cabin, the noise and light serving to accentuate the darkness and stillness under the trees.

Shadows stirred within shadows, and eyes that gleamed softly from within, stared hungrily toward the laughter.

Let us take them now.

Fool, have you learned nothing?

But we must kill them.

It is only the child that is important. Without her, they can do nothing.

But she has gone. They search for her.

They only make a show of searching. The enemy knows where she is. They sent her there.

Then let us go there ourselves and kill the child. If she heals the worlds, we are lost.

We cannot go there alone. The enemy must take us.

They will never do that.

They will not know they have done it.

When?

Very soon.

How will we know?

They do not suspect the presence of one of our number in their Council. They will tell us everything, we will act on this knowledge and destroy them. Then our world will be safe.

And if we fail?

We cannot fail.

The story concludes in *Looking Glass*
Book 3 of the *Glass* trilogy

About the Author

Max Overton has travelled extensively and lived in many places around the world-- including Malaysia, India, Germany, England, Jamaica, New Zealand, USA and Australia. Trained in the biological sciences in New Zealand and Australia, he has worked within the scientific field for many years, but now concentrates on writing. While predominantly a writer of historical fiction (Scarab: Books 1 - 6 of the Amarnan Kings; the Scythian Trilogy; the Demon Series; Ascension), he also writes in other genres (A Cry of Shadows, the Glass Trilogy, Haunted Trail, Sequestered) and draws on true life (Adventures of a Small Game Hunter in Jamaica, We Came From Königsberg). Max also maintains an interest in butterflies, photography, the paranormal and other aspects of Fortean Studies.

Most of his other published books are available at Writers Exchange Ebooks, http://www.writers-exchange.com/Max-Overton.html and all his books may be viewed on his website: http://www.maxovertonauthor.com/

Max's book covers are all designed and created by Julie Napier, and other examples of her art and photography may be viewed at www.julienapier.com

If you want to read more about other books by this author, they are listed on the following pages...

A Cry of Shadows
{Paranormal Murder Mystery}

Australian Professor Ian Delaney is single-minded in his determination to prove his theory that one can discover the moment that the life force leaves the body. After succumbing to the temptation to kill a girl under scientifically controlled conditions, he takes an offer of work in St Louis, hoping to leave the undiscovered crime behind him.

In America, Wayne Richardson seeks revenge by killing his ex-girlfriend, believing it will give him the upper hand, a means to seize control following their breakup. Wayne quickly discovers that he enjoys killing and begins to seek out young women who resemble his dead ex-girlfriend.

Ian and Wayne meet and, when Ian recognizes the symptoms of violent delusion, he employs Wayne to help him further his research. Despite the police closing in, the two killers manage to evade identification time and time again as the death toll rises in their wake.

The detective in charge of the case, John Barnes, is frantic, willing to try anything to catch his killer. With time running out, he searches desperately for answers before another body is found...or the culprit slips into the woodwork for good.
Publisher: http://www.writers-exchange.com/A-Cry-of-Shadows/

Adventures of a Small Game Hunter in Jamaica
{Biography}

An eleven-year-old boy is plucked from boarding school in England and transported to the tropical paradise of Jamaica where he's free to study his one great love--butterflies. He discovers that Jamaica has a wealth of these wonderful insects and sets about making a collection of as many as he can find. Along the way, he has adventures with other creatures, from hummingbirds to vultures, from iguanas to black widow spiders. Through it all runs the promise of the legendary Homerus swallowtail, Jamaica's national butterfly.

Other activities intrude, like school, boxing and swimming lessons, but he manages to inveigle his parents into taking him to strange and sometimes dangerous places, all in the name of butterfly collecting. He meets scientists and Rastafarians, teachers, small boys and the ordinary people living on the tropical isle, and even discovers butterflies that shouldn't exist in Jamaica.

Author Max Overton was that young boy. He counted himself fortunate to have lived in Jamaica in an age very different from the present one. Max still has some of the butterflies he collected half a century or more ago, and each one releases a flood of memories whenever he opens the box and gazes at their tattered and fading wings. These memories have become stories--stories of the Adventures of a Small Game Hunter in Jamaica.
Publisher: http://www.writers-exchange.com/Adventures-of-a-Small-Game-Hunter/

Ascension Series, A Novel of Nazi Germany
{Historical: Holocaust}

Before he fully realized the diabolical cruelties of the National Socialist German Worker's Party, Konrad Wengler had committed atrocities against his own people, the Jews, out of fear of both his faith and his heritage. But after he witnesses firsthand the concentration camps, the corruption, the inhuman malevolence of the Nazi war machine and the propaganda aimed at annihilating an entire race, he knows he must find a way to turn the tide and become the savior his people desperately need.

Book 1: Ascension

Being a Jew in Germany can be a dangerous thing...

Fear prompts Konrad Wengler to put his faith aside and try desperately to forget his heritage. After fighting in the Great War, he's wounded and turns instead to law enforcement in his tiny Bavarian hometown. There, he falls under the spell of the fledgling Nazi Party. He joins the Party in patriotic fervour and becomes a Lieutenant of Police and Schutzstaffel (SS).

In the course of his duties as policeman, Konrad offends a powerful Nazi official who starts an SS investigation. War breaks out. When he joins the Police Battalions, he's sent to Poland and witnesses there firsthand the atrocities being committed upon his fellow Jews.

Unknown to Konrad, the SS investigators have discovered his origins and follow him into Poland. Arrested and sent to Mauthausen Concentration Camp, Konrad is forced to face what it means to be a Jew and fight for survival. Will his friends on the outside, his wife and lawyer, be enough to counter the might of the Nazi machine?

Publisher: http://www.writers-exchange.com/Ascension/

Book 2: Maelstrom

Never underestimate the enemy...

Konrad Wengler survived his brush with the death camps of Nazi Germany. Now, reinstated as a police officer in his Bavarian hometown despite being a Jew, he throws himself back into his work, seeking to uncover evidence that will remove a corrupt Nazi party official.

The Gestapo have their own agenda and, despite orders from above to eliminate this troublesome Jewish policeman, they hide Konrad in the Totenkopf (Death's Head) Division of the Waffen-SS. In a fight to survive in the snowy wastes of Russia while the tide of war turns against Germany, Konrad experiences tank battles, ghetto clearances, partisans, and death camps (this time as a guard), as well as the fierce battles where his Division is badly outnumbered and on the defence.

Through it all, Konrad strives to live by his conscience and resist taking part in the atrocities happening all around him. He still thinks of himself as a policeman, but his desire to bring the corrupt Nazi official to justice seems far removed from his present reality. If he is to find the necessary evidence against his enemy, he must first *survive...*

Publisher: http://www.writers-exchange.com/Maelstrom/

Book 3: Dämmerung

Konrad Wengler is captured and sent from one Soviet prison camp to another. Even hearing the war has come to an end makes no difference until he's arrested as a Nazi Party member. In jail, Konrad refuses to defend himself for things he's guilty and should be punished for. Will his be an eye-for-an-eye life sentence, or leniency in regard of the good he tried to do once he learned the truth?

Publisher: http://www.writers-exchange.com/dammerung/

Kadesh, A Novel of Ancient Egypt

Holding the key to strategic military advantage, Kadesh is a jewel city that distant lands covet. Ramesses II of Egypt and Muwatalli II of Hatti believe they're chosen by the gods to claim ascendancy to Kadesh. When the two meet in the largest chariot battle ever fought, not just the fate of empires will be decided but also the lives of citizens helplessly caught up in the greedy ambition of kings.

Publisher: http://www.writers-exchange.com/Kadesh/

Fall of the House of Ramesses Series,
A Novel of Ancient Egypt
{Historical: Ancient Egypt}

Egypt was at the height of its powers in the days of Ramesses the Great, a young king who confidently predicted his House would last for a Thousand Years. Sixty years later, he was still on the throne. One by one, his heirs had died and the survivors had become old men. When Ramesses at last died, he left a stagnant kingdom and his throne to an old man--Merenptah. What followed laid the groundwork for a nation ripped apart by civil war.

Book 1: Merenptah
The House of Ramesses is in the hands of an old man. King Merenptah wants to leave the kingdom to his younger son, Seti, but northern tribes in Egypt rebel and join forces with the Sea Peoples, invading from the north. In the south, the king's eldest son Messuwy is angered at being passed over in favour of the younger son...and plots to rid himself of his father and brother.
Publisher: http://www.writers-exchange.com/Merenptah/

Book 2: Seti
After only nine years on the throne, Merenptah is dead and his son Seti is king in his place. He rules from the northern city of Men-nefer, while his elder brother Messuwy, convinced the throne is his by right, plots rebellion in the south.

The kingdoms are tipped into bloody civil war, with brother fighting against brother for the throne of a united Egypt. On one side is Messuwy, now crowned as King Amenmesse and his ruthless General Sethi; on the other, young King Seti and his wife Tausret. But other men are weighing up the chances of wresting the throne from both brothers and becoming king in their place. Under the onslaught of conflict, the House of Ramesses begins to crumble...
Publisher: http://www.writers-exchange.com/Seti/

Book 3: Tausret
The House of Ramesses falters as Tausret relinquishes the throne upon the death of her husband, King Seti. Amenmesse's young son Siptah will become king until her infant son is old enough to rule. Tausret, as Regent, and the king's uncle, Chancellor Bay, hold tight to the reins of power and vie for complete control of the kingdoms. Assassination changes the balance of power, and, seeing his chance, Chancellor Bay attempts a coup...

Tausret's troubles mount as she also faces a challenge from Setnakhte, an aging son of the Great Ramesses who believes Seti was the last legitimate king. If Setnakhte gets his way, he will destroy the House of Ramesses and set up his own dynasty of kings.
Publisher: http://www.writers-exchange.com/Tausret/

Glass Trilogy
{Paranormal Thriller}

Delve deep into the mysteries of Aboriginal mythology, present day UFO activity and pure science that surround the continent of Australia, from its barren deserts to the depths of its rainforest and even deeper into its mysterious mountains. Along the way, love, greed, murder, and mystery abound while the secrets of mankind and the ultimate answer to 'what happens now?' just might be answered.

GLASS HOUSE, Book 1: The mysteries of Australia may just hold the answers mankind has been searching for millennium to find. When Doctor James Hay, a university scientist who studies the paranormal mysteries in Australia, finds an obelisk of carved volcanic rock on sacred Aboriginal land in northern Queensland, he realizes it may hold the answers he's been seeking. A respected elder of the Aboriginal people instructs James to take up the gauntlet and follow his heart. Along with his old friend and award-winning writer Spencer, Samantha Louis, her cameraman, and two of James' Aboriginal students, James embarks on a life-changing quest for the truth.
Publisher: http://www.writers-exchange.com/Glass-House/

A GLASS DARKLY, Book 2: A dead volcano called Glass Mountain in Northern California seems harmless...but is it really?
Andromeda Jones, a physicist, knows her missing sister Samantha is somehow tied up with the new job Andromeda herself has been offered to work with a team in constructing Vox Dei, a machine that's been ostensibly built to eliminate wars. But what is its true nature, and who's pulling the strings?
When the experiment spins out of control, dark powers are unleashed and the danger to mankind unfolds relentlessly. Strange, evil shadows are using the Vox Dei and Andromeda's sister Samantha to get through to our world, knowing the time is near when Earth's final destiny will be decided.
Federal forces are aware of something amiss, so, to rescue her sibling, Andromeda agrees to go on a dangerous mission and soon finds herself entangled in a web of professional jealousy, political betrayal, and flat-out greed.
Publisher: http://www.writers-exchange.com/A-Glass-Darkly/

LOOKING GLASS, Book 3: Samantha and James Hay have been advised that their missing daughter Gaia have been located in ancient Australia. Dr. Xanatuo, an alien scientist who, along with a lost tribe of Neanderthals and other beings working to help mankind, has discovered a way to send them back in time to be reunited with Gaia. Ernie, the old Aboriginal tracker and leader of the Neanderthals, along with friends Ratana and Nathan and characters from the first two books of the trilogy, will accompany them. This team of intrepid adventurers have another mission for the journey, along with aiding the Hayes' quest, which is paramount to changing a terrible wrong which exists in the present time.
Publisher: http://www.writers-exchange.com/Looking-Glass/

Haunted Trail A Tale of Wickedness & Moral Turpitude
{Western: Paranormal}

Ned Abernathy is a hot-tempered young cowboy in the small town of Hammond's Bluff in 1876. In a drunken argument with his best friend Billy over a girl, he guns him down. Ned flees and wanders the plains, forests and hills of the Dakota Territories, certain that every man's hand is against him.

Horse rustlers, marauding Indians, killers, gold prospectors and French trappers cross his path and lead to complications, as do persistent apparitions of what Ned believes is the ghost of his friend Billy, come to accuse him of murder. He finds love and loses it. Determined not to do the same when he discovers gold in the Black Hills, he ruthlessly defends his newfound wealth against greedy men. In the process, he comes to terms with who he is and what he's done. But there are other ghosts in his past that he needs to confront. Returning to Hammond's Bluff, Ned stumbles into a shocking surprise awaiting him at the end of his haunted trail.

Publisher: http://www.writers-exchange.com/Haunted-Trail/

Hyksos Series, A Novel of Ancient Egypt

The power of the kings of the Middle Kingdom have been failing for some time, having lost control of the Nile Delta to a series of Canaanite kings who ruled from the northern city of Avaris. Into this mix came the Kings of Amurri, Lebanon and Syria bent on subduing the whole of Egypt. These kings were known as the Hyksos, and they dealt a devastating blow to the peoples of the Nile Delta and Valley.

Book 1: Avaris

When Arimawat and his son Harrubaal fled from Urubek, the king of Hattush, to the court of the King of Avaris, King Sheshi welcomed the refugees. One of Arimawat's first tasks for King Shesi is to sail south to the Land of Kush and fetch Princess Tati, who will become Sheshi's queen. Arimawat and Harrubaal perform creditably, but their actions have far-reaching consequences.

On the return journey, Harrubaal falls in love with Kemi, the daughter of the Southern Egyptian king. As a reward for Harrubaal's work, Sheshi secures the hand of the princess for the young Canaanite prince. Unfortunately for the peace of the realm, Sheshi lusts after Princess Kemi too, and his actions threaten the stability of his kingdom...
Publisher: http://www.writers-exchange.com/Avaris/

Book 2: Conquest

The Hyksos invade the Delta using the new weapons of bronze and chariots, things of which the Egyptians have no knowledge. They rout the Delta forces, and in the south, the unconquered kings ready their armies to defend their lands. Meanwhile in Avaris, Merybaal, the son of Harrubaal and Kemi, strives to defend his family in a city conquered by the Hyksos.

Elements of the Delta army that refuse to surrender continue the fight for their homeland, and new kings proclaim themselves as the inheritors of the failed kings of Avaris. One of these is Amenre, grandson of Merybaal, but he is forced into hiding as the Hyksos sweep all before them, bringing their terror to the kingdom of the Nile valley. Driven south in disarray, the survivors of the Egyptian army seek leaders who can resist the enemy...
Publisher: http://www.writers-exchange.com/conquest/

Book 3: Two Cities

The Hyksos drive south into the Nile Valley, sweeping all resistance aside. Bebi and Sobekhotep, grandsons of Harrubaal, assume command of the loyal Egyptian army and strive to stem the flood of Hyksos conquest. But even the cities of the south are divided against themselves.

Abdju, an old capital city of Egypt reasserts itself, putting forward a line of kings of its own, and soon the city is at war with Waset, the southern capital of the Nile Valley, as the two cities fight for supremacy in the face of the advancing northern enemy. Caught up in the turmoil of warring nations, the ordinary people of Egypt must fight for their own survival as well as that of their kingdom.
Publisher: http://www.writers-exchange.com/Two-Cities/

And More (7 books total).

Series Page:
https://www.writers-exchange.com/hyksos-series/

Scythian Trilogy
{Historical}

Captured by the warlike, tribal Scythians who bicker amongst themselves and bitterly resent outside interference, a fiercely loyal captain in Alexander the Great's Companion Cavalry Nikometros and his men are to be sacrificed to the Mother Goddess. Lucky chance--and the timely intervention of Tomyra, priestess and daughter of the Massegetae chieftain--allows him to defeat the Champion. With their immediate survival secured, acceptance into the tribe...and escape...is complicated by the captain's growing feelings for Tomyra-- death to any who touch her--and the chief's son Areipithes who not only detests Nikometros and wants to have him killed or banished but intends to murder his own father and take over the tribe.

LION OF SCYTHIA, Book 1: Alexander the Great has conquered the Persian Empire and is marching eastward to India. In his wake he leaves small groups of soldiers to govern great tracts of land and diverse peoples. Nikometros is one young cavalry captain left behind in the lands of the fierce, nomadic Scythian horsemen. Captured after an ambush, Nikometros must fight for his life and the lives of his surviving men. Even as he seeks an opportunity to escape, he finds himself bound by a debt of loyalty to the chief...and his own developing love for the young priestess.
Publisher: http://www.writers-exchange.com/Lion-of-Scythia/

THE GOLDEN KING, Book 2: The chief of the tribe of nomadic Scythian horsemen is dead, killed by his son's treachery. The priestess, lover of the young cavalry officer, Nikometros, is carried off into the mountains. Nikometros and his friends set off in hard pursuit.

Death rides with them. By the time they return, the tribes are at war. Nikometros must choose between attempting to become chief himself or leaving the people he's come to love and respect to return to his duty as an army officer in the Empire of Alexander.
Winner of the 2005 EPIC Ebook Awards.
Publisher: http://www.writers-exchange.com/The-Golden-King/

FUNERAL IN BABYLON, Book 3: Alexander the Great has returned from India and set up his court in Babylon. Nikometros and a band of loyal Scythians journey deep into the heart of Persia to join the Royal court. Nikometros finds himself embroiled in the intrigues and wars of kings, generals, and merchant adventurers as he strives to provide a safe haven for his lover and friends. With the fate of an Empire hanging in the balance, Death walks beside Nikometros as events precipitate a Funeral in Babylon...
Winner of the 2006 EPIC Ebook Awards.
Publisher: http://www.writers-exchange.com/Funeral-in-Babylon/

Sequestered
By Max Overton and Jim Darley
{Action/Thriller}

Storing carbon dioxide underground as a means of removing a greenhouse gas responsible for global warming has made James Matternicht a fabulously wealthy man. For 15 years, the Carbon Capture and Sequestration Facility at Rushing River in Oregon's hinterland has been operating without a problem...or has it?

When mysterious documents arrive on her desk that purport to show the Facility is leaking, reporter Annaliese Winton investigates. Together with a government geologist, Matt Morrison, she uncovers a morass of corruption and deceit that now threatens the safety of her community and the entire northwest coast of America.

Liquid carbon dioxide, stored at the critical point under great pressure, is a tremendously dangerous substance, and millions of tonnes of it are sequestered in the rock strata below Rushing River. All it would take is a crack in the overlying rock and the whole pressurized mass could erupt with disastrous consequences. And that crack has always existed there...

Recipient of the Life Award (Literature for the Environment): "There are only two kinds of people: conservationists and suicides. To qualify for this Award, your book needs to value the wonderful world of nature, to recognize that we are merely one species out of millions, and that we have a responsibility to cherish and maintain our small planet."
Awarded from http://bobswriting.com/life/
Publisher: http://www.writers-exchange.com/Sequestered/

TULPA
{Paranormal Thriller}

From the rainforests of tropical Australia to the cane fields and communities of the North Queensland coastal strip, a horror is unleashed by those foolishly playing with unknown forces...

A fairy story to amuse small children leads four bored teenagers and a young university student in a North Queensland town to becoming interested in an ancient Tibetan technique for creating a life form. When their seemingly harmless experiment sets free terror and death, the teenagers are soon fighting to contain a menace that reproduces exponentially.

The police are helpless to end the horror. Aided by two old game hunters, a student of the paranormal and a few small children, the teenagers must find a way of destroying what they unintentionally released. But how can they stop beings that can escape into an alternate reality when threatened?
Publisher: http://www.writers-exchange.com/TULPA/

Strong is the Ma'at of Re, A Novel of Ancient Egypt
{Historical: Ancient Egypt}

In Ancient Egypt, C1200 BCE, bitter contention and resentment, secret coups and assassination attempts may decide the fate of those who would become legends...by any means necessary.

Book 1: The King

That *he* is descended from Ramesses the Great fills Ramesses III with obscene pride. Elevated to the throne following a coup led by his father Setnakhte during the troubled days of Queen Tausret, Ramesses III sets about creating an Egypt that reflects the glory days of Ramesses the Great. He takes on his predecessor's throne name, names his sons after the sons of Ramesses and pushes them toward similar duties. Most of all, he thirsts after conquests like those of his hero grandfather.

Ramesses III assumes the throne name of Usermaatre, translated as "Strong is the Ma'at of Re" and endeavours to live up to the sentiment. He fights foreign foes, as had Ramesses the Great; he builds temples throughout the Two Lands, as had Ramesses the Great, and he looks forward to a long, illustrious life on the throne of Egypt, as had Ramesses the Great.

Alas, his reign is not meant to be. Ramesses III faces troubles at home--troubles that threaten the stability of Egypt and his own throne. The struggles for power between his wives, his sons, and even the priests of Amun, together with a treasury drained of its wealth, all force Ramesses III to question his success as the scion of a legend.

Publisher: http://www.writers-exchange.com/The-King/

Book 2: The Heirs

Tiye, the first wife of Ramesses III, has grown so used to being the mother of the Heir she can no longer bear to see that prized title pass to the son of a rival wife. Her eldest sons have died and the one left wants to step down and devote his life to the priesthood. Then the son of the king's sister/wife, also named Ramesses, will become Crown Prince and all Tiye's ambitions will lie in ruins.

Ramesses III struggles to enrich Egypt by seeking the wealth of the Land of Punt. He dispatches an expedition to the fabled southern land but years pass before the expedition returns. In the meantime, Tiye has a new hope: A last son she dotes on. Plague sweeps through Egypt, killing princes and princesses alike and lessening her options, and now Tiye must undergo the added indignity of having her daughter married off to the hated Crown Prince.

All Tiye's hopes are pinned on this last son of hers, but Ramesses III refuses to consider him as a potential successor, despite the Crown Prince's failing health. Unless Tiye can change the king's mind through charm or coercion, her sons will forever be excluded from the throne of Egypt.

Publisher: http://www.writers-exchange.com/The-Heirs/

Book 3: Taweret

The reign of Ramesses III is failing and even the gods seem to be turning their eyes away from Egypt. When the sun hides its face, crops suffer, throwing the country into famine. Tomb workers go on strike. To avert further disaster, Crown Prince Ramesses acts on his father's behalf.

The rivalry between Ramesses III's wives--commoner Tiye and sister/wife Queen Tyti--also comes to a head. Tiye resents not being made queen and can't abide that her sons have been passed over. She plots to put her own spoiled son Pentaweret on the throne.

The eventual strength of the Ma'at of Re hangs in the balance. Will the rule of Egypt be decided by fate, gods...or treason?

Publisher: http://www.writers-exchange.com/The-One-of-Taweret/

The Amarnan Kings Series, A Novel of Ancient Egypt

Set in Egypt of the 14th century B.C.E. and piecing together a mosaic of the reigns of the five Amarnan kings, threaded through by the memories of princess Beketaten-Scarab, a tapestry unfolds of the royal figures lost in the mists of antiquity.

SCARAB - AKHENATEN, Book 1: A chance discovery in Syria reveals answers to the mystery of the ancient Egyptian sun-king, the heretic Akhenaten and his beautiful wife Nefertiti. Inscriptions in the tomb of his sister Beketaten, otherwise known as Scarab, tell a story of life and death, intrigue and warfare, in and around the golden court of the kings of the glorious 18th dynasty.

The narrative of a young girl growing up at the centre of momentous events--the abolition of the gods, foreign invasion, and the fall of a once-great family--reveals who Tutankhamen's parents really were, what happened to Nefertiti, and other events lost to history in the great destruction that followed the fall of the Aten heresy.
Publisher: http://www.writers-exchange.com/Scarab/

SCARAB- SMENKHKARE, Book 2: King Akhenaten, distraught at the rebellion and exile of his beloved wife Nefertiti, withdraws from public life, content to leave the affairs of Egypt in the hands of his younger half-brother Smenkhkare. When Smenkhkare disappears on a hunting expedition, his sister Beketaten, known as Scarab, is forced to flee for her life.

Finding refuge among her mother's people, the Khabiru, Scarab has resigned herself to a life in exile...until she hears that her brother Smenkhkare is still alive. He is raising an army in Nubia to overthrow Ay and reclaim his throne. Scarab hurries south to join him as he confronts Ay and General Horemheb outside the gates of Thebes.
Publisher: http://www.writers-exchange.com/Scarab2/

SCARAB - TUTANKHAMEN, Book 3: Scarab and her brother Smenkhkare are in exile in Nubia but are gathering an army to wrest control of Egypt from the boy king Tutankhamen and his controlling uncle, Ay. Meanwhile, the kingdoms are beset by internal troubles while the Amorites are pressing hard against the northern borders. Generals Horemheb and Paramessu must fight a war on two fronts while deciding where their loyalties lie--with the former king Smenkhkare or with the new young king in Thebes.

Smenkhkare and Scarab march on Thebes with their native army to meet the legions of Tutankhamen on the plains outside the city gates. As two brothers battle for supremacy and the throne of the Two Kingdoms, the fate of Egypt and the 18th dynasty hangs in the balance.
Finalist in 2013's Eppie Awards.
Publisher: http://www.writers-exchange.com/Scarab3/

And More (6 books total).

Series Page:
https://www.writers-exchange.com/the-armarnan-kings/

The Pyramid Builders, A Novel of Ancient Egypt

The third dynasty of the Old Kingdom of Egypt saw an extraordinary development of building techniques, from the simple structures of mud brick at the end of the second dynasty to the towering pyramids of the fourth dynasty. Just how these massive structures were built has long been a matter of conjecture, but history is made up of the lives and actions of individuals; kings and architects, scribes and priests, soldiers and artisans, even common labourers, and so the story of the Pyramid Builders unfolded over the course of more than a century. This is that story…

Book 1: Djoser

King Khasekhemwy has two sons, Djoser and Imhotep, but their destinies are very different. One will become king and the other his architect and the power behind the throne. Together, they plan to build something new, a great tomb that will be the wonder of the world. But not all is peaceful within the kingdoms of Egypt. Djoser's son Sekhemkhet will inherit the throne, but there are others that seek power and set their plans in motion, and they care nothing for the architectural ambitions of their king.

Ordinary men and women inhabit Djoser's Egypt too, living their own lives, dreaming of power or simple happiness, but sometimes these dreams do not harmonise with the plans of kings…

Publisher: http://www.writers-exchange.com/djoser/

Book 2: Sekhemkhet

Sekhemkhet faces the daunting prospect of following on from the glories of his father's achievement. He desires an even bigger pyramid than that of Djoser and orders Imhotep and Den to build it. However, the king finds it easier to build a tomb than to raise heirs to follow him on the throne, and a cousin seeks to take advantage of Sekhemkhet's precarious position and challenge the king.

Not all is well within Den's family. He is married, but love from an unexpected source threatens to destroy the success he has so laboriously built up. Will he sacrifice love for ambition, or can he find a way to have both?

Publisher: http://www.writers-exchange.com/sekhemkhet/

Book 3: Khaba

The throne of Egypt has passed to Khaba, an old man who seeks only to secure his family's position. Construction of a pyramid tomb is a secondary consideration, and the fortunes of those who desire to build them languish as he refuses further innovations. It is left to his grandson and heir, Huni, to dream of greater architectural glories.

Architect Den has achieved love, but at the cost of ambition. He and his burgeoning family struggle to survive, his relatives seeking out love of their own even as they look for opportunities to further their careers. The promise of a return to fulfilment is offered, but will they be able to grasp it?

Publisher: http://www.writers-exchange.com/khaba/

And More (10 books total).

Series Page:

https://www.writers-exchange.com/the-pyramid-builders-series/

We Came From Konigsberg
{Historical: Holocaust}

Based on a true story gleaned from the memories of family members sixty years after the events, from photographs and documents, and from published works of nonfiction describing the times and events described in the narrative, *We Came From Konigsberg* is set in January 1945.

The Soviet Army is poised for the final push through East Prussia and Poland to Berlin. Elisabet Daeker and her five young sons are in Königsberg, East Prussia and have heard the shocking stories of Russian atrocities. They're desperate to escape to the perceived safety of Germany. To survive, Elisabet faces hardships endured at the hands of Nazi hardliners, of Soviet troops bent on rape, pillage and murder, and of Allied cruelty in the Occupied Zones of post-war Germany.

Winner of the 2014 EPIC Ebook Awards.

Publisher: http://www.writers-exchange.com/We-Came-From-Konigsberg/

You can find ALL our books up on our website at:
http://www.writers-exchange.com

All Max's Books:
http://www.writers-exchange.com/max-overton/